C'EST LA VIE

Jaime...
Enjoy the finale of
the Unbroken Series. Organized
chaos of their messy, exciting
lives.

xoxoxo
Melody

For information:
Melodious Enterprises, Inc.
P.O. Box 2400
Fort Lauderdale, Florida 33303

For information about signings or personal appearances:
info@melodiousenterprises.com
melody@melodysaleh.com

Cover design by 17 Studio Book Design
Editing by Revision Division

C'est La Vie: Such is life...
ISBN: 978-1-7333897-4-7 (paperback)
ISBN: 978-1-7333897-5-4 (ebook)

Deja Vu: Here we go again...
ISBN: 978-1-7333897-3-0 (paperback)
ISBN: 978-1-7333897-2-3 (ebook)

Facade: Things aren't always as they appear...
ISBN: 978-1-7333897-0-9 (paperback)
ISBN: 978-1-7333897-1-6 (ebook)

Unbroken Series
Book I - Facade - Release Date 12/31/2019
Book II - Deja Vu - Release Date 6/23/2020
Book III – C'est La Vie - Release Date 12/1/2020

For Prince Charming

INTRODUCTION

Welcome to book III of the Unbroken Series. By now you've read *Facade* and *Deja Vu.* If not, please go back and do so; these should be read in order—they are not stand alone books and you might find yourself lost otherwise. You've become invested in Amber's, Debra's, Dominque's and Zya's lives. Not to mention their love interests and family. I know you have lots of questions; you'll find these answers, and more, in the next 350+ pages.

As in the first two books, I didn't know what was going to happen until—it *actually* happened. I let my characters take me along for the ride as I took dictation for their story. I never knew where we were going each day. I wrote the first draft rather quickly, in two weeks. Some days I wrote over 10,000 words because they just wouldn't stop. My writing has been described as being 'very visual,' and that's because the movie plays in my head. Do I see these books as a TV series or movies? I already have. I just didn't get to enjoy the popcorn.

C'est La Vie starts August 2018 and ends on February 15, 2020; just before the COVID-19 pandemic swept our planet. This year has been quite the challenge; I don't think any of us need a reminder. However, if a spin-off or two from the series comes out, *(hint, hint, something big is happening in April 2020 in C'est La Vie)* I will have to include similar experiences and how it relates to them. You'll see what I mean. My brain is already creating the twists and turns that *could* happen. I hope you'll let me know what you think and what you'd like to see more of. These books would stand on their own—not as part of the series. My email is listed in the back.

I hope you enjoy the finale to the series. Bittersweet—I'm not ready to say goodbye; they've all become my closest friends; and I theirs. So let's just say until we meet again.

ACKNOWLEDGEMENTS

Writing and publishing a book is not for the faint of heart. It takes a lot of work—and patience. My husband, Ali, my Prince Charming, has been super supportive and understanding. Especially on those days I questioned why I was doing this to myself. I love to write! It's definitely when I'm at my happiest. It's everything else that comes along with this gig that's hard and time-consuming; and keeping me away from my keyboard. PC has been there to encourage me during my dark days and to celebrate my successes. Thank you, baby, for being my rock.

My daughter has recently begun helping me with my social media. It's made such a big difference taking that off my plate. Aside from being one of my beta readers and my social media administrator, Tiffany is also one of my biggest fans. Thank you for being so supportive and wanting to be involved. Thanks for my two beautiful grandchildren as well. I love you!

My friends—my sisters have been the inspiration behind the bonds of Amber, Debra, Dominque, and Zya. As you read *C'est La Vie*, you'll feel it even more so than in the previous two books. I miss seeing my friends—it shows in my words. If you think they have an amazing friendship, this is the blessed life I have with my tribe. Cherie, Holly, Linda, Lisa, Marie, Nancy, and Tammy, I love you all so much. Your friendship is so important to me. Our bonds are forever *unbroken*.

While I'm busy taking dictation for my characters, my fingers don't always fly fast enough to catch every detail. Without my editor, Kimberly Hunt from Revision Division, those holes would not get plugged. Thank you for your expertise and advice as I work at becoming a better writer.

I had lots of *questions* regarding the opening courtroom drama. I know what I wanted to happen, but I wasn't sure if legally it was possible. Thank you, Frank Morgan, my Twitter writer/lawyer friend, whose knowledge and expertise helped me find a way to realistically keep Amber safe.

My incredible cover designer, Anjanee from 17 Studio Book Design—OMG, you are so talented. These covers are amazing. You've been such a delight to work with and so patient with my perfectionistic personality. Thank you for always going above and beyond.

Finally, thank you to my readers. I do this for you. As long as you want to come along for the ride and escape with me, I'll keep telling stories. Thank you for your support, encouragement and sharing your thoughts with me. I hope I continue to live up to your expectations.

Stay tuned...my next project is a thriller; lots of twists and turns. I hope you like roller coasters.

Melody Saleh

C'EST LA VIE

A Novel

CHAPTER ONE

"I did it! I killed Paul Brettinger—Amber didn't do it." The mysterious woman in the front row throws off her sunglasses and walks up through the center of the courtroom toward the judge. "You can't arrest her—take me," she says, as she continues forward with her wrists together.

Amber's mind whiplashes between being found guilty of murdering the man who raped her and seeing her identical twin sister come forward, taking the blame. The same sister she wrote out of her life years ago.

"Brandy, what are you doing here?" Amber says, shaking her head in confusion. "Wait! Wait! You killed Brettinger? And pinned it on me?" Sudden clarity strikes and Amber's hands ball into fists and daggers fly from her eyes, slicing at her sister. The table between them is preventing her from lunging at her.

Brandy turns and walks back toward where Patrick is standing next to her. "No! Yes! I mean no…" she says, shaking her head. The tough facade she always wears, shredding before their eyes.

"I didn't go to kill him, honest—I went to ruin your reputation." Brandy's eyes dart up and then back down quickly. "I went to have sex with him, and that's it. I knew about his reputation, and I was pretty sure he'd try to get into your pants. But I knew you wouldn't go for it. So, I set up to go back and take your place." Brandy's eyes settle on Amber's as the tough-girl persona reappears. She sashays the rest of the way over to the table and leans on it with one hand. Looking over her shoulder and after licking her lips, she says, "You suddenly changed your mind and decided you wanted to pound him. It was pure luck you forgot your portfolio."

Patrick catches Amber as she lunges across the table toward Brandy.

Brandy never flinches. She raises her hand and examines her fingernails and says, "He asked if you came back for another round, so I knew I was too late. I couldn't believe my sweet little innocent, carbon copy, would willingly have sex with that fat slob."

Brandy's exterior cracks again. She pivots, walking toward the judge, shaking her fists. "He raped her—I knew it, and I just got so mad. No man has the right to force themselves on a woman—EVER!"

Spinning back around facing Amber, her face red and her eyes wide, she continues. "I saw an ice pick on the floor in the bathroom. I planned to put it on the vanity, but when I heard him spouting off at the mouth—I couldn't believe my ears. It was in my hand when he said I must have loved it. I *did* put it down, just not where I had originally intended. That disgusting pig. He deserved it. I'd kill him again if I could."

Amber drops heavily into her chair. Her shoulders slouch as her eyes glaze over, gazing at an invisible spot somewhere on the floor in disbelief.

"I'm sorry it got this far. I thought Patrick was going to get you off."

Brandy shifts her eyes, now with hatred toward Patrick. "I thought you were a better attorney. You should have been able to save her—not me."

She turns again to the judge, pleading, "Your Honor, take me—she didn't do it."

"Bailiff, can you please come and take this woman into holding and get a statement," the judge responds, shaking her head, in disbelief.

As the Bailiff is escorting Brandy away, Patrick chases after them. "Don't say anything to anyone until I can get in to see you."

Amber and Brandy jerk their heads up, staring at him.

Amber says, "You're going to represent her? After she set me up for murder? Whose side are you on?"

Brandy drops her head back and laughs hysterically. "No way in hell you're going to be my lawyer. She didn't even do it, and you couldn't get her off. This is rich—so rich!"

Patrick rushes back to Amber and grabs her hand. "She's your sister. I know she meant to ruin your reputation, but she stood up and is taking responsibility for her actions—she didn't have to do that."

"Don't worry sis, I've been through the system many times; they'll get me an attorney—a better one," Brandy says as they remove her from the courtroom. She's shifted entirely back to the hellion she's always been. With her shoulders pulled back, she looks at every person she passes directly in the eye, defying them to say anything or look at her wrong.

Patrick rushes back to the judge. "Your Honor, in place of this confession, can we drop the charges against my client?"

"Nice try, counselor, you know that's not the way this works. Your client has been found guilty of second-degree murder. She will go to the Broward County Jail, where she'll await sentencing."

"Please, your Honor, don't make her go there—she didn't do it," Patrick begs the judge.

"Mr. Simpson—Patrick, I understand how you feel; however, right now, we have someone who *claims* to be the murderer. Until we can investigate, your client is guilty, and we will follow procedure. Do you understand?"

"Yes, your Honor," Patrick replies as the vein pops out of his forehead and his jaw tenses.

Hearing the judge's words, the room begins to spin, and the floor feels as if it's falling out from under Amber's feet.

Patrick turns toward her, watching her face turn white, and her eyes bulge like a deer caught in headlights. "It's going to be okay. I'll immediately file an appeal, and I'll be on the detectives' backs to get through the investigation as quickly as possible."

Amber slowly looks up at him. Or rather, she's looking through him, trying to digest everything that's happened in the last ten minutes. She's going to prison. The only other time she's been this afraid was being pinned beneath the very man who not only took her body against her will, but who is now taking away her way of life.

The bailiff walks over to Amber and gently puts the handcuffs on her. As they leave the courthouse, Amber's eyes never leave Patrick's.

Her best friends, Debra, Dominque, and Zya, watch, with tears streaming down their faces, as they usher her away.

Amber is numb and dumbfounded; she doesn't hear the ding on her phone from a text.

You should have taken me up on my offer; you wouldn't be going through this right now. But then again, maybe this is better than the agony and terror you'll feel when I get you. You will be mine, Amber. In the meantime, your Patrick has thoroughly pissed me off! He's gonna have to pay now that I have to wait.

CHAPTER TWO

Amber goes through the motions, yet she hasn't come to terms with what's happening. Not sure if it's the 98°F temperature plus high humidity, or the fear of what lies ahead, that has her clothes drenched with sweat. She keeps replaying the morning over in her head when her security guy at her building told her everything was going to be okay. She believed him. Everything is definitely not okay.

Once they arrive, she allows herself to be pulled along, not wanting to think beyond each step, for fear of the next. The female prison guard assigned to her smiles and takes her the rest of the way. Everyone was filled in about the theatrics in the courthouse, but then again, they all say they're innocent. To actually have one, has the whole prison abuzz.

One of the holding cell occupants sits next to Amber and picks at locks of her hair, telling her how pretty she is and offers her protection. Amber's eyes never move from the tiny black spot on the wall directly across from her.

The guard yells, "Keep your fingers to yourself, or you might be the one needing protection."

Amber's admirer slinks away to the other side of the cell.

Amber slowly turns her head toward the guard and nods, acknowledging her.

The guard leaves, returning just moments later with her file. "Amber Fiore," she calls out.

Amber turns her head and says nothing.

"Come with me. Let's get you processed and out of this cell with the wolves. I'm in uncharted territory here, but I'm sure this is not where you need to be."

Amber does as instructed, at a pace slower than a snail. As she shuffles along, her eyes never rise above anyone's knees. Keeping her eyes at this perspective blocks out the world she finds herself in, the one she's still unwilling to accept. Although she knew this was a possibility, never in a million years did she dream this would happen. She didn't kill him. He raped her, and she's the one being punished. She can't get her mind to wrap around that this is happening—to her.

"Personal belongings go here," she says as she points to a white rectangle plastic bin.

As Amber pulls her phone from her pocket, she glances at it and sees the first few lines of the text. She drops the phone as if it were a hot coal. Her knees buckle as she folds to the floor. She quickly scoots backward to the wall like a spider. She finds a corner and wraps her arms around her knees, hugging them tightly, making herself as small as possible. Her eyes are as big as saucers—her breath comes in short bursts, bringing her to the verge of hyperventilation.

The guard picks up the phone and reads just a few lines she can see while the screen is locked. Her face turns pale as she reaches her hand out to Amber. "Come with me."

Amber looks up at then reluctantly takes her hand. Once she does, she doesn't let go. She pulls her body up as close to the guard as possible, making it difficult for either of them to walk.

The guard pulling Amber tight against her escorts her into a small, empty room and asks her to sit.

Reluctantly Amber lets go and fits herself in a corner, again pulling her knees up, squeezing her eyes as tight as possible, taking shaky breaths.

The guard sits down next to her. "Breathe—take some breaths for me. You're safe here."

Amber, keeping her eyes glued shut, slowly takes in a few deep breaths as the guard instructs her, "In and out."

Once she's certain Amber will not pass out from lack of oxygen, she asks, "Who is this from?"

Amber shakes her head.

"Is it okay if I read the rest of it?"

Amber nods.

The guard attempts to give her the phone, but Amber pulls her knees in tighter, tucking her head down further as if the phone were poisonous.

"Then give me your code."

"1213," she says in a tiny voice, never lifting her head.

The guard punches in the code and reads the rest of the text.

Amber peeks up after a few seconds of silence, recognizing the look of shock on the guard's face as her eyes rapidly go back and forth across the screen, rereading the words.

They both jump when the phone in the holding cell area rings.

The guard, after taking a deep breath, answers it. "Yes, it's okay. Send him back."

"Your attorney is here to see you. We don't normally let them in until you've been through processing, but I think he'll want to see this," she says, pointing to the cell phone.

Amber shrinks again when eyes move to her stalker's terror tool.

Amber can hear the guard introduce herself to Patrick on the other side of the door. "Before we go in, I think you need to read this."

As Amber continues to rock back and forth in the corner, behind the door, she hears his reaction and their conversation.

"Shit! Sorry."

"No need to apologize."

"Has she seen this?"

"Just the first few lines. She didn't kill him, did she?"

"No, her sister did. We knew she was the only one that could pull it off. She made sure we couldn't find her to be summoned."

"So, what's her next step?"

"Why the interest? Don't get me wrong, it's refreshing, but I'm not used to strangers going out of their way for us."

"She's not like the others I see come through here. Even the ones that claim to be innocent. I can tell—she is."

She claims ignorance as Patrick fills her in on the details from the courtroom—his side of the story.

When they open the door, Amber panics and runs to the farthest corner. She allows her mind again to go numb as Patrick rehashes the afternoon's details, not wanting to relive them.

"Amber—Amber, it's me, Patrick."

She stops and turns around and runs instead into his open arms, collapsing into them. Her gut-wrenching sobs reverberate off the walls.

After crying her eyes out for several minutes, just being in his arms, she feels some newfound, temporary strength. She pulls back from him. "You have to get me out of here. He's coming for me. He's gonna get me. I can't stay here."

He pulls her tightly back into his arms as he guides her back to the bench. "I'm working on it. I've been speaking to the judge."

Amber looks up, her pleading eyes swollen and red as tears continuously flow down both cheeks.

He shakes his head. "I'm sorry I don't have an answer yet. I don't want her to start the sentencing phase until they finish with Brandy's investigation. She can dismiss your charges once they convict Brandy." Patrick pulls her back into arms. "I'm so sorry. I promised you wouldn't be here. It wasn't supposed to be this way."

The guard exits the room, giving them privacy.

Amber says, through tears, "It's not your fault. You tried everything. It's her fault. That BITCH—she got me."

"I know you don't like the idea of me representing her. I need to make sure this goes perfectly, and quickly, so you two can change places."

Amber wipes her eyes and nose while nodding and says, "You're right, she came forward—she didn't have to. It doesn't excuse her though—there's no forgiving this. Even God himself would understand. I swear, if I ever thought there was a chance we could have a relationship, it's gone. I never thought she would stoop this low. Look at what she did to me. I'm in prison because of her. How does family do this—to family?" Amber's eyes spit out fresh tears as she buries her face into his damp shoulder.

Patrick strokes her hair as his eyes look skyward. "I get it, and I promise you, I'll never bring it up again. I certainly don't have a great track record with family either. I was just hoping maybe you two could have something I never did. I get she was so mad he raped you, she stabbed him. Hell, I would have if she hadn't. She went there to ruin your reputation in the first place, there's no excuse for that."

Amber shakes her head as fresh tears fall.

After a few moments, the guard taps on the door and enters. "I just spoke with the detective assigned to Brandy's case. He's a good friend of mine. I, uh, turned in a favor, so he's coming down now to speak with Brandy and get her full statement and confession. I hope that helps."

Amber looks up, shocked, and grateful. She jumps up from the bench and throws her arms around the guard. "Thank you. Thank you so much. I don't know why you're being so kind to me, but thank you."

"You don't belong here. This is not a nice place. You've got a world of hurt going on between your sister and that text. You deserve a break. I'm glad I can help. It feels good."

Patrick gets up and shakes the guard's hand. Then at the last second, he surprises her with a hug. "Thank you. We'll never forget this."

He turns back to Amber. "I need to be there when the detective talks to her. We need this to go smoothly—and quickly."

Amber nods with her head hanging down, searching for answers on her fingernails. She doesn't want him to leave; she's so afraid here. However, she knows to leave this hellhole, he must.

"Are you okay to sit in here by yourself?" the guard asks. "I need to get back to my wild ones."

Amber looks up and nods while inside her mind she's screaming, *NO!*

Amber crawls back to the corner and pulls her knees up and becomes lost in her thoughts. How could her sister—her own flesh and blood, do this to her? Brandy was always so jealous of Amber's accomplishments. No matter how hard Amber tried to include Brandy, she pulled back and caused even more trouble. While Amber did well in school and excelled in extracurricular activities, Brandy was failing, doing drugs, and sleeping with just about any male that could get a hard-on. She's done some really nasty things to Amber, but this takes the cake. And then she confesses? That makes little sense. Why the sudden conscience?

Amber's thoughts are distracted as a drop of blood drips from her finger. Her heartache is far greater than the throbbing in her fingers from biting her nails down below the quick. A habit she dropped after high school, right after Brandy left home.

The guard passes one of her peers and asks if it's okay to take a quick break, dancing, rubbing her legs together.

As she enters the bathroom, she pulls out her phone. "It's all set. Patrick is on his way over to the Fort Lauderdale Police Station to meet with Brandy."

CHAPTER THREE

"Patrick, can you give us an update? Is Amber going to prison?" Zya asks. She, along with Amber's best friends, are all together on the phone.

"I'm on my way to the station now to meet with Brandy and a detective. A guard is helping us." Patrick fills them in on the plan to get the confession and statement, and Amber, out of prison tonight. And about the text, she received in the courthouse.

Debra's voice comes through the phone. "How's Amber? Is she okay?"

Amber is always so strong. Watching her crumble these last few hours has been very hard for him. The tightness in his chest has only gotten worse since he heard the verdict. He can't tell her friends just how bad she is. Hopefully, one day they'll forgive him.

"She's as good as can be expected. She's in shock. We were so sure she would get a not-guilty verdict; we didn't prepare for anything else. And then Brandy…"

Dominque's voice comes through next. "Tell her we love her, please. We're here for her. If there's anything we can do, anything at all, consider it done."

"I know she'll appreciate that. You all have one amazing friendship; I know it will brighten her up."

"Sisterhood, Patrick," Zya says. "We're more than friends —we're sisters."

After Patrick hangs up the phone, he thinks about the promise he made his father so many years ago. He would never love a woman to the point she'd be able to hurt him. No woman would ever get close enough to destroy him. He realizes it's a promise he couldn't keep as his heart rips to shreds over Amber. And it's not her fault—it's his, he failed.

☯

Debra sits on the couch as tears silently stream down her cheeks, thinking about Amber being at that awful place. Zya sits beside her, arms wrapped around her. They are all waiting at Patrick's house. That was the plan; they would meet there and celebrate after the trial. Several unopened bottles of champagne are still sitting on the counter, the condensation pooling around the ice buckets next to them. Unsure what would happen after Brandy's courtroom confession, they moved forward with the location—the celebration part eliminated. "I know, it seems like this is all a bad dream."

Dominque and Tad are sitting on the other side of Debra. Dominque says, "Amber is always the one who fixes us. I don't know how to make this better for her."

"There has to be something we can do. I know Patrick is beating himself up but he'll keep fighting for her. He will not rest until she's back home. Think girls, what would Amber want us to do?"

Debra wipes her eyes and says, "She'd want us to keep investigating her stalker. We have to find him."

"You're right!" Zya says. "Okay, let me grab some paper."

The girls gather around the island in the kitchen. Zya puts a pad of paper and a pen down in the middle and says, "Let's start by listing those we've eliminated while I open up a bottle. Deb, you good to have wine?"

"Yeah, I pumped enough until tomorrow morning, I'm good."

"Okay, Roberto and Brandy were the first two names on our list. Can we safely cross them off?" Dominque asks as she picks up the pen, ready to write them down.

Zya comes back with the bottle and three glasses. "Yes, I think we can remove them. Roberto is back in Italy. He's still on the run; I don't see how he can get back here."

"But couldn't he still send the texts? Even if he's in Italy?" Debra asks as she has the most to lose if he ever comes back.

"I guess he could, but it doesn't make any sense. It would be costly and traceable since he's using burner phones."

"And didn't Patrick say the phones were purchased here in Florida and Georgia?" Dominque adds.

"That was before they deported him. Who knows where the phones are coming from now."

"Okay, let's leave him, but he's not our number one anymore. Brandy's in prison, and that text Patrick just told us about came while both of them were in the courthouse."

"Could she have an accomplice?" Debra asks.

"Doesn't seem like her style," Zya adds.

"You're probably right," Debra responds.

"Okay, then it has to be someone she profiled in one of her articles. Dom, you know them better than anyone, and you were looking into them; did anyone jump out at you?"

"Amber was fearless. She always thought South Florida was home to too many people looking to make a quick buck. If she found a sliver of a story where someone needed justice, she followed it to the end, no matter where it took her. She wound up in Liberty City and Overtown way too many times. She didn't care; she went wherever she had to."

"Gangs? Do any of them involve gangs?"

"She did with one in Little Havana. The cops have an ongoing investigation into the leader. She's been giving them information—helping them."

"Okay, that's helpful. His name goes to the top. What other ones?"

The four continue discussing names and possibilities of who would want to cause bodily harm to their friend over the next two hours and two bottles of wine.

That nagging feeling of helplessness urges them on to at least help solve this mystery. Individually, when their minds began envisioning what she is through, they'd quickly redirect that energy into the list.

Chapter Four

Patrick finds his way over to detective Ackerman's desk in the police station. As he sits waiting, he absentmindedly sifts through his emails and texts.

"Patrick Simpson?"

"Yes, and you must be detective Ackerman," Patrick says, standing and extending his hand. "Thank you for helping us get through this process so quickly."

"No problem. I understand your client—your girlfriend was convicted today, and her sister has since confessed. You're trying to get her out on bail."

"Yeah, pretty much. I need the report and written confession so I can see the judge. I'd prefer it if she didn't have to spend the night there."

"I hear you. Let me see what I can do," the detective says as he motions for Patrick to follow him.

Once Patrick catches up, he says, "Your friend at the prison, it's pretty nice of her to set this all up; she doesn't even know us. You two must be good friends."

"Nope, I barely know her. She was a guard in Belle Glade, where my sister has been residing. When she found a joint in her cell, she called me to say she discreetly disposed of it. My sister swears it wasn't hers; someone set her up. I guess I owe her for taking care of it regardless of who it belonged to."

They enter a small windowless gray room with a matching metal desk and chairs. A red dot blinks above a camera in the corner. "Take a seat. I'll go get our murderer."

Brandy struts through the door, cocky and full of confidence. "Hi handsome, come to play? You know, liquor may be quicker, but Candy is dandy. And as you may remember, Candy knows how to tease and make it last. All. Night. Long." Brandy licks her lips as she stretches out these last three words, then winks at him.

The guard gives Patrick a sideways look.

"It's nothing…ignore her, it's nothing," Patrick says, shaking his head and running his fingers through his hair.

"You didn't think it was nothing when you were eating whipped cream off my nipple," Brandy says as she gets close enough to lick the side of his face.

The guard yanks her handcuffs, pulling her to the other side of the table as Patrick wipes his face.

When he stops by her chair, Brandy rubs her body up against the detective and coos, "Oh, you like it rough, do you, baby? I love handcuffs. You, I'd let tie me up and fuck me all night long. In fact, while I'm here, why don't you come visit me. I'll ride you like a bronco."

The guard ignores her and continues about his business, securing her hands to the steel ring attached to the table. "Sit," he instructs.

"Brandy, if you're through playing around, we need to get down to business," Patrick says, embarrassed for the detective.

"What business? I told you I don't want you for my attorney. You couldn't keep Amber out of prison, and she didn't even do it. How stupid are you? You must feel so worthless. The woman you love—she's in prison because of you."

Through gritted teeth, Patrick replies, "No, she's there because of you. Now, shut up and listen. This detective is going to help us get through the process, with no delays, to get your written confession."

"So you can get my baby sister out of prison," she says with her lower lip puckered out. Before he can reply she continues. "I was born before her. Did she tell you that? By two and a half minutes, I should have been the one to have it all. The brilliant career, the one our parents adored, cheerleader, and now you. On second thought, you're no prize—she can keep you."

One of Brandy's many talents is pushing buttons, and she's doing a superb job right now as Patrick's face turns red, and the vein in his neck visibly throbs. Inside, he feels like he's about to explode, but his heart—his love for Amber—keeps his temper in check. He takes several deep breaths before he opens his mouth again. "Ahem, Brandy, please will you cooperate?"

Brandy doesn't answer. She stares at Patrick a moment, then turns her attention to the room's other occupant. "Now the detective here, he's one fine piece of ass. Did you notice those rock hard thighs on him?" With a suggestive gaze, she continues. "I bet it's rock hard between them too."

The detective walks over to the video recorder and presses record, causing the red light to blink. "Okay, Miss Fiore, we are not here to get our jollies. You confessed to murdering Mr. Paul Brettinger on January 16 of this year. Is that correct?"

"Mmm, hmm," she says seductively.

"Are you giving this confession of your own free will?"

"Mmm, hmm." She licks her lips and leans up on the table. With her hands still in cuffs and secured to the table, she rubs one of her breasts with her fingertips.

The detective continues, ignoring the scene. "You understand, by giving this confession, you are not receiving anything in return. No plea bargains or special arrangements; is that correct?"

"Yes! Yes! Yes!" she says panting, and breathless.

"Miss Fiore, do you understand how serious this is? Because you don't seem to take any of this to heart."

Sitting back suddenly, she says, "Oh, I totally understand. I killed him. I stabbed him in the neck with the ice pick. It's a good thing he was taking a shower because of the blood, there was so much of it. The mess it would have made all over his cream carpet."

"Let's go back to the beginning, shall we." After the standard names, case number, and location details, the detective continues. "Miss Fiore, can you please tell me when you first thought about setting your sister up for the murder of Mr. Paul Brettinger?"

Brandy attempts to sit back and cross her legs, however, the ring securing her hands prevents her. The playful grin and booming laugh suddenly change as her eyes narrow and fix on the detective. Her fingers curl under tightly, causing her knuckles to turn white. Speaking through clenched teeth, she says, "First, I did not set out to kill him. I planned to ruin my sister's life."

She takes a deep breath, settling in to tell her story. "It all started years ago. She was our parents' favorite; she could do no wrong. I was the black sheep while she was Little Miss Bo Peep. No matter how hard I tried, I was never good enough. In school, she was the cool kid, and I was in the principal's office all the time. Did she tell you I screwed the dean pretending to be her? He kept calling me Brandy because he couldn't believe it was Amber spread eagle on his desk, begging for him to bury his face between my legs. Oh, how his mustache tickled so good. I'm a fan of facial hair ever since. He did scream out her name when he shot his wad. I thought he was going to have a heart attack."

Patrick swallows hard. He knew things were rough for Amber when she was in school, and he heard about the evil ways Brandy tried to destroy her. To sit here and watch as she spews out all this ugliness, he can't imagine this is her sister saying these things—her identical twin. She doesn't resemble Amber at all.

"Let's come forward a bit and talk about the murder of Mr. Brettinger."

"Like I said, I didn't plan on killing him; I was going to fuck his brains out. I knew he was a womanizer, and if he met his match, it would get around quickly. Oh, the shit I planned to do to him. I was going to suck his cock like it was a popsicle, taking long, slow licks, then with the Ben-Wa balls I had tucked inside my bra, I was going to push them into his asshole slowly and pull them out when he came, making him scream my name. I mean, Amber's name."

She sits back as far as her tethered wrists will allow. "They were releasing me early from jail, and my dear sister wouldn't return any of my calls. This time, I was determined I was going to get out and stay out, but I needed her help. She offered it to me before, so I couldn't understand why now she couldn't be bothered this time. I was more determined than ever to ruin her. When I got out, I hitched down to Fort Lauderdale. My last ride lives here, so I repaid him by returning the ride. He let me crash there as long as I kept his dick happy.

"I had been researching Little Miss Perfect the whole time I was locked away, knowing one day, I'd get even. I came across the article she wrote about you," she says, addressing Patrick. "I have to say, an attorney with ethics, now come on, who are you kidding?"

Patrick doesn't move a muscle. The vein in his forehead pulses in sync with one in his neck. They say there are three sides to every story—his, hers, and the truth. He's starting to believe there's Brandy's warped take of it all; Amber's washed down, embarrassed version because the real one is too horrible to share; and the appalling truth.

"I knew the way to destroy her was to get to you, so I decided I needed an attorney. The reason Amber needed an attorney was so horrible, she had to wear a disguise so I wore a scarf and sunglasses. I walked in the front door and overheard your sexy roommate tell his secretary how he hired a stripper for your birthday. This tidbit of information gave me an even better idea. I went over to Ladies, Ladies, Ladies to see about a job, and to cancel your birthday present so I could take her place. Since you knew what Amber looked like, I had to put on a disguise. Not too much—I wanted you to think you knew me, but couldn't quite place my face. Remember when you unbuttoned my top with your teeth? And how hard you got when I was grinding my hips into you? Did you smell the crotch of my panties when you opened them?"

Patrick jumps up and storms out of the room. She was an expert seductress, and she looked familiar, if only he had known. She made his body respond in ways it hadn't in years.

It makes his stomach turn to think it was Brandy all along—not Amber.

He sees a water dispenser down the hall and makes a beeline for it. He needs to keep her talking, but he needs a break; he can't let her get under his skin. After guzzling two triangle cups, he turns on his heel, determined to finish and get Amber released.

"Oh goody, you came back to me," Brandy says, wriggling around in her seat. "My juices just started flowing again."

Standing next to the table, Patrick punches his fist onto the surface, causing Brandy to jump. "Just get to it already, will you. Not interested in your games."

"Cool your jets, Ace, I'm getting there," she says, sitting up straight.

"I needed to infiltrate her life, so, after your little birthday delight, I changed clothes and went up to see your receptionist. I thought the timing would be perfect since you thought you knew who Candy was. I was hoping you'd put two and two together. Your roommate Stewart conveniently came out of your office at the same time. Did I mention he's one hot, sexy dude?" She closes her eyes as her tongue circles around, licking her lips. "I like danger and I can take the heat so I decided a little extra toying wouldn't hurt. Being an expert in disguise and seduction, all I had to do was blink my eyes a few times and he was putty in my hands. He stopped me and introduced himself. I knew he was a Pharmaceutical rep so I pretended to work in the office of the top surgeon at Broward General Hospital. He explained how he had been trying to get an appointment to see the good doc; I promised to help.

"You're going to love what happens next." Brandy sits forward with her eyes gleaming and says, "So he calls me the very next day for a booty call and the opportunity to get in to see the head dick—I mean doc. I get him all riled up; hot and horny on the phone. I swear I've got him about to cum in his pants when I give him the number he needs to make the appointment. As I give him the number, I throw in how hard I'm going to fuck him and how I love to suck cock between digits. I distract him to utter confusion. Finally, I give him one of my numbers because I was just having too much fun. When he finally calls, he gets a phone sex friend instead. Oops, I guess he got it wrong after all." She brings her mouth down to her hands with a fake surprised look on her face.

It stuns Patrick. He and Stewart thought it was pure coincidence. Amber told him not to underestimate her; she's much smarter than she lets on. He never realized only how true that statement is—until now.

"Why Stewart, and wouldn't he have recognized your voice?" Patrick asks.

"Really? You don't think I'm that dumb, do you?" Brandy disguises her voice into a throaty, sexy tone and says, "Remember, I'm the master of disguise. At first it truly was for the sex, but then I decided I had already waited this long, I'd use him for information to get closer to you. You two would be my new playthings."

"Amber and I weren't even dating on my birthday."

"I didn't need you two doing the horizontal mambo—I decided I'd take my time to plant the seed. I was going to create the perfect crime she'd need you for. Being her carbon-copy has its advantages."

The detective interrupts. "So what happened next?"

"I had phone sex with Stewart during the day, and screwed my ride to Fort Liquordale at night, while I did more research on dear old sis. I paid a lot of attention to the good-deed articles she wrote about. I was piecing together how to plant evidence, proving she only reported the ones who didn't grease her palms to keep quiet. It's tedious work.

"The deeper I dug, the madder I got. What about those poor people who were just trying to get by and earn a buck? Who looks out for them? One man lost his job, and his apartment, when she turned him in for taking sex in exchange for rent. What's wrong with that? Everybody deserves to get laid. Suppose she couldn't afford the roof over her head. What's wrong with blowing him for it? How hard is that? Fucking bitch went and complained. I got even for him. My girlfriend in the slammer was a computer geek; she taught me a few things that would be helpful when I got out. I made it look like she lied because he dumped her. Oh. My. God. If you could have seen the look on her face when the reporters showed up on her doorstep with pictures of them together and copies of the receipts for the lavish gifts she bought to win him back. Karma is a bitch—just like for Amber.

Patrick, running his fingers through his hair, says, "Brandy, you stood up and confessed to murdering Paul Brettinger so Amber wouldn't go to prison. If you hate her so much, why?"

"I know, I know—right? What was I thinking?" Brandy looks down at her hands as her fingers pick at each other. She stares at them for a long time before she continues. "Prison was never my intention; Little Miss Perfect wouldn't last a night in jail. Plus, I can't torment her when she's sitting in a 5x8 cell. I'm anxiously waiting to find out who her stalker is. Can I get popcorn in jail when that plays out?" she says, looking at the detective, failing miserably at playing the tough act.

The hair on the back of Patrick's neck stands up at the mention of Amber's stalker. Listening to the coldness in her voice every time she mentions her sister's name, he's convinced, tormenting Amber with those texts is exactly something Brandy would do.

"I'm getting tired. Think we can call it quits for today?"

Patrick, red-faced, scoots forward in his chair and says, "No, we can't—continue."

"Oh! You playing tough guy? Does Amber like that? Nah, probably not, I bet she's a cold fish in bed. I bet she just lies there and lets you do all the work. Does she just stare at the ceiling? Does she even moan or breathe heavy?"

"Miss Fiore, I can promise you, this will go a lot quicker, and better, for you if you'll just stick to the story. Please continue," the detective says.

"Okay, okay, you're no fun either. By now, Stewart and I have had kinky phone sex all over the house, so he's bugging to meet in person. I figure it's time for me to come out of the woodwork."

Patrick chuckles, remembering when Amber said those exact words when Brandy suddenly appeared. Only she compared Brandy to the large brown creepy-crawly insect Florida is well known for.

"I wanted to see if I could pass muster pretending to be her so I accidentally left my keys upstairs on day. Her security guard couldn't help me fast enough. He is so nice; did you know he made me an extra copy to keep in my purse just in case I did it again. You better watch out Patrick, I think that man has a thing for your girl."

Patrick doesn't take the bait. He remains calm—on the outside.

"One day, once I'm ready to put my plan into action, she finds me sitting on her couch. You should have seen the look on her face! It was like she had seen a ghost! I pretended I wanted to bury the hatchet, when actually, I was sharpening the edge," Brandy says, as her eyes narrow. Her head remains pointing down, just her eyes glancing up.

"I found out from my Phone Sex buddy Amber had a big interview coming up. When he's got his pants down around his ankles, he'd answer any question I asked."

"Why would you and Stewart be discussing me and Amber? That doesn't make sense."

Brandy leans forward again as her eyes and lips narrow to thin lines. "You have no idea how brilliant I am, do you? Amber is smart, but common sense is the one area I exceed. We may have identical IQs, she just doesn't have the street smarts I do. It was easy to get Stewart to spill all about his roommate and how you two just couldn't get it together. The hot tub? Priceless! Oh, he has no idea how much of a pawn he was in all this. I couldn't have done it without him."

"I did almost have one hiccup when the time on her big interview got pushed back. I didn't find out about it until the day before. PHEW! We all wouldn't be here otherwise."

"The clothes, the shoes, how did you do all that?" Patrick asks. That was one question that kept coming up when they were in the discovery phase before the trial. Neither he nor Amber could figure out how she would have the exact replicas of everything.

"Once I knew what my plan would be, I had to get into her closet. I realized a long time ago, her navy blue suit with the light pink blouse was her go to ensemble for important meetings. I knew I had to duplicate it. I was pretty shocked when I saw her get in her car that afternoon wearing that sexy red dress. I kept eyeing it in her closet; I almost stole it from her. But I didn't want her to know I was in her place. She's so busy, she typically shops at one store—creature of habit. She has her own personal saleslady who contacts her when the new season's business attire arrives. I might have listened to a message on her home recorder explaining her latest purchases were ready and they would send them over unless she wanted to come pick them up. It was another opportunity for me to go undercover as Amber.

"When I arrived, the saleslady rushed over to me like I was the Queen of England. I'm betting the commissions she earns on Amber's purchases keep her in the lifestyle she's accustomed to. I saw the red dress and just couldn't resist. It's a good thing it didn't need altering. She advised me to be more careful at parties and added it to Amber's account. Since I was there, I took her recent altered purchases and delivered them myself. I was sure she'd never see the dress on the bill—and I was right."

Patrick keeps his arms crossed to keep the body odor from his sweat-stained shirt from being detected. It's not hot in the room; it's his body's reaction listening to how easily Brandy invaded Amber's life. The more she talks, the faster his heart beats, and the intense heat flushes through his body.

"How did you get into Amber's parking garage? You need an opener."

"I broke into a car and stole one. Good thing the building is still operating in the stone age and not using the windshield stickers, those don't come off without destroying them.

"I had to go home to get the dress and then Ubered over to Brettinger Holdings. I used the lobby restroom to get everything ready. I took it over and left it locked so no one would disturb my masterpiece.

"Anyway, I knew Paul baby would make a pass at Amber. It's common knowledge that's the only way you'll get anywhere with him. And since that last published article was such a disaster, I knew he'd offer his dick for her article—and she'd decline. Once she left and I went back and fucked his brains out, she'd get the interview without knowing why. Well, at least initially, she wouldn't know. Eventually, Prickinger would spill the beans, and her reputation as Miss Goodie Little Two Shoes was as good as gone. She'd be known as a professional slut who screwed her way to the top. Kind of like her friend Dominque. Didn't she suck and fuck her way into the wonderful world of modeling?"

Patrick's knuckles turn white from clenching his fists so tight. He would never hit a woman; heck, it would take a lot for him to punch a man—this bitch is asking for it.

"I knew I'd have to drug her to take her place, so I waited outside for her. Getting close to her would be easy—I'm her sister. I wanted her to see me in the dress just as I injected her so she'd pass out knowing I was up to no good so I put on a trench coat so she wouldn't see the flash of red until the very last moment.

"She got a little turned around and ended up exiting just as a group of people were entering. I had a syringe of GHB; all I needed was just to touch her. Her bursting through the crowd at the exit the way she did, allowed me to jab her forearm through the pocket in my coat. I thought for sure she would recognize me, or my smile at least, but her mind was elsewhere. She never saw the dress either. Hindsight—now I know why.

"I watched her for about ten minutes, waiting for the drug to take effect. She got out of her car at one point and threw up several times. I wondered at that point if she fucked him after all and was disgusted with herself. But I couldn't take the chance. I had to go up and follow through, anyway.

"Once I saw her head bob, I jumped into action and pushed her over in her car. She looked at me with these blank eyes and kept saying, 'my portfolio,' over and over. That's when I noticed it wasn't there; the perfect excuse to go back.

"Amber is a creature of habit. She always twisted her hair the same way since we were in high school, so creating the perfect facade was easy peasy. After she passed out, I logged into the security camera for the parking lot. Remember that girlfriend I had in prison? She taught me that as well, only I was interested in it more for ATM cameras. In this wonderful world of technology, they had an antiquated camera that was so easy to hack. During my research on that make and model, I found lots of complaints about how the numbers were indistinguishable. The three and the eight were the simplest to work with, so I just found a time splice using those two numbers to delete five minutes so you'd never see me coming the first time.

"After I finished with the camera, I sashayed my sweet little ass back upstairs to seduce Mr. Paul, and as I said earlier, I found his fat ass singing in the shower. I slipped out of my dress and shoes and joined him. I could fuck him and wash his disgustingness off me at the same time. As I walked in, I found an ice pick on the floor. I intended just to put it on the vanity, but then he started shouting, 'you come back to get more of this cock. You want me to fuck you hard again? I knew you liked it, didn't you?' I lost it. She didn't throw up because she had sex with him—he raped her," Brandy says with clenched teeth, her body pulsing to each word in the last sentence.

She takes a deep breath and sits back as far in her chair as her chained wrists will allow. Her face instantly transforms, showing a calm demeanor with a sweet smile.

"I did put the ice pick down, just not on the vanity as planned. Instead, it found a nice little place"—she bolts upright as her jaw tightens—"right in his neck. One jab and he was squirting his hot red blood all over the place. Hollywood always makes you think when you hit a major artery, blood spurts six or seven feet in the air; in reality, it only goes about one. Not what he was hoping to squirt all over the place, that's for sure," she says, cackling.

"You should have seen his eyes. He couldn't believe I—or rather, Amber—would kill him. It was priceless. Oh, how I wish I had my camera. Now that's an image I will forever cherish in my mind. He tried to grab me, but oops, as I stepped out of his way, my foot might have got tangled up in his. He fell hard—THUD! Did that fat fuck crack the floor? Oh, never mind. I stood there and watched as the blood squirted less and less, down to barely a trickle. I watched until his miserable, ugly life drained out of his eyes. Did you know you bleed out in about thirty seconds when your carotid artery is severed? That is if your heart's not racing at the time—then it's much faster.

"I rinsed, dried myself off, fixed my hair, put on my dress and shoes, and grabbed Amber's portfolio. Then I left."

The detective had been quietly listening; his face devoid of any emotion. "Did anyone see or talk to you when you left his office?"

"His sweet secretary asked me if I wanted to schedule the interview. I told her to call me."

"Why did you put a pencil on her desk when you left?" Patrick asks, remembering that detail at the trial.

"Well, you see, it's my trademark. Amber didn't tell you about it?"

Patrick shakes his head.

"My little princess sister always had these fancy sticks and pins to secure her little bun. I got none of those, so I'd pick up anything I could get my hands on to put mine up with. I pranced around, saying I was just as pretty as her—maybe even prettier."

"That makes little sense. Why does Amber use a pencil now to put up her hair all the time if it was your thing?"

Brandy's hard features soften again. "There was a time when Amber tried to help me; I guess it was like a peace offering. She tried everything. I told her I wanted her fancy pins and sticks, and she had to put her hair up with pencils for the rest of her life. My giving the secretary a pencil was a vital clue. I'm disappointed my smart double didn't catch on."

The detective goes over and shuts off the recorder. He turns to Patrick and says, "I'm sure I have enough for you to get Amber out on bail tonight. It will take me a few hours to get this transcribed. I'll call the judge myself and let her listen to the important parts, promising to follow up with the full written confession tomorrow. You head on back over to the prison. I'll call the guard and make sure they keep Amber in transition, so she doesn't get processed tonight."

Patrick jumps to his feet; that's music to his ears. "Thank you, thank you so much," he says, shaking the detective's hand, preparing to flee.

"Make sure you send my sister my love. She has to visit me every week. You tell her that. It's the least she can do since I confessed for her."

CHAPTER FIVE

"**O**kay, I think we've got an impressive start for our research tomorrow. What time is it? Shouldn't Patrick have called with an update by now?"

"Yeah, I wish he would too; I have to leave. Little George is giving Megan a hard time. He's had enough of the bottles—he wants momma. Tracey's tried to help, but there's only so much a seven-year-old can do. How late are you all planning on staying?"

"I'm not leaving until we hear something, or Amber walks through that door—whichever comes first," Zya responds.

"Yeah, us too," Dominque adds, referring to her and Tad.

"Please let me know as soon as you hear anything. I don't care how late it is. I won't sleep anyway."

Zya hugs Debra and walks her to the door. "I'll let you know as soon as I hear—promise."

Tina comes out from the study to say goodbye to Debra just as she's leaving.

"Where have you been, babe? You should have been out here with us."

"No, you needed to be here with your friends. I didn't want to intrude," Tina responds.

"You saw Tad was here, right?"

"Yes, and I also saw he sat on the couch on his phone while you three drank wine and worked out names on the list."

"Were you eavesdropping?"

"Maybe? Just a little. Watching you three feverishly working on finding who's been terrorizing her was pretty awesome. You four have an incredible bond."

"That we do. There's nothing we wouldn't do for each other."

"Nothing?"

Just as Zya is about to answer, her phone buzzes; they all look over in anticipation. "It's Ashanti; sorry guys."

"Hey, honey, what's up?"

"Have you heard anything yet?"

"No, not yet; Patrick sounded sure he could get her out on bail tonight. We're still waiting to hear. How are you and Stacey holding up? Did you eat dinner?"

"We ordered pizza. I hope that's okay."

"Yes, of course it is. Did you have homework? Gosh, I'm sorry I wasn't home with you to help."

Ashanti, laughing, says, "Mom, you know you can't help me with calculus and chemistry, but thanks for the offer. Besides, you need to be where you are. We're okay, I promise."

Tina says into the phone, "Tell Stacey I love her, and we'll be home soon."

"I'll tell her. Mom, have *you* eaten tonight?"

"Who's the mother and the daughter here?"

"I guess I got my answer—nothing, right?"

"When did you get so damn smart? No, I haven't, but we will," she says, looking around to everyone as a cue. "We'll order something; I promise."

"Okay. Love you, Mom, and please don't worry about us. We won't open the door for anyone—we're fine."

"You opened the door for the pizza guy?"

"No, we didn't. We paid for it, including his tip on your credit card. Then we put a note on the door asking him to leave the pizza on the table on the porch. We got it after he left," Ashanti says, very proud of herself.

"You really are something, you know that. Smart and beautiful. Watch out world."

"No, you're not biased, are you?" Ashanti laughs as she says goodbye and hangs up.

Click. Click. Click. The shutter noises on the camera just outside Ashanti's living room window. He pulls back, looking at the screen and her smiling face. *Such a shame; you have a promising future. Too bad everything Amber loves must die.*

A janitor is mopping the floor down the hall from the room where the guard left Amber. The guard asks him, "Did you see where the girl in that room went?"

"Oh, yeah, she went to processing. Bossman was mad too when he found her."

Patrick follows behind the guard at a clipped pace toward what he hoped was processing.

She turns and stops him as they come upon a barred door. "Wait here. I'll go find her."

Patrick turns around and nervously walks back and forth while running his fingers through his hair. He feels like he's failed her at every turn today. Once she starts processing, he won't be able to get her out until they're done. It includes a very impersonal shower, a possible body cavity search, and a doctor's exam. It's not uncommon for inmates to wait days, even weeks, for the doctor to do this last step.

Patrick can see the guard through the bars at the far end of the hall, addressing someone using her arms to express the urgency.

She turns and begins the long walk back toward him, with her head hanging when the phone behind her rings. The guard runs back, hoping it's for her.

After several nods and listening to words Patrick is too far away to make out, the guard shakes hands with the person behind the wall and hustles back toward him.

"They began processing her, but nothing is filed in the computer yet. Detective Ackerman has made good on his promise. He called the judge; she's waiting for your call right now to discuss bail." The guard smiles wide, showing her pearly white teeth.

Patrick thanks her, then turns around, scanning his phone for the judge's number. As he puts the phone up to his ear, waiting for his call to connect when he hears the guard speaking in a hushed tone. He turns around to find her phone up to her ear, slowly walking away. She's whispering, but he swears he hears her say, "It's all done. She'll be home tonight."

☯

Amber slowly exits the jail holding her arms across her chest and her head hanging down. Her long brown hair hangs loosely, hiding most of her face.

Patrick puts his arm around her shoulders as he walks her to his car. She's still in shock—in a fog, so he pulls her tight against him. He feels so helpless; he can't take it all away and make her smile again—what he wouldn't give to see that beautiful face light up.

Amber says nothing in the car; she just stares out the window with her fingers in her mouth.

While waiting at a traffic light, Patrick pulls her hand away. Another ten pounds just got added to the heaviness in his heart as he notices the dried blood across the tips of her fingers.

When they enter Patrick's home, Zya runs to the door throwing her arms around Amber, nearly knocking her down. Zya has only cried this hard once before; the day she found out her dad died.

Amber stands just inside the door, looking blankly across the room while her friends surround her, taking turns wrapping their arms around her, so happy she's with them. Her arms don't move; they stay hanging at her side. It's only when Dominque pulls away to wipe her tears, she notices the emptiness in Amber's eyes. Her pupils are as large as her iris', making it impossible to tell them apart. It's startling. Her eyes look almost dead.

Patrick grabs Amber's hand and pulls her toward the bedroom. It's late, or relatively early, the next morning.

"Do you want to take a shower or just crawl into bed?"

She turns her head, slowly meeting his gaze. Her vacant stare sends shivers through his body. She doesn't answer him—no response.

"Come on, let's get you undressed and under the covers."

Amber allows him to lead her toward his bedroom when she glances over at the wet bar. She heads for a bottle of vodka, pulling it to her lips the second she has the top off. She takes three full swigs before Patrick gently pushes the bottle down and takes it from her hands. No one sees the single tear escaping before he quickly wipes it away.

Amber gives him no assistance or resistance as he removes the clothes she's been wearing since yesterday morning. She sits on the edge of the bed, staring into space as he maneuvers her out of most of her clothing. Once he gets her under the covers, she doesn't move. Her eyes stare wide and blank at a spot on the ceiling.

As he closes the door behind him, another cold shudder strikes his body. *Is she broken?*

Patrick intends to put the cap back on the bottle of Vodka; instead, he tips the bottle over his mouth and takes one, two, three, full swigs first.

"She's okay," he says, to the tear-stained faces anxiously waiting for him. He's never been a good liar. Time to see if he would ever make it in Hollywood. "She's in shock, as you can see. Brandy has stooped to an all-time low. Amber's trying to wrap her head around it all."

"Does she have to go back to prison?" Dominque dares to ask.

"She's out on bail. Once the judge hears Brandy's statement, I'm positive she'll dismiss the case."

Zya's head snaps and tilts as she asks, "You can dismiss the case after a verdict?"

"Sometimes, yes, but it's rare—there is precedent. We're piecing this all together as we go along. The guard at the jail last night was a godsend. Amber wouldn't be here with us tonight if she hadn't stepped in and helped."

CHAPTER SIX

"Babe, please eat something," Patrick pleads. It's been three days since Amber's trial, and she's barely moved from the indent in the mattress. Her friends have been over to visit only to leave broken-hearted as she just lay on the bed either asleep, faking it, or staring at the ceiling. She's yet to utter a word.

"I know it's all surreal, and I can't pretend to know anything about how you feel, but I don't want to see you waste away, or get sick. Please eat something. If not for you, please do it for me."

Amber turns her head to look at him. The tenderness in his eyes helps to break the spell. "I could stand to lose a few pounds."

Patrick smiles widely, hugging her shoulders. "There you are. You look perfect to me."

"They say love is blind," she says as she scoots to sit up in the bed as he lifts the tray from the nightstand.

Patrick stands beside her, clasping and unclasping his hands as she picks at a turkey sandwich he lovingly piled way too high. She has no appetite, yet she has to try, so she flips the bread over and picks at the meat.

He sits down on the bed beside her and says, "I'm so sorry. I was sure the jury wouldn't find you guilty. You wouldn't be in this nightmare if you had a better lawyer."

"Are you kidding me? You did what you could—you can't control everything. The evidence pointed to me being guilty. Hell, my exact double *did* it! Any other attorney would have had me pleading guilty for a lighter sentence."

Patrick looks down at his hands.

"Babe, I love you. This sucks, I will not lie to you. The hardest part is what my sister was trying to do to me. I don't know why she suddenly grew a conscience and confessed. I'm sorry I've been in another world these last few days; I've been trying to make sense of all this. I don't think for one second she did it for me—there's something in all this for her. I don't know what, but I *will* find out."

"How's Amber doing? Any better?"

"Patrick just sent us a group text. She's finally eating—and talking," Zya responds while washing the dinner dishes.

"You going to the studio tomorrow? Your summer collection will not finish itself, you know," Tina says playfully, wrapping her arms around Zya's waist, kissing her on the neck.

Zya's shoulders relax as she takes a deep breath. She didn't realize just how tense she was until the moment she knew Amber was no longer comatose.

As she looks around the house, at her partner and fiancé Tina, and the girls still sitting at the table, everything suddenly looks lighter even though it's dusk. The smiles on everyone's faces suddenly brightens up her world.

"Oh, I almost forgot," Tina says as she runs out of the kitchen and back in with an envelope. "Cassie dropped this off the other day. I didn't want to give it to you until things got a little better. I'm sorry."

Zya tears open the envelope from the attorney Ashanti's father forced her to hire. Doug filed a petition for full custody when he found out about her alternative lifestyle. He couldn't handle her turning down his marriage proposal for a woman.

"That bastard! He's going forward with it. I can't believe it. Why in the hell would he do this to Ashanti? Why move a fifteen-year-old from Fort Lauderdale to New York, away from her friends?"

Tina hugs Zya and says, "I'm sorry. I hope I didn't cause all this. The last thing in the world I want to do is hurt you…or Ashanti."

"It's not you—he's an ass. His ego is bigger than his balls, and those are pretty big. We have to be careful how we tell Ashanti," Zya whispers. "I don't want her to think she's responsible for this—because she will. She already feels bad about causing my sudden coming out on national television."

Zya grabs Tina, holding onto the second best thing that's happened to her; dreading what has to happen next. "It's probably going to get ugly. I'm going to make a copy of the drug deal I witnessed a few years ago and send it to him. So we're all safe, I'll carry out our plan for the original. His boss would probably kill him to make this all disappear rather than come after us. I hate the thought of this, but losing Ashanti isn't an option. If I have to choose, it's her life I'll save every time."

"Do you think it will get that far?" Tina asks, surprised.

"I didn't think we'd be here," Zya says as she blows out a breath causing her bangs to fly.

"Mrs. Johnson, it's nice to see you again. Congratulations on your recent nuptials," the doctor says, shaking her hand, then smiling and shaking Tad's.

"Thank you. I needed something wonderful in my life after dealing with breast cancer."

"How are you doing? Feeling okay?"

"Not too bad. You said the chemo was residual, and I would gradually feel worse with each treatment. I do wish the opposite was true at the same pace. I feel a little better each day, but it's been slow progress."

"It's only been a little over three months since your surgery. Your body is still healing from that and the treatments. Be patient; you'll feel like your old self before you know it."

Tad adds, "Only better—she'll be cancer-free."

"Your blood tests look great. Still a little anemic; I suspect this may become your new normal. All your other numbers look great."

"How about her tumor markers?"

"Ah, someone's been doing his homework," the doctor says with a chuckle. "Her CA125 markers are well below range. I don't go solely by those numbers; I look at much more."

"So, they don't detect tumor cells?"

"They do, but they're not always accurate. Besides, they're used more for ovarian cancer, and a raised marker doesn't necessarily mean cancer. Endometriosis, fibroid cysts, even pregnancy could cause them to elevate. I'll watch them, but most times, there are other indicators."

Dominque jumps at the opportunity to discuss the subject that's been on her mind since her whole cancer nightmare began. "Since you brought it up...when can we try to get pregnant?"

"We'd like you to wait at least two years."

"I'm thirty-seven. If I wait two years, I'll be thirty-nine before we even start; and I want two kids."

"I understand. We base your survival statistics on two and five years post-treatment. If you are going to have a recurrence, it will most likely happen within the first two years. The numbers gradually improve as time goes by. Your safest bet is to wait at least two years."

The color on Dominque's face drains, making her cheeks appear more red than usual. She looks down at her hands; she was hoping they could start right away. Knowing there are risks after the age of thirty-five, and more so after forty, wanting to have two kids, she was hoping to start sooner. And if the stars are aligned, have the second right around that magic number.

"Please don't think I'm being stubborn, I hear you. Could I start earlier if I'm willing to take the risk?"

Tad's head snaps over at her, his eyes wide in surprise.

She puts her hand over his. "Would the obstetrician be willing to move forward since my cancer was triple-negative?"

"That's a question for your doctor. I've advised you against it. However, if you choose to move forward anyway, the decision is between you and your obstetrician."

"If I have a recurrence, will I have to end the pregnancy?"

"Triple-negative breast cancer is very aggressive, especially in a young woman. If you were to get pregnant and your cancer reoccurs, chemo during the first trimester might harm the fetus. Second and third trimester, not as harmful, but they are possible."

As they leave the office, Dominque's eyes tear up. She's been holding it in, not willing to break down in front of an audience.

Tad turns to address the elephant Dominque dropped in the room. He decides against it once he sees the pained expression on her face and the stream steadily flowing down her cheeks.

☯

As Brian is locking up his office door, he hears a car door shut behind him. He turns around to tell whoever's there he's closed for the night. He's surprised to see Debra quickly approaching him.

"Quick, back inside," she says.

A flip of the key, and he's inside punching the keys on the alarm panel. Just as his fingers reach the fourth number, Debra's body is up against his back, her hands up his chest, and unbuttoning his shirt.

"Whoa, what's gotten into you?" He turns around to face her just as her lips meet his. Her lips drown out his words as her tongue searches, making him forget he was even leaving.

The battle rages on in her mind. She's never been forward like this—she's very shy. Her friends told her she needs to spice things up a bit. Heck, she's not even sure she's ever had an orgasm. Brian has been very patient; it's time for her to be more confident, more forward, sexier.

His arms wrap around her as he returns her kisses with more fervor. He backs her into his office and up against his desk, then he quickly lifts her, sliding the contents on the surface to the floor with one arm sweep. He pushes her dress up against her hips and spreads her legs wide while pulling her forward.

Her mind is screaming for her to push her dress down and close her legs. The other part, where the fire is raging, wraps her legs around his waist while her hips unconsciously grind into him.

He tears at the wrap front dress, releasing her full breasts. No bra! His eyes wide with surprise, and he bites his lip. His lips encircle one of her nipples as her hands grab his head, pulling him closer.

"Now! Now! I want you now!" she says, as she fumbles with his pants.

"Who are you and, hello?" he says, grinning as they both get them down as quickly as possible, getting in each other's way.

He barely has the zipper down when her hand reaches inside and wraps around him.

His knees slightly buckle, and he lets out a loud moan.

The magazine Debra picked up at the purple store has some great articles explaining step-by-step on how to please a man. They explained how much control a woman has over a man during oral sex. Her late husband George was not adventurous in the bedroom—he was, I guess you could say, standard. Debra was a homemaker, taking care of Tracey, dinner was hot on the table every night, the house was always immaculate; she played the Suzy Homemaker role to a tee. Now she wants more, and this man makes her want to learn. The article said by wrapping her fingers around a man's penis, he would become putty in her hand. She's finding out—it's true.

Brian puts both of his hands on the desk to steady himself as she works the one wrapped around him, back and forth.

Unsure at first, she looks for clues if she's doing it right. His moans, quick gasps, and closed eyes tell all and encourage her to take longer strokes, squeezing a little tighter.

His moans get louder and louder while his hips buck as her hand continues to stroke, twisting as it moves up and down. The experts in print also mentioned gently cupping his testicles, so she reaches down and gently does as instructed.

Brian's eyes go wide as the sensation instantly takes him over the edge. He quickly grabs a tissue from the box next to them, holding it over him.

She continues cupping, stroking, while gently twisting and turning, as he moans and pumps his hips, the tissue in place as he ejaculates with full force into it. His body shudders as he takes one last thrust, groaning loudly, then drops his head forward.

She watches in total amusement. *Yes, it feels good to be in control.*

He wipes the tip and slowly takes a few steps backward until he's sitting in the chair by the window. He locks eyes with her, taking deliberate deep breaths. "I'm not complaining, but where did that come from?"

"I thought I would give you a little surprise. I missed you today."

"Um, surprise, yes—you have succeeded. And you can do that anytime." Holding up one finger, he adds, "Allow me to clarify, anytime I don't have clients."

She jumps down off his desk and saunters over toward his chair, flipping the sides of her dress up as she takes each step.

"Seriously, who are you, and where is my woman?"

She suddenly gets worried; maybe it's too much. She's kind of digging this new sexual persona she's discovering, but she doesn't want to scare him. "Too much?"

"Hell no! Every man wishes his woman was a little slutty sometimes. I'm not saying you're a slut!"

She laughs. That's almost word-for-word what the article said. *Hmm, maybe he's been reading the same one.*

She gets on her knees and crawls up his thighs with her fingertips, watching as his manhood spring back to life, dancing and bouncing as each finger steps closer. She wraps her lips around it and takes as much of him as possible before her gag reflex kicks in.

Brian moans again, not expecting her to put him in her mouth. She hasn't done that yet. He's even more surprised by what she does next.

She quickly straddles him and slides herself down onto his now thoroughly lubricated erection.

Brian's eyes spring wide open—another surprise—she's commando. No bra and no panties!

She pulses, up and down. With her hands on his chest, she looks deeply into his eyes. "I love you, Brian Phelps. You make me feel safe and loved. I want to do these things for you—with you. I want to do so much more."

She was madly in love with George—this is different. Love, yes, but not the same. There are so many similarities. It's as if they've known each other their entire lives; yet it's not possible. If their meeting was fate, then George's death was inevitable. To get here, with him, she had to endure the agony and pain of losing George. Has it been worth it? Tears spring into her eyes as her heart gives her the painful answer.

It's not just sex; this the Webster's definition of making love. Two hearts, beating in sync and in tune. She feels a wave swell through her heart, then crashes through her body from her toes to her fingertips. Her body quivers uncontrollably. Tears spring from her eyes unexpectedly from the pure joy in her heart.

Still wrapped in his arms, she lets the tears flow—sheer happiness.

Brian feels a drop hit his shoulder. "Babe, did I hurt you? Are you okay?" he says, as he pushes her away to look into her eyes.

"I can't remember when I was this happy," she blubbers, as a wave of fresh tears spills out.

Brian pulls her close, hugging her tight.

After a few moments, he laughs while holding her tight.

"What's so funny?" she asks, leaning up and wiping her eyes.

"I don't want to spoil this tender moment—you went from June Cleaver to Playboy Bunny in like sixty seconds. I can't wait to see what you come up with next."

CHAPTER SEVEN

"It feels so good—so normal—to be out. I've missed you all so much."

"We've missed you too Amber. We can't imagine how you must feel, or how you're keeping it together," Debra says, as she reaches across the pub table and squeezes Amber's hand.

"It has been a nightmare."

"What's the next step?" Dominque asks.

"Patrick and I have to go before the judge for my sentencing. However, considering Brandy's confession, he's sure she'll dismiss the case. We have an appointment on the twenty-fifth to meet with her. If we're successful, most of this nightmare will be over."

"Most? What's left?"

"Patrick wants me to sue Brettinger's estate. And then there's the subject of Brandy."

"Are you hesitating on the lawsuit?" Zya asks as she motions to the waiter for another round of drinks.

"What do I gain by suing his estate? I don't want his money; it won't undo what he did. It will just make me relive that horrible day again. And I don't think I want to."

"Didn't Patrick say something about helping the other women? And, won't it help his secretary with child support for her son?"

"I know, no need to remind me. Those are the only reasons I'm even considering it. I want to help—I really do, but at what cost to me." Amber's mind dares to travel back to that day in January, testing the waters to see if she's strong enough to handle it. While her friends continue to talk around her, she sees their mouths move, but the images flashing inside her mind drown their voices. *She's on his couch, underneath him. He's so strong; the more she struggles, the further she slides underneath him. She can't move. She can't fight. His hand is over her mouth. She can't breathe. She can't get in any air.* She jumps in her seat, her body convulsing, willing herself to MOVE! Her heart is beating so fast; it feels like it's going to come right out of her chest. Her skin feels flushed as a thin layer of sweat forms over it.

"You okay?" Zya asks.

Amber looks around and realizes it was all in her head. It was so real—she was frozen, locked in place—it was all in her mind. "I'm good," she says, unclenching her fists and bringing her shaking drink to her lips, draining it as her fingertips regain feeling.

"What about Brandy? You don't have to do anything with her, do you?" Debra says, oblivious to the sweat pouring down Amber's back.

Amber takes a napkin, wipes her face and eyes, and fans herself. "Is it hot in here, or am I having a hot flash? Don't answer; I'm too young for that. Brandy, I don't trust her. She didn't confess to murder to save my ass, there's something else up her sleeve, and I'll be damned if I'm going to let her get away with it. If she thinks she's the only one that can play games, she's got another thing coming."

Zya twirls the stirrer around in her drink, listening intently as Amber's voice rises when she talks about her twin. "I wondered that myself. She's been too evil for too long to grow a conscience suddenly."

"People change," Debra says, forever naïve in the nicest—sweetest way. She's always looking for the good when there's none to find. "Maybe she realized she went too far this time. Isn't that possible?"

Amber sitting next to her, puts her arm around her, and pulls her close. After a kiss her on the forehead, she says, "I love your optimism, but not her; she has no morals. She's got more at play here, and I want to find out what it is."

"I hate to bring this up, could she be partnering with your stalker?" Dominque asks.

Debra jumps in before Amber can respond and says, "Have you had any more texts since she went to prison?"

"She may be my stalker; none since she went to jail."

"How could she text you when she was confessing?" Zya asks, as one of her eyebrows arches in suspicion.

"The timestamp is pretty much the same as when the jury was giving my verdict. She may have had it ready to go and sent it before she stood up."

"Did they find her phone? Was the text on it?" Dominque asks, leaning in.

"They didn't find one. Patrick checked the lost and found to see if she intentionally left it behind. There were over forty phones there, all locked. He'd need a warrant to break into them, and he'd have to know which one was hers. He asked Stewart what kind she had, but he doesn't remember. Plus, if she was the stalker, she used burner phones; it would have been a throwaway. It still would have been a dead end."

"If the texts have stopped, then it looks like she was it. I don't need more proof," Zya says right before she drains drink number two.

"Whoa, lady. You're sucking those down pretty quickly. What's up?" Amber asks when she hears the ice cubes rattle against the empty glass.

While motioning the waiter back over, Zya says, "That bastard Doug is moving forward with the petition for full custody."

When the waiter comes back, she points around the table to see if anyone else wants one.

Everyone shakes their heads with full glasses in front of them.

"I'll take another—and a glass of water, please."

"What does Ashanti think about this?" Amber asks, glad to have the conversation steered away from her.

"I haven't told her yet."

"WHAT?" Dominque asks, causing the patrons at the other tables to turn and look.

The tequila bar, a Las Olas hot spot, is hopping. The high-gloss shine on the bar top is barely visible because of the clutter of wine glasses, beer mugs, margarita glasses, and pitchers. Most of the pub tables are full. The room is so loud; it's impressive they can hear each other.

"I know she's going to feel responsible for this mess. If she hadn't blurted out on Helen, Tina and I were more than just friends, I wouldn't be here right now. I don't want to hurt her."

"Her father wants to take her away from you, and you're trying to protect her when you have an opportunity to teach her a very valuable lesson?" Dominque asks, but it's more of a statement.

Zya turns to Dominque with daggers in her eyes.

Dominque puts her hand up and says, "Before you say anything, I don't mean any disrespect. Ashanti shouldn't be ashamed of what she said—you and Tina love each other. She wasn't embarrassed when she said it, and she shouldn't be now either. Loving a woman isn't a sin, and I don't care who thinks it is. Love is love. It doesn't know gender, skin color, or religion. If Doug wants to play hardball, you get a bigger bat. I bet you, Ashanti will be right there behind you, catching for you. Give her a chance—I think she'll surprise you."

Zya's shoulders slump as she looks down into the glass of water that's magically appeared. She picks it up, then gently sets it back down. She spins it around in the condensation puddle that's quickly formed beneath it. "I wish I could keep her young and innocent forever. That's the hardest part of having children—they grow up. You're right; I don't want either of us to be ashamed. I'll tell her tonight," she says, grabbing her drink from the waiter's hand as he's putting it down. She drinks half of it before she releases it from her fingers.

"How 'bout you tell her tomorrow? Tonight, let's get everything off our chest. So much has happened these last months, and as much as we promised we'd always be there for each other, life has a way of taking over. Let's get it all out in the open," Amber says, sliding the drink away from Zya's hand.

Debra turns to Amber and says, "Getting back to Brandy, how are you going to find out what she's up to? And if she's your stalker?"

Amber takes a deep breath. When she said get everything out in the open, she meant all of them—she needs to focus on other people's problems instead of hers. "I'm going to play along and be thankful she saved me. We may not have spent a lot of time together these last few years, but she hasn't changed; I know her tells. I'm going in with my eyes wide open."

Dominque covers Amber's hand with hers and says, "I'm so glad those texts have stopped; it must be a relief. I have to ask you though, why haven't you responded to any of my texts?"

Debra and Zya both respond as well in unison, "Yeah, mine too?"

"I'm sorry, I had a lot of anger and took it out on the phone, so I threw it against the wall. Patrick just got me a new one. I got all your messages today. I figured I'd see you, so I didn't need to respond. But there are no messages from him, or her, either."

"I think I just peed my pants a little with excitement knowing that part is over," Dominque says as she runs toward the far wall and the door that reads, *'Damas.'*

"OMG!" Amber says, laughing so loud the table next to them looks over. "I haven't laughed like that in a while. Phew, that felt good."

Amber, looking at Debra, says, "How's Brian?"

"He's amazing. I can't believe how lucky I am. Tracey and Little George just adore him. We've kind of grown into this nice little happy family."

"You deserve to be happy. Talk about someone who's been through some shit. That smile on your face says it all," Amber says, squeezing Debra's hand.

"How's the sex?" Zya blurts out.

Debra's cheeks immediately flush bright pink. She picks up her drink and takes a long sip. "It's great. He's great. He's replaced my washing machine."

Zya and Amber erupt into hysterical laughter again, hands flying to their faces trying to muffle the screams, knowing full well, all eyes are once again upon them.

Dominque comes around a group of people and rushes back to the table, seeing the hysterics. "What'd I miss?"

"Brian has replaced the washing machine," Zya says, in a hushed voice, between bursts of laughter.

Debra's cheeks burn brighter as Dominque looks over at her confused.

"Brian is doing your laundry? What's so funny about that?"

"No, silly, remember the spin cycle? The bumping and knocking her machine does," Zya says, thrusting her hips while sitting in her chair.

Dominque's eyes go wide. "Oh? Oh. Oh! Do tell."

"I don't kiss and tell. Let's just say he's done things to me I couldn't even begin to dream up. But then again, maybe I've done some things to him." Debra's cheeks flush bright red, causing her to hide behind her hands.

"Honey, you've lived the life of Suzy Homemaker, how wild can you get? You been watching porn?" Dominque says playfully.

Amber smacks her on the arm. "Be nice Dom."

"The big question is, have you experienced the big O?" she asks, forming the letter with her lips.

"You mean, O. O. O?" Debra answers, her cheeks still glowing.

"Multiples! I'm so proud of you. I might get you that sex swing after all," Dominque says, winking at her.

Most of the surrounding noise suddenly dies down. The words *sex swing* are loud and exciting enough to halt all other conversations. Eyes from at least two rows over, in all directions, are on them.

Debra's cheeks burn even brighter. She drops her head and lowers her voice as she says, "He has this thing he does with his tongue."

The girls lean in close.

Debra giggles and keeps her eyes cast down in her lap. "It comes out to a point at the end."

Dominque and Zya immediately stick out their tongues, mimicking what Debra's describing.

Debra glances up and laughs. "No, not like that, Dom—and not even close Zya."

"Damn, I was hoping," Zya says, still trying to get her tongue to come to a point, but the sides keep curling up.

They all look over at her, stunned.

"What! Don't look at me like that. I gotta keep a girl happy. I'm just learning all this shit."

Dominque reaches across the table for Debra's hand. "Go on, what does he do with his unusually shaped muscular organ?"

"You make it sound so dirty, Dom," Debra says.

"You're about to tell us how he uses it to pleasure you— who sounds kinky?"

"Now shush and let her tell us," Zya says to Dom, eager to get the details.

"You guys crack me up. Okay, he flicks the tip super fast." Debra flicks her hand back and forth quickly, trying to mimic the motion.

"Like this," Dominque says, showing her almost pointy tongue. "I can't make it go fast though."

"Looks like you're trying to have a bowel movement," Zya adds.

Amber busts out laughing so hard, her eyes tear up.

They all stop what they're doing and stare at her.

"OMG, you'll are hysterical. I have missed this so much. Thank you! Thank you!"

"What are you thanking us for? She hasn't told us what he does yet!" Dominque squeals.

They all laugh and clasp hands across the table. It feels good to have her friends together. No judgments, just pure love, understanding, and friendship.

"Okay, can we get back to the tongue now?" Zya asks.

They all sit forward, leaning toward Debra.

"So obviously, he can only flick it fast for so long before it gets tired."

Amber tries to hide her giggling.

Debra looks up at her and smiles. "He's been working on it. It is, as you said Dom, a muscular organ, so he's been building it up," Debra says, herself now plagued with the giggles.

"And I'm assuming you've been the willing participant?" Amber asks between chuckles.

Debra pauses, looks around the room, then back down at her hands before answering. "Sometimes, even when I'm in the kitchen making dinner, and Tracey is in her room playing while Little George naps."

They all fall back in their chair, holding their abdomens, squealing. The other patrons have become used to their antics now and just smile at them.

Amber looks over and mouths 'sorry' to the table next to them.

"No, we're not. This is some good shit here," Zya says to them.

"It's a game. Every chance we have a minute or two, we hide, and he—works out."

They are dying. Zya is stomping her feet and covering her mouth, trying not to disrupt the other patrons. The bar and restaurant are now at full capacity, and the noise level at its highest. But they are still at the highest-pitched, loudest table in the bar.

"Who are you, and what have you done with Mrs. Cleaver?" Dominque asks.

Debra's cheeks flush deeper red as she says, "I might, from time to time, disrupt his paperwork when he brings it to my house. He's been doing that a lot lately."

"Do you get under the table and give him a blow job while he's trying to concentrate?" Dominque asks, her eyes flashing.

Debra's eyes dart from side to side while her hands still fumble in her lap. "Maybe."

Dominque's mouth opens wide with shock. "You've given him a blow job! I'm so proud of you!"

"Shh, don't need to tell the entire world."

Dominque jumps over and hugs her tight. "Okay, details, please," she says as she bows and backs away.

She tells them about the magazine article and how she surprised him at his office. She drank two shots of tequila in her car before she got out to work up the courage. "Now when he's working, I'll either crawl under the table when he's deep in thought or I just sit on his lap, in a dress, with no panties on. I like going commando—easy access."

Amber jumps in, her eyes open wide with excitement. "What? I can't believe it. You might be having more sex than me."

"I doubt that," Dominque says. But then she whips her head around and looks at Debra with an invisible question mark on her forehead.

"Every day, sometimes twice—or three times."

"Okay, I'm getting depressed now. Deb, I'm thrilled for you. I remember just before George passed, you were trying to be more adventurous, and now look at you. I'm impressed, proud, jealous, damn girl—I may have to call you for some pointers," Zya says.

"You won't need tips from me. Tina doesn't have the same equipment for me to give you any guidance."

All three heads snap at once in Debra's direction.

Amber looks at Debra and says, "What are you talking about?"

"This article, there are some great pointers on how to give a blow job."

"Oh, please share," Dominque says.

"Well, first I had to find something to practice on, a banana or something similar."

Amber still has the giggles.

Dominque hits her leg under the table, engrossed in what Debra has to say.

"There are a few ground rules. No teeth, not even gently, and no bending."

A brief silence at the table as each woman who's broken either of those rules is silently cringing inside.

"What did you pick, a banana?"

"No, Hebrew National hot dogs."

"Brian's not Jewish. And even if he was, it wouldn't matter," Zya says.

Dominque adds, "He's not circumcised? I'm lost."

Debra's cheeks instantly flush. "No, their jumbo hot dogs are about the right size," she says, positioning her hands about six inches apart in front of her.

Their table erupts in hysterics again.

Amber holds her abdomen as she wipes tears away. "I think I may have to stop at the 24-hour supermarket on the way home and pick up a pack." The last few words come out with a burst of laughter as her body folds upon itself from laughing so hard.

"I'm never going to look at a hot dog the same way again," Zya says, as she tries to control her hysterics.

All four of them are uncontrollably cackling, snorting, and chortling.

As the hysterics tone down, the waiter brings the food over. Zya orders another round of drinks. This time, they're ready.

Amber looks over at her as she picks it up, promising to take an Uber home.

"I haven't laughed in a long time. I'm proud of you, girl," Amber says as she picks up her slow-roasted pork tacos.

Debra nods. Perfect timing, she's just taken a bite of her deep-fried, smothered in cheese, Chimichanga. No diet when she's out with the girls.

"Dom, you look great. I know cancer patients hate it when people say that, but you really do," Amber says.

"It's okay; I think it's when we're in the middle of treatments, with gray skin and bald heads, we don't want to hear it. I feel terrific. I went for my three-month checkup a few weeks ago, and everything is great. Slightly anemic, but what's new."

"When do you see him again?" Debra asks.

"Every three months for the first two years, then I graduate to every six. At some point, it will be once a year."

"You and Tad settled into married life well?"

"That man is a dream. I'm just sorry I wasted my life chasing what's hanging between men's legs, and not more time getting to know what's inside. I've lost so much time I could have had with him."

"Let's be thankful you found him. Many never do," Amber states.

"You're right. I've decided. I haven't even told Tad yet. He has an idea because we talked about it at the doctor's office. Or rather, I asked."

The other three lean in closer, not wanting to miss a word.

"We're going to start trying for a baby next May; one year from my surgery date."

"That's so exciting," Debra says as her lower lids fill.

"Isn't that too soon?" Zya asks.

Dominque fills them in on her conversation with her doctor. "I've done some research on my own. If I wait two years and have my first child at thirty-nine, I have more of an increased risk of gestational diabetes, preeclampsia, and other complications. Let's face it; with my history, those are a real possibility. If I have a recurrence during the first three months, I'll end the pregnancy; chemo for the baby in the second and third trimester is okay."

Amber reaches across and takes Dominque's hands in hers. "Can I ask the hard question?"

Dominque nods as her eyes turn glassy.

"What's the survival rate for Stage II, triple-negative breast cancer?"

The teardrops fall as she lowers her gaze. "Sixty percent in the first five years," she says, not able to meet any of their eyes.

Zya reminds her, "Your doctor told you when they diagnosed you, if your cancer comes back, it will most likely happen within the first two years, right?"

Dominque nods, looking down in her lap as the tears steadily drip in a constant stream.

The table is quiet for a moment, then Dominque looks up, wiping her eyes. "So I don't want to wait two years. What if I don't survive past five? I want to leave a piece of me behind— a baby—our legacy. I've thought a lot about this, so please don't try to talk me out of it. I've weighed all the options carefully, and this is what I want to do."

"Will you really be able to end if you have a recurrence during your first trimester?" Zya asks.

"Yes. Well, I plan to. I think I can."

"And if Tad doesn't agree?" Amber asks.

"He will. He may not like it, but he will."

"You know we'll support you, no matter what you decide Dom; regardless of what the future holds, we've got your back," Amber says, feeling better now the focus is off her. She not comfortable being the one to need; always she prefers to be needed.

CHAPTER EIGHT

"Wakey—wakey!"

"What are you doing here?" Patrick asks, after being awoken from a deep sleep.

"I decided not to go home after all. I thought I'd come visit you—and you," Amber says as her hand travels from his chest down between his legs, causing him to jump.

"Humph! Boy, aren't we a little frisky at…"—Patrick looks at the clock beside the bed—"1:30 in the morning."

"I had such a great time seeing the girls, and I didn't want the night to end. So, here I am!"

Turning over and bringing her hand up to his mouth and gently kissing it, he says, "I can see you had a good time. Are we a little drunk?"

"Maybe just a little," she says, bringing her fingers together, squinting her eyes.

"I can't believe I'm about to say this, but don't you think we should wait until you're feeling more, um, like yourself?"

"No, we haven't made love in weeks—I know it's all my fault. I don't want to wait anymore. It's time," she says, slurring her words.

"Okay. Let me go to the restroom first before I get any more excited," he says, looking down at his growing erection. "I'm going to have to stand on my head already as it is."

She giggles as he kisses her on the forehead and rushes to the bathroom.

He stands over the toilet cursing those three beers he had with Stewart before he crashed. It's like they've multiplied into six as they've passed through his kidneys.

He hasn't pressed Amber, although they've shared the same bed every night for the past two weeks. Amber refused to succumb to fear and allow anyone to have power over her. After her attack, she would not play the victim. Her stalker couldn't bring her to her knees, either. But somehow, her sister did. They haven't talked about it; he's just glad to have her close. Tonight she was going to sleep at her place; he's glad she decided against it—even if she is tipsy. When she's ready, she'll let him know. He didn't think she would need alcohol as a stimulant—he's not complaining.

Finally, finished, he doesn't bother pulling up his trunks. He yanks them off, throwing them behind as he runs to the sink, washing his hands quickly.

He cracks open the door and sticks out his erection, making it bounce. He says in a squeaky voice, "I'm ready for you, my little flower. Are you ready to play?"

Not sure what response he expected—silence was not one of them. He peeks into the bedroom and finds Amber sound asleep in precisely the same position he left her. Snoring loudly, with a big grin on her face.

Chuckling, he turns back to find his trunks and heads back to bed. He gets her shoes off and pulls the covers over her.

Still asleep, she cuddles up next to him on his pillow and says, "I love you so much. I don't know what I would do without you."

"Good morning, Miss Fiore." John, the building security manager greets her when she arrives at 8:45 a.m. that same morning.

She winces, although his voice is relatively soft.

"Morning, John," she mutters, shuffling a coffee, her phone, and her keys between her hands.

Lowering his voice, he says, "A package arrived for you yesterday. I haven't taken it upstairs. Let me get it."

Amber stops and turns around, walking toward his desk, balancing the coffee on top of her phone. "I'm not expecting anything. I'm sure it's not important; it can wait until later."

"It's no trouble, I have it right here," he says as he reaches across his desk to grab it. He turns just as Amber is walking toward him, causing them to collide.

Her coffee goes flying as her phone drops to the ground, and his heel steps on it, all in perfect synchronization, as in a well-rehearsed ballet.

Amber cringes at the crunch sound.

"Oh, Miss Fiore, I'm so sorry," he says as he picks it up. A large light brown stain slowly spreads across the front of him and matching drips trail down the side of his desk. "I'm such a klutz; please let me replace this for you."

"It's not your fault John; it was an accident. And see, it still powers up," she says, showing him it works. She just has to look around at the six cracks running through the screen.

John hangs his head. "Please let me pay to have it fixed—please."

"Nonsense, really. I have a friend at the mall who will take care of it. It only costs me a dozen bear claws. It's no problem;

69

I need to go there today, anyway." She kisses him on the cheek. "It's okay, really. No harm."

She picks up the package. "Sorry about the coffee."

"Really?" he says, with his hands on his hips.

An hour later, she heads downstairs for her shopping excursion.

John stops her on the way and hands her a box. "I hope he likes the glazed ones."

❧

"Thanks for staying with the kids, that was really sweet of you."

"You have fun?" He says, with a sly grin on his face, knowing full well she did, from the non-stop giggling.

"I had a great time. We laughed so much. I think Amber did too. It's been so long since we'd spent time together catching up. There's been so much drama. I hate to jinx it—I think things might settle down."

"You're right, don't say it!" Brian says, kissing her.

"Watching the kids *and* sleeping in…you know, a girl could get used to this."

"I was hoping you might say that," he says with his head tilted and his eyebrows lifted.

Debra's heart pounds, knowing a segue when she hears one. Brian is everything she could ever hope for. No one can ever replace George. He's not trying to. He's different—in a good way. She loves him so much, but is she ready? George left her just fifteen months ago. What will people think?

She looks up, seeing his wrinkled brow. "Brian, I love you so much. More than I could have thought after such a short time. I know it shouldn't matter, it just seems like it's too soon after George's passing. It's an ongoing battle in my mind and my heart. I don't want to lose you, can we just keep things the way they are for now, please?"

Brian picks up her hand and kisses it. "Yes, we can. And I understand. Part of me doesn't, because who cares what anyone else thinks except who's right here in this house. I know you do, I get it, society says it's too soon. I know what we feel in our hearts. I think George would approve."

Debra chuckles, knowing he's right.

"I'm not going anywhere. However, I have been here almost every night since Dom and Tad's wedding. Tracey is calling me Uncle Brian, and I'm sleeping with her mommy. I'm okay with it, but it's a little strange," he says, chuckling. "I think I need to spend a few nights at home until we're ready to take the next step."

Debra swallows as a knot forms in the pit of her stomach at the thought of him going back to his place. Debra nods as she looks into her coffee cup for answers. After a long awkward silence, she asks, "What does the next step look like to you?"

Brian pulls out a red ring box with a gold etched design on it and places it in front of her.

Chapter Nine

"Thanks for meeting me," Zya says, trying desperately to sound genuine and not allow venom to seep into her words.

"No problem, I was in town taking care of business, anyway. Are you ready to talk about dumping your blond whore and accepting my proposal?" he says, leaning back in the chair.

Zya takes a long draw on her glass of wine to stop herself from lashing out at him. She has to get the words out calmly. Cassie, her attorney, begged her to do this in a certified letter, but Zya insisted. Doug was the father of her daughter and deserved to have this conversation face to face. Plus, she wanted to watch him squirm.

"I'm assuming your business must be with the Cuban drug cartel here in Miami. Your boss know you're dealing with them?"

Doug sits up in his seat and leans in real close. "What I do with my time is none of your business. And if I were you, I'd be very cautious about what I accuse people of. You might just say the wrong thing to the wrong people and get yourself in a whole heap of trouble. You could get yourself in so deep, even I can't help you out."

Zya leans in even closer, invading his personal space, causing him to lean slightly back. Her heart is pounding as a layer of sweat appears on the back of her neck. There's no turning back now. "Humph, funny, that's not how I see it. It's not an accusation; I have actual proof." She stares him down, not blinking or looking away until he sits all the back in his chair.

He looks long and hard at her with a fake smile showing his bright white teeth. He glances down and nervously chuckles, then adjusts his tie as the joke becomes less funny. He takes a swing of his drink, and staring down into the chunks of ice, he says, "I forgot just how funny you are. That was good; I almost believed you there for a second. If you're trying to frighten me into dropping the case, you know I don't get scared..."—with his other hand, he suddenly reaches out and grabs her wrist, squeezing hard—"I get even."

The pain shoots up through her arm, but she refuses to give him the satisfaction of knowing how much it hurts. Keeping a relaxed expression, she blows a puff of air at his hand then locks eyes with him. Her smug grin is hiding the screaming inside her head.

He finally releases her. He sits back, never breaking eye contact, and makes a church steeple with his fingertips.

She wants to rub her wrist so badly, but she doesn't dare. She wills it not to give out as she uses that hand to pick up her wineglass and slowly take a drink, knowing his eyes are still locked on her with contempt. Not only does her wrist hold firm, it's also steady. While his eyes appear to be looking for the slightest sign of weakness, she's proving he may need Kryptonite to find some.

"Doug, you've unknowingly taught me many things over the years; to always protect yourself and those you love. You won't be getting full custody of Ashanti, and you will drop the petition; this isn't a threat—it's a promise."

She places a flash drive on the table in front of him. "You'll find a nice vacation memory there. Six years ago, when Ashanti and I came to New York to visit you in Manhattan, remember?"

Doug doesn't respond. The smug grin vanishes, replaced with clenched teeth, his eyes slicing through her.

"You stepped away on business while we were admiring the Cohan statue in Times Square. Ashanti was playing around, trying to pose like him while her momma was filming her. I didn't notice you in the background until I got home. Actually, no, it wasn't just you," she says, wagging her finger at him. "That urgent business you needed to take care of was there too. I could be mistaken, but they looked very Cuban to me, especially wearing their guayabera shirts." The nervousness and pain a thing of the past. The more she thinks about her daughter, the angrier the fire rages. Her eyes never drop from his. She leans further toward him, the more daggers he attempts to throw from his. The tougher he tries to be, the stronger she proves she is. "I thought you did business with Nicky? Now you're here in South Florida—coincidence? Maybe. I wonder what Nicky would think about these pictures and your trips here. Do you tell him it's to see Ashanti?"

Doug sits upright and reaches for her wrist again.

Zya pulls it back just in time. "Touch me again, motherfucker, and you'll get my stiletto up your ass."

Doug drags his hand back as a pompous grin reappears. "You don't know who you're playing with. You're in the big leagues now. You're going to get yourself killed; you know that?"

"Oh, you won't touch me or my fiancé, Tina—the one you called a whore. This is a copy. The original is safe in the bank. I've sent instructions to my lawyer, and a few key people in my life have copies with instructions. If you hurt so much as one tiny hair on either of us, or any of our friends, a copy of this drive will be sent to the cops. And because there's a chance your Cuban contacts may have connections with the local police department, the Miami Herald and the New York Times will also get copies. It won't be our lives at stake—it will be yours. If Nicky ever finds out you're doing business with the Cubans, he'll slit your throat. Do I have your attention now?"

☯

Tina rushes outside when she hears Zya's car pull up. "How did it go? You okay?" Tina hugs her tight, not waiting for an answer.

Once she got in her car, everything she had bottled up came flooding out. Her body shuttered in convulsions as the tears ravaged her the entire drive home. Tina has been against this play, but Zya knows this is the only way to get Doug out of their life—for good. He takes what he wants. He's not taking Ashanti—no way in hell!

As Zya closes her car door, she forgets about the injury until it's too late. "Ow!" she screams.

"What's wrong with your hand?"

"My wrist, not my hand. Doug's trying to play big-man."

"He hurt you?" Tina asks her face changes from concern to protective momma cat. "That creep. First, he grabs my crotch because he thinks what's yours is his, and now he intentionally hurts you. Think Amber will let me borrow her gun? Never mind, you were going to get one anyway, weren't you?"

"Honey, it's okay. I didn't expect him to take this quietly. I met him somewhere public, so he couldn't make too much of a scene. I didn't realize he was that strong. I thought he was going to crush my bones."

"How did he take it?"

"Not well—he doesn't have a choice. The fact he's here again is more proof. I don't know how often he comes to Miami, but I bet it's more than Nicky's aware of. He'll save his own skin. I expect Cassie will call us soon to tell us the petition's being pulled."

Tina goes to the freezer and puts ice in a zip-lock bag. "Here, put this on your wrist. Of course, he'd tried to hurt you so you couldn't work. Is this going to affect your schedule?"

"I think it's just bruised; the ice will help, thanks. I'm way ahead of schedule, and Stan will help. That man is a godsend. I'll be okay. Come here."

Tina sits in the chair next to her. Zya pulls her close with her left hand and kisses her on the lips. She pulls back, keeping their foreheads touching. "I'm so damn lucky to have you. Every day you surprise me. Thank you for not giving up and giving me the time I needed to accept your love."

Tina pulls Zya's head up with her hands, cradling her face. "You never have to thank me. I can't imagine my life without you. I knew you would come around, eventually. You were worth the wait." Tina kisses Zya sweetly on the lips. Quickly, gentleness becomes pure heat.

"Where are the kids?"

"Babysitting for Debra and Brian."

That's all the encouragement Zya needs. She pulls Tina over to her lap, being careful with her hurt wrist.

Tina curls up, wrapping her legs over the chair and her arms around Zya's shoulders. "What do you have in mind?" Tina asks, her nipples stiffening in anticipation.

Zya notices and reaches out and lightly pinches one, making Tina squirm.

"Wow, no romance, just going for the gusto?"

"You want me to?" Zya moves between Tina's legs and cups her over her jean shorts, causing Tina to throw back her head and let out a low moan.

Zya loves to watch Tina when they make love. Doug, Zya's only other lover, always made the ugliest faces when they were together, especially when he orgasmed. His face screwed up tight as if he was taking a bowel movement; she couldn't watch. Tina, on the other hand, always has the sweetest smile, and her eyes are so dreamy when she orgasms. The moment they hold Zya's, they are full of love and hope; she can see her soul through them.

Tina spreads her legs wide as Zya works her palm into the seam which by now has worked its way further down, causing friction against her more sensitive spots.

Making love to Tina has come naturally to Zya. Pleasing her, loving her, is something she never has to think about. Her finger slips inside the leg of her shorts. As soon as her fingertip touches her skin, Tina jumps in anticipation of where she's heading.

"Kiss me," Zya says.

The moment their lips touch, Zya's finger finds its way under the edge of her panties and teases just inside.

Tina lets out a muffled moan as Zya's tongue dances inside her mouth. She squirms, moving her hips just enough to nudge Zya's fingers further in—enough teasing.

Zya knows what she's trying to do, so she does the opposite, playfully running her fingers in the opposite direction causing Tina to moan louder, only this time in frustration.

"Get on the table," Zya instructs.

Tina opens her eyes slightly, her head still in a fog. "What? You want me to get on the table? We eat there."

"That's exactly what I plan to do."

Tina's eyes open wide as Zya's words create a shock wave through her body. She jumps off Zya's lap. With her head tilted down slightly, lustfully gazing into Zya's eyes, she slowly lowers her shorts to the floor, never breaking eye contact. Intentionally, her drenched lace panties stay in place.

She takes her time getting up on the table, one cheek at a time, licking her lips. She's as good a player as Zya. Facing her, she extends one leg straight up in the air, her hands starting at her ankle, moves down to her knee as she bends it and places her foot on the arm of the chair. She slowly does a repeat performance on the other leg.

Zya puts her hands behind Tina's hips and yanks her to the edge of the table, causing Tina's eyes to go wide and her hands to drop behind her to stop from falling backward. "Lie back, that's exactly how I want you."

Zya pushes Tina's legs wide apart and buries her face between them. The heat from those words escaping into the fabric causes Tina to comply, sliding back; her hands bury themselves in her hair as Zya expertly nibbles away, soaking the material further.

Tina's head thrashes back and forth as her moans grow in intensity. The slow burn becomes a quick sear when Zya pulls the fabric aside. Her tongue dives between Tina's engorged lips, searching out her swollen clit simultaneously as her finger inches inside her. The sudden, expert sensations cause her hips to thrust and buck violently, as she screams for the Almighty.

Both feet on the arms of Zya's chair hold her weight as she thrusts her hips high into the air.

Zya hangs on, her lips locked in place while her finger continues to thrust and twist as Tina yells out one last time, much louder than usual. Zya places feathery kisses as the bucking ebbs, and the roller coaster car clicks to a stop.

There has been so much stress and tension working up to today's meeting with Doug, more than either cared to acknowledge. The release was long overdue.

Zya stands up, licking her lips. "Mmm, did someone have chocolate ice cream today?"

Tina looks up and says, "I did, but now that you mention it, I forgot the syrup. I've already had my dairy quota…can you think of anything I can lick the hot fudge off of?"

If pleasuring Tina is an aphrodisiac for Zya, dirty talk is oral sex.

"I think I do—and no extra calories. Let's go." Zya reaches out for Tina's hand.

"Can my little pink friend come along? You know, the one with the rabbit ears."

Chapter Ten

Amber sits quietly at the table while Patrick works his magic in the kitchen. The bacon is sizzling in the skillet when hot, light brown bread pops up in the toaster. He flips the eggs over medium, to keep the yolks runny, just the way she likes them. The mixture of delicious aromas fills the kitchen, but Amber doesn't notice. Her mind replays the dream—nightmare—that woke her at 3 a.m. It terrified her so much she never fell back asleep.

Patrick puts her plate in front of her and refills her mug with strong Colombian coffee.

The steam swirls up in front of her face, yet her eyes never waver; they're locked on an imaginary spot in the backyard.

Patrick waves his hand in front of her eyes. "Hello there, earth to Amber. You in there?"

After a moment, she sees it and jumps back, startled. "Sorry, my mind was somewhere else."

"Really? I couldn't tell. Want to share?"

She takes a deep breath. Her hands grip her mug as her eyes drown in the caramel-colored liquid. "I had this awful dream last night, and I'm trying to make sense of it."

"What was it about?"

"Brettinger…and the day he raped me."

Patrick immediately drops his fork and puts his arm around her shoulders. "I'm so sorry, babe."

"It's just so weird. I'm not dreaming about the rape; it's about killing him."

"What?"

"It's just bits and pieces, not everything. I've got the ice pick in my hand, and I'm stabbing him repeatedly."

"It's probably your mind trying to get revenge. Now that you know Brandy did it, maybe you're seeing it through her eyes."

"Here's the bizarre part—I'm enjoying it. It's like I can't kill him enough!"

"He deserved it!"

"Maybe, who are we to be judge, jury, and executioner? Don't get me wrong, it's horrible what he did to me, and these other girls, but I shouldn't want to mangle him like that."

"You're working through your emotions; shouldn't anger be part of them? You've been seeing a therapist, and working through all this shit might help you get it all out in the open. It hasn't been that long—give yourself a break."

Amber nods, thinking maybe he's right, but she can't shake how much pleasure she took each time she sank the pick into his flesh. The dream felt so real, she could feel the resistance as the ice pick hit tissue, and the heat as his blood oozed around her hand. And not just the temperature; she could feel how thick his blood was as it ran through her fingers. Her body shivers as she relives the sensation.

"By the way, have you thought more about the lawsuit? You'd be helping a lot of other women, especially Maryann and her son."

"I have, and honestly, I still don't know."

"Maybe it's time to go back and see the hypnotist. She did offer to help you get through the attack sequence. Maybe it will help with your dream too."

"Yeah, you're probably right. I'll call and make an appointment." As Amber thinks more about the last time she sat with the hypnotist, she thinks now might be the perfect time to see her.

"Now, eat your breakfast before it gets…colder."

She laughs and pushes the corner of her toast into her egg to break the yolk as her phone dings. She picks it up, expecting it to be one of the girls.

How sweet, your man made you a yummy breakfast. Make sure you eat it all up now; you're going to need your strength. And keep that white tee handy. I think your blood will look lovely stained all over it.

Amber throws the phone across the room as her hands go up to her hair, grabbing at it—almost pulling it out. She leans way back in her chair with her mouth wide open. Her wide eyes dart between the phone and outside. *How does he know what I'm wearing?*

Patrick runs over and picks up her phone and reads the text. "Shit! I thought he was gone."

Amber pushes away from the table, running away with Patrick in hot pursuit.

"This doesn't make sense. You haven't heard from him in almost three weeks. Why suddenly now—and how?"

"I don't know. And how can he see me?" She says, her words stuttering in between brief gasps of air. She grabs the robe that's lying across the bed, wrapping it tightly around her to help ward off the feeling of being violated.

Patrick wraps her in his arms and pulls her onto his lap. "Let's think this through. My yard is secure—you know that. There's no way he's here. Between the gate, the cameras and alarms, it's like Fort Knox here, so you're safe, okay?"

Amber pulls away, confused. "Then how does he know what I'm wearing?"

Patrick's eyes go wide. "Of course! He has to be hacking in somehow? The TV? Our computers? Our phones? They all have cameras and microphones. Somehow, he's tapping in, seeing and hearing you—us. If he's got access, he knows where you are all the time. That would make sense, why he knows things so quickly."

"So what do we do? Turn everything off?"

"I think we have to do more than that. If he's put spyware anywhere in my home, I'll bring in someone today to sweep it. They'll need access to your condo too."

"John can let them in."

"Can we trust him? Because he rubs me the wrong way."

"That's just because you're a guy. I think he kind of has a little crush on me. We can trust him."

Shivers run down her spine again. *How much has he seen—or heard?*

"We'll get him babe—don't you worry. This has to be how he's getting his information."

"It's not that. I'm just picturing everywhere we've made love with phones, TVs, and computers, right there." She runs to the bathroom and fills the toilet with the coffee she drank.

"My, my, I wasn't sure you'd ever come by and thank me. I mean, it's been what, three weeks already."

Amber takes a deep breath to steady the anger and hurt within. She has to play the game.

"I'm sorry—no excuse. Although I have been pissed, you let me go through that awful trial until you confessed."

"We've never been buddy-buddy, so I'd say it would be the least you would expect from me."

"You're right. I'm actually surprised you confessed at all."

Brandy's face softens, but only for a split second before it hardens again. "I kinda rather like it here in the slammer. Meals cooked for me, a great exercise facility, and all the pussy I can eat, 24-7."

Amber flinches at the last part. She's trying not to let Brandy get under her skin, yet she knows exactly what buttons to push.

"What about Stewart? I think he genuinely cares about you."

For the second time in the last sixty seconds, Amber notices a break in Brandy's armor. As quickly as it cracks, it seals again.

"He was great fun. I think he learned a thing or two from me. Hey, if things don't work out between you and Legal Eagle, you should take a ride on old Stew—you'll never go back to boring Mr. Ethics. He's quite the stud, you know. What a cock on that guy—phew!" Brandy closes her eyes and leans back in her chair. After licking her lips, she slides her hand down between her legs. With her eyes still closed, she continues. "I was at an advantage though, when we had our phone fun. I knew exactly how hot he was when we were getting each other's rocks off."

Amber's eyebrows shoot up, not understanding how that would be possible.

Brandy cackles as she sits back up. "When I was grinding my crotch all over your handsome's hard dick. Remember, when I was his birthday stripper?"

Amber's fingers clutch the arms on the wooden chair so hard; she bends back the tiny bits of her fingernails that have just grown back, almost flipping them backward.

"I couldn't help myself. When I had my tits in Patrick's face, I glanced over at hottie and found him rubbing himself through his pants. You know how tight he wears them—nothing to the imagination. That's the moment I knew one day I would see that cock up close and personal." Brandy licks her lips again.

Amber is not sure what Brandy means by this; she has not been privy to her statement, yet. What she knows is she has to keep playing the game. Somehow, she has to get Brandy to let her guard down enough to slip up. "Well, he keeps asking Patrick about you. Would that be okay if he and Patrick came to see you?"

Brandy's face hardens as she sits up straight. "No, I don't want to see him—or Patrick either. I don't need an attorney. And certainly not one that sucks. Boy, you two have thick skulls. I don't want him, got it?"

Amber nods.

"And as for hottie, I'm not into cocks. It was all an act. I'm into hot and juicy pussies. I can take my pick here, even from some guards. You know I've got a reputation to uphold—my tongue is legendary; I can make you cum in under sixty seconds. Too bad you weren't nicer to me; we could have had some great fun. Just think, identical twins, lesbians, sixty-nine, eating each other out. We could have made a mint with a video like that. What would we have named it?" Brandy puts her head on her hand, drumming her fingers along her cheek, staring at the ceiling.

"Hey, I've got to run. I've got an interview I have to do. It's been great seeing you, Brandy. I'd like to come by next week if that's okay," Amber says, gathering up her purse without meeting Brandy's eyes. Brandy crossed the line; she can't allow her to continue, or she's sure she would have lost it—precisely what Brandy wants. This time, Amber is going to set the rules, and Brandy will learn to play along.

"Yeah, next week. Sure."

"Okay, bye."

"Hey, Amber."

She stops and reluctantly faces her.

"They catch your stalker yet?"

Amber doesn't dignify Brandy with an answer.

Chapter Eleven

"Would it be weird if I asked you to be my girlfriend?"

"Yeah, it would."

"Would you want to anyway?" Mitch asks.

"I don't know. I like you—I really do, but..."—Ashanti shrugs her shoulders—"you should hate me."

"Your mom brainwashed you—it wasn't your fault." Ashanti reassures him, touching him on the shoulder.

"I know the difference between right and wrong. I should have known better," he says, looking down at the ground.

Ashanti, standing next to him, also looks down at the ground. There was so much blood. A tremor shoots through her as she remembers watching the life drain out of him.

Mitch puts his arm around her, pulling her close. "I'm so sorry for ever hurting you. You didn't deserve it. You're one of the smartest, kindest, and prettiest girls I know."

Ashanti looks up at him, feeling the tips of her ears flush. "You're full of it; you know that."

"I mean it." He gently tilts her head back and kisses her tenderly.

She doesn't pull back, and she doesn't return the kiss either. He pulls away and looks at her.

Her eyes dart back and forth between his eyes, looking for answers.

His eyes turn glassy—begging for forgiveness.

She puts her hands behind his head and kisses him.

"Does that mean you'll be my girlfriend?"

She looks down at her hands in her lap, not sure of anything, except she wants to be near him; she does like him. "It's taken me nine months to get used to the friend part. How 'bout you give me some time to add girl?"

The ring box has sat on the kitchen counter for five weeks now...unopened. She still has the ring Roberto gave her in January, the day she realized she said yes to the wrong man.

She found the ring in the top drawer of her nightstand two days later when there were still trying to piece it all together. She has told no one she has it. It's tucked away in her closet, wrapped in the Louis Vuitton leopard scarf he bought her in Milan when they first met. She's pulled it out several times since this red box has appeared as a fixture in her kitchen, wondering what's the right thing to do.

Brian comes up behind her hugging her, kissing her neck, jolting her out of her thoughts. "Good morning gorgeous." When he looks up noticing her eyes are glued to the box. "You can look inside, you know."

"I know. I'm just not ready yet."

"It's not going anywhere. Of course, I'd much rather see my pricey investment placed on your beautiful finger." He kisses her left-hand ring finger. "I know it will only increase in value."

She turns around, kissing him, and says, "That is the corniest thing anyone has ever said to me."

"Well, stick around honey, I'm just getting warmed up," he says, mimicking Groucho Marx with a make-believe cigar.

Tracey comes running into the kitchen, slamming into Brian's leg, hugging tightly. "Morning, Uncle Brian."

Brian picks her up and swings her around, causing a bucket of giggles.

"Tracey, honey, you know Brian is not your uncle, right? He's more than that." Debra cringes every time she hears her call him uncle.

"I know. One day he's going to be my daddy. You freaked out when I called that other nice man daddy, and you smile when I call him Uncle Brian. So I'll just keep calling him Uncle Brian until you don't freak out anymore," the seven-year-old says matter-of-factly.

Brian and Debra both look up at each other, surprised. Out of the mouth of babes.

Tears spring into Debra's eyes. *How much do you tell a young child? How much do they pick up on, anyway? They don't come with instruction booklets—how are you supposed to know?*

Debra picks up Tracey and hugs her. It's often said, there's nothing like the love of your own child. You can't explain it—it's indescribable. They're a part of you. You'll do anything, give everything, sacrifice all day, every day, and gladly give your life for theirs, without hesitation. Before you have a child, you know in your head—of course you're going to love them.

When you hold them in your arms the first time, that's when you know it—full force—in your heart. You'll protect them at all costs. There is nothing more precious, no gift more valuable.

"Sweetheart, you are just too smart for your own good." She puts her down and leans down to her level.

"When daddy passed away, mommy was hurt and very confused. I'm sure you were too."

Tracey nods.

"I'm sorry I wasn't a very good mommy for you then; it was so hard for me. I'm grateful nana was here for you, and your Aunt Megan."

"And Auntie Amber, and Auntie Zya, and Auntie Dom too!" Tracey enthusiastically adds.

Debra smiles. "Yes, and them too. My heart was broken, and Roberto made it feel better for a little while. I shouldn't have let him into our lives so quickly, and that's"—Debra makes finger quotes—"my bad."

Tracey giggles as those are her new favorite words to say lately.

"Brian"—she extends her hand toward him—"I love him very much. I'll always love your daddy, that will never go away. He'll never replace your daddy in your heart, but he'll love you just as much. And I know your heart is so big, there's enough room in there for all of us."

Brian seizes this opportunity to say a few words. "I'll always be here for you, your brother, and your mom. And to shower all of you with lots and lots of love."

"You'll never go away like my daddy did?" Tracey asks in a tiny voice, looking down at her swinging feet.

Brian looks at Debra, who shrugs. Although he's not a child psychologist, he lets his years of training guide him.

"Come here." He motions for her to jump up on his lap. "There's a saying I like to live by. Yesterday is the past, tomorrow is unknown, and today is the present—it's a gift. You like gifts, don't you?"

Tracey's eyes light up as she nods vigorously.

"Me too. What we have..."—he motions to all of them —"is a gift. And I promise you today, I'm here—you have me. I'll be whatever you need me to be. If it's within my power, I'll do the same every day."

"You're going to give me a gift every day?" Tracey asks.

Chuckling, he says, "Is loving you a gift?"

She nods again and adds, "And Little George, and mommy too."

"Absolutely—it's a package deal."

It's that exact moment Debra decides she doesn't care what society thinks.

She walks over and picks up the box and hands it to Brian. "Ask me."

☯

Amber runs into her office fifteen minutes late for a meeting with her boss. South Florida afternoon traffic seems to get worse every year. It's season, so all the snowbirds are back. The number of out of state plates match those with the outline of the sunshine state, one to one, as they idle in all three lanes from the New River Tunnel south, back to the airport exit on US1. The only other way around is through downtown; that's just as bad. The price you pay for living in paradise.

The negative media attention has died down since the Brettinger debacle. Her boss felt it best if she stayed out of the limelight, and the front page, as much as possible. She won't be interviewing any CEOs, top philanthropists, or celebrities again soon. As a South Florida native, and Las Olas Boulevard being her playground, it's decided she'll work on a story about the new restaurants popping up. Microbreweries and gastropubs mixed in with alfresco fine dining and waterside casual eateries. An eclectic mix to whet anyone's appetite. It's funny how everything has come full circle. Her very first article with NeoQuest involved food. She interviewed Jack Jackson, one-half of the name of the once-famous Burt & Jack's restaurant nestled in Port Everglades. The other half was Burt Reynolds— the famous actor who lived in Jupiter, Florida.

She was so nervous. She wanted to do the article justice, and it was her first big interview. Jack being one of the most successful restaurateurs in South Florida, she was hoping to get his secret to share. He was very gracious and warm when he greeted her and immediately began introducing her around to the Who's Who of Fort Lauderdale. By the time they arrived at a table by the kitchen, and the Intracoastal Waterway, her head was spinning.

The chef himself delivered one small plate after another, having her taste every seafood, pasta and veal dishes the restaurant served. Why every single one isn't considered a house specialty is beyond her. The mouthwatering stuffed lobster came on its own full-size plate, because how do you cut down a full lobster? She ended up taking most of it home and ate it the next day—and the next. When she thought she couldn't eat another bite, a slice of double chocolate cake came out by none other than, Burt Reynolds himself. The *slice* was really one-fourth of a cake. It was a very sad day for South Florida when the restaurant closed its doors in 2002. The heightened security after 911 made it difficult for their patrons to dine there. Because security was extremely tight, or they were avoiding scrutiny altogether, who knows. It was the closing of an icon.

As she drives down Las Olas, she passes by what is now called the Lobster Bar Sea Grille situated on a prime piece of corner real estate on the west end of the boulevard. Six years earlier, it was the popular Jackson 450 Steakhouse, owned by none other than the same, Jack Jackson. She decides that's a great place to start. It's not a new restaurant, but what a great comparison this luxury seafood restaurant will make to the lighter bites as she makes her way east down the famous boutique and eatery lined path.

As Amber jumps out of her car at valet, a car pulls into a spot across the street.

You think you're so smart; you figured me out, huh? I'll play your game, sweetheart, because I want to watch you mess up. I want you to think I'm gone, and everything in your little bubble has gone back to being perfect. I'll never forget what you did to me—what you did to us. You're going to pay—I promise you will suffer. Feel safe for now, Amber.

CHAPTER TWELVE

"Oh, I love this place. I'm so glad you picked it, Debra, I haven't been here in ages," Dominque says as she grabs her seat, breathing in the salty air.

The sun is setting, casting a dark orange glow on the patrons sitting along the Intracoastal. The boats are docked two- and three-deep, gently rising and falling from the small waves caused by the boats passing in the no wake zone. Three restaurants are side by side along this portion of the waterway, always full of seafood- and sunshine-lovers.

A round of drinks hits the table within thirty seconds of Dom's cheeks hitting her seat.

"These are compliments of a secret admirer, ladies," the waitress says as she drops the last one in front of Zya, then turns to leave before they can object.

Dominque grabs to take the first sip when Amber grabs her wrist, stopping her. "We don't know who they're from; shouldn't we just throw them away?"

"Honey, I doubt the bartender or waitress would poison us. I'm sure no one else touched our drinks. But if it makes you feel more comfortable..." Zya throws out the contents of her glass into the Intracoastal.

Dominque brings her drink back up to her mouth and says, "I'll take my chances." After downing it in three sips, she says, "Oh, this brings back memories; Tad was so romantic—heck, he still is!"

"Maybe it's that cop? The one that had a thing for you? You thought he was your secret admirer there for a while," Zya teases.

Dominque playfully slaps her on the shoulder. "I've totally forgotten about him, and I'm sure he's done the same. Anyway, it's kinda nice being admired from afar."

Zya's laugh stops mid ha when a flash blinds her. She looks for the culprit and grabs Debra's hand. "Is that what I think it is?"

Dominque and Amber both gasp as their mouths fall open. Debra blushes.

They all start talking at once and grabbing at her left hand to look at the brilliant stunner.

Debra laughs at the excitement. "Okay, okay, he wanted to ask me in September. Stupid me, I let what others think hold me back. It sat on my kitchen counter for five weeks."

"What?" Zya says, shocked.

The others' eyes open wide in surprise.

"I know. Well, I grabbed the box two weeks ago and told him I was ready."

"Two weeks? You've been engaged for two weeks, and we're just now finding out?" Amber asks.

"I couldn't get you all together. You're all so busy. I didn't want to tell you on the phone. Besides, I knew you'd want to see it," she says, flashing her hand.

Debra fills them in on the morning between Brian and Tracey that prompted her to pick up the box.

Amber sits back and listens to laughter and excitement coming from her three closest friends. Funny how things can change so quickly. Over the past year and a half, Zya has gone from one of the up-and-coming designers to one of the few labels people know just by looking at the pieces. 'Is that a Zya?' can be heard in the trendy social circles. Magazines now have actresses side by side in her pieces asking, 'Who wore it better?' Plus, she found love—finally, and with a woman. It took her a while, but she finally came around. Almost left it all and went back to S. Africa after Ashanti's brush with Mitch and his goons. Thankfully, her levelheaded mini-me set her straight.

And then there's Dominque—oh, Dom. She's made the most significant changes. She always felt so insecure and worthless. No matter how much love they gave her, it was never enough to undo all the hurt and pain she endured being shuffled in and out of foster homes. *I sometimes wonder what would have happened if you hadn't answered my ad for a receptionist and you'd responded to the adult film industry ad instead. Every time you retell that story, and how close you were at going the other way, I get the shivers.*

Her self-esteem was so low, she nearly starved herself so she'd look perfect—or her version of it. They came so close to losing her just last year at Zya's show in Milan. They did not understand the extreme lengths she was going to. *You were so skinny—you couldn't see it.* Amber's eyes tear up as she remembers her gray skin, hollow eyes, and bones sticking out at her elbows and knees. Her skin was so thin, Amber swore she could see the bones themselves. And now here she is, a cancer survivor, married to the perfect man, and glowing.

And finally, there's Debra, as bright as the sun showing off her next step in happiness. Just last year, she lost George, the love of her life. After trying for years to have a second child, she was so excited to tell him they finally did it. She never got the chance. *I remember that night so vividly; it was horrible.*

Then came along the hunky Italian, Roberto, and her therapist Brian, who both fell madly in love with her. Who wouldn't? She's perfect, as George would always say. She was so torn between grieving for her husband, taking care of Tracey, being thrilled for her unborn child, and confused when two men started competing for her hand in marriage. It's no wonder she felt stretched in every direction. *And now you've got it all again. I'm just so sorry you had to go through all that pain to get here.*

☯

Zya is sitting on the couch, working on the hem of a sample dress while Ashanti is at the breakfast table, trying to focus on her calculus. She keeps staring off into space, tapping the end of her pencil quickly against the book.

"Does that annoy your teacher when you do that in class?"

Ashanti jerks out of her trance, turning her attention back to her textbook. "Sorry, mom."

"Homework, or something else on your mind?"

Ashanti puts her pencil down and crosses her arms over her book. "Are you giving up your Muslim faith?"

Zya puts the dress down and takes off her readers. "I've chosen to go back to the Christian beliefs my parents raised me with. Why do you ask?"

"I think I might give it up too. I love most parts of being Muslim; especially helping others. But I'm conflicted with other areas."

"Such as?"

"Well, according to the Quran, homosexuality is haram; it's not allowed. I was wondering if that's why you gave it up—for Tina."

"That's not why I chose. Before I explain, your faith is your choice. No one can make that for you. And no one should force you into believing something that doesn't sit right with you.

"When I met Tina, I did a little more digging into the Quran and lesbianism. Many claim, according to the story of Sodom, sex between men is prohibited. That didn't help me any, and I assumed the same goes for women. So, I dug even deeper and found the Quran mentions sex between men several times. Some translate it as consensual, others as rape. Not getting a concrete answer, I finally went with what was in my heart. I loved going to church with my mom and dad. There was so much love and kindness—and giving. I, too, love helping others, and there's no reason we can't keep doing that; regardless of what we believe. Last time we talked about this, you were going to study different religions; what did you come up with?"

"Mostly, they believe in a higher power, giving hope, and spreading love and kindness. Do the right thing like the ten commandments. Some have rules—really strict ones."

"How do you feel about that?"

"I think they're controlling. Just because I can't follow one of their rules doesn't mean I don't love God any less than they do. God is very forgiving, yet they're not. Break a rule, and you're shunned. It's conflicting to read one thing in print and hear something completely different during a sermon."

"You have done your research. Like I said before, follow your heart. You're very smart, you'll make the right decision. And as far as forgiveness goes, you've got that part down pat. Some might even say you're on your way to sainthood."

Ashanti laughs. "Mom, how did you know you were in love?" she asks, staring at a dot in her book.

Zya's head snaps to Ashanti at the abrupt change in subject. She takes a deep breath, calming the heavy feeling that's spontaneously appeared in her gut.

"You asking for yourself—or a friend?"

After a long pause, she says, "For me."

"Someone I might know?" Zya asks, although she's sure she knows the answer.

"Yeah, Mitch."

Zya puts the dress over the arm of the couch and motions for Ashanti to come to sit by her. "Honey, you're what fifteen, almost sixteen now? I'm glad it's taken you this long to ask me this question, but are you sure you want to ask—about Mitch?" Zya asks as her face twists, and her eyes squint.

"You'll be honest with me, even if he was my bully."

"You are not going to make this easy for me, are you?"

Ashanti smiles and shakes her head.

"There was a time, not so long ago, I wanted to wring that boy's neck. I don't hate anyone, but you know my feelings for him were as close as they come."

Ashanti opens her mouth, about to say something when Zya holds up her finger, stopping her.

"However, he has done an amazing transformation these past eleven months. I never knew the other side of him, and he's damn lucky because if I had, he'd never step foot in this house. I only know what you told me. They say going through a near-death experience can change a person, and I'd like to think that's exactly what's happened to him. I am your mom, so I have my suspicions—it's my job. I will always be wary of him."

"He's been so sweet, and I think he's genuinely sorry. Mom, you should hear him speak—it's from the heart. I listen to him, and I'm in awe. He inspires so many. I sometimes wonder if everything happened exactly the way it was supposed to. I feel like this is his calling; he's exactly where he's supposed to be.

"His dad took him down to Miami, and they asked me to tag along. Micki came too. Sorry, I know you don't like her."

Zya can't help herself. "How is Micki—Officer Sanderson? She and Cassie still doing well?"

"Smooth mom—real smooth," Ashanti says, chuckling. "They're doing great; they're thrilled and grateful you and Tina introduced them."

Zya nods with a satisfied smug. Another bullet dodged.

"I keep reminding myself who he was before, but it's getting harder and harder. I don't want to like him—I want to hate him; I just can't. I want to be near him—feel him touching me," she says, the last sentence in almost a whisper.

Zya squeezes Ashanti's hand.

"Ow, mom, relax—not like that. He's held my hand a few times. And we've kissed too, but that's it," she says, yanking her hand out of her mother's vise-like grip.

Zya doesn't like Mitch having any part of Ashanti's life, but she's so proud of the lessons they're learning and teaching others; the difference they're making. *Why does she have to have feelings for this boy—why him?*

"I'm going to advise you as if he was any other boy—I'll do my best. Follow your heart, but don't leave your head too far behind. Falling in love is one of the most beautiful experiences you'll ever have. And to enjoy love, let yourself fall and not get hurt—that's the trick."

"Mom, that's an oxymoron."

"You're just too darn smart for your own good. Oh, you're gonna hurt, just be prepared. If you go in with the mindset you're going to enjoy it, for however long it lasts, and allow yourself to learn whatever lessons you can from it, it will always be a positive experience, no matter what. We all want love to last forever; we see ourselves growing old together. But things don't always go the way we plan. Look at Debra and George. Live your life and have no regrets. Love deeply. If you go in with both feet, and no expectations other than enjoying every moment, then you'll have no regrets.

"Relationships take two people; you can't *make* someone love you. From what I've seen, people mostly get hurt when they try to change others or try to force them to love them. It shouldn't be that hard. If you and Mitch truly care for each other, then go for it. Take each day as it comes and see what happens. I think you both know people are going to talk. Not only because he was your bully but also because he's white, and you're a lovely caramel color."

"That's partly why I'm struggling with being Muslim."

"You know you can date him and be Muslim, right?"

"I do. Would he have to convert if we get serious?"

"Are you maybe getting a little ahead of yourself? Why not take it one day at a time and see where it goes?"

"Mom, why did you become Muslim in the first place? Was it because of dad?"

"Yes, I thought it would win him over. I made a lot of mistakes when I fell in love with him, ones I can never take back. While parts of me regret following him here, I would not have had you otherwise. And honey, I wouldn't be who I am today if you hadn't come into my life."

"Thanks for the talk, Mom. I know it's going to be tough. Heck, I don't think we know how to do easy, do we? If we ever had a normal life, it would probably bore us to death."

"Normal? Why be normal?"

CHAPTER THIRTEEN

"How's the article coming?"

"Great—I think. My favorite part is sampling all the food. As soon as I sit, my table is suddenly covered with every delicacy they serve. Johnny V's closed their doors, but there are so many new places now. We need to go back—soon."

"How about tonight?"

"I was thinking about something else. I've been spending a lot of time at your place so why don't we stay at my place tonight? We can make dinner and have a fun evening in…"

"I'm getting déjà vu. Is there a banana split for dessert in your immediate future?"

She laughs, remembering the elaborate tray of toppings he arranged when he offered himself up for dessert. She's been a fan ever since.

"I was thinking more, nine and a half weeks."

Without missing a beat, he shouts over the phone, "Count me in! What time?"

Laughing, she says, "How about six?"

"I'll be there wearing my blindfold. Wait, no I won't, then I won't see where I'm going. I'll bring it, though."

She continues to laugh as she hangs up, sensing the excitement in his voice. She's been staying at Patrick's because of her stalker. She's attempted several nights to go home, but she's come up with every excuse in the book why it was easier to stay with Patrick. Her condo building is safe; it's her parking garage that spooks her. You need an opener to get in, but if you are thin enough, you could fit through the rails on the gate. And the door stays open long enough for someone to slip through. She timed it one night; forty-five-seconds before the door began closing. A full fifty-five before it was secure. Plenty of time for someone to slip in.

Patrick's house, as he says, is like Fort Knox. He has security cameras all around the perimeter and an electric gate that closes immediately. When Stewart became his roommate, and Patrick realized he was sleeping with most of South Florida's female population, he was sure those with spouses would eventually come knocking on their door.

Patrick never made time to invest in a relationship, and he wasn't into one-night stands; finding a roommate seemed the best way to have companionship. Plus, Stewart was funny and easy to get along with; he lived vicariously through him. He just wanted to be sure he didn't accidentally get shot because of him.

☯

"Miss Fiore, your guest has arrived," her security manager says in a short, clipped manner.

Amber has always described John as sweet and helpful; this doesn't fit the description of the person standing in front of him. Patrick's only met him briefly, coming in or leaving her building together. This is the first time he's been alone with him.

"Amber has told me a lot about you. Thank you for taking such great care of her."

With tight lips, he replies, "It's my job, and Miss Fiore is a real special lady and deserves to be treated as such."

Patrick feels as if he's just been gut-punched.

"Whoa, man, who do you think you are? I love Amber very much. I treat her very well; and I don't answer to you."

John opens his mouth just as Amber steps off the elevator. Patrick watches as he transforms into a mild-mannered, sweet man complete with a genuine smile.

"Miss Fiore. It's so nice to see you at home. We've missed you."

"Thanks, John. It's nice to see you too. I'm sorry I didn't see you when I came in earlier. Must have been just before your shift."

She takes Patrick by the arm and leads him back to the elevators.

Patrick looks back at John to see slitted eyes of steel staring back.

Once inside and the doors have closed. "You sure John is sweet and innocent?"

"Yeah, why?"

"Nothing—never mind." He keeps their conversation to himself. He is very protective of her; which may not be a bad thing, under the current circumstances.

Amber prepared her meat lasagna—Patrick's favorite. It takes several hours to prepare, but it's worth it. The trick is adding heavy cream when sautéing the meat and letting it soak in until just the fat remains. Fresh basil, full-fat ricotta, freshly shredded mozzarella, and parmesan cheese layered between Italian lasagna noodles and the meat sauce created with only the finest of crushed San Marzano tomatoes. Her grandmother taught her years ago. If you're going to cook anything Italian, the tomatoes make all the difference. The béchamel sauce she fussed over for thirty minutes, covering the top, was the literal icing on the dish. Amber requested Patrick bring two bottles of the costly Opus One wine she loves so much. Never being cheap, he still cringed on the inside when she asked.

To tease him, she set one hard fast rule...no dessert until the dishwasher is loaded and running. He waits on the couch, listening to the sound of running water as she rinses the dishes, the clanking of silverware as she drops them in their appropriate place. He offered to help; she told him he'd only be in the way. In his mind, she's going in slow motion and can't get out to him fast enough. He's rubbing his hands together, anxiously awaiting to see what sweets are on the menus. He knows he's getting lucky—but how? Nine and half weeks; blindfold—check, and food from the refrigerator. He's letting his imagination get carried away when the lights dim, and the music changes to a sexy, sultry tune.

His heart thumps wildly in anticipation.

Suddenly, a red stiletto peeks out from behind the double-swung kitchen door. After a few twirls of her ankle, her leg extends out, covered in a thigh-high black fishnet stocking. A red silk gloved arm slithers out like a snake, then down to her ankle. She seductively glides her hand up to her hip that's now appeared, covered in a tiny piece of silk—the same shade as her gloves. One breast appears as her fingernails tease around the edges of the bra cup.

Patrick instantly gets a rise as Amber plays the seductress. He's immediately drawn into the scene she's playing out, momentarily forgetting who she is.

Half of her face is now visible as she blows him a kiss and winks. She steps out from behind the door and leans her back against its edge. She playfully slides up and down, leaning her weight into the door, not thinking about its ability to swing easily on its hinges. Luckily, she catches herself before she falls over. After a few giggles, she opts for the more stable door frame by wrapping one leg on each side and creates a wave with her body, starting with her chest until eventually she thrusts her groin into the jamb—a trick she picked up watching a stripper movie.

Patrick can't believe his eyes. Subconsciously his hand moves to the front of his pants, intending to reposition himself, allowing his erection to extend fully. However, the show causes his hand to stay in place as he rubs himself, thinking how damn lucky that frame is right now.

With her eyes closed, she lets the music fully take her. Turning around, she moves her hips side to side around the edge of the doorjamb as her hands explore her breasts. Her lips pout as her fingers trace over her hard nipples. A moan escapes her as she gently pinches one. Her other hand quickly moves between her legs, causing her breaths to become short and ragged.

Patrick's hand slips inside his pants; she's getting him so aroused. He can't believe this vixen in front of him is Amber. He's throbbing, the desire for her more urgent than ever—

every nerve ending dancing and on fire. He groans loudly, bringing her out of her trance.

She slides down to the ground, crawling slowly toward him, arching her back with each long stride like a cat. Their eyes lock as his hand continues to take long, deliberate strokes in tune with each step she takes.

Across from the couch is a desk. She stands up and leans across the chair sitting behind it, away from him, bending over much further than necessary and making sure the string in her thong pulls tight while she nudges a pencil off and to the floor. She looks over her shoulder at him, putting a finger to her red pouty lips and says, "Oops."

Slowly, she sashays over to retrieve it. Bending over again, making sure he gets a splendid view of the string pulled taut.

Still turned away, she drops back to her knees just a few feet in front of him and spreads her knees wide apart. The action has caused the thong to work its way further up, dissecting her in two. She glances over her shoulder at him, and without losing eye contact, puts her finger in her mouth, sucking on it. Starting at her lower back, she slips her thoroughly lubricated finger under the edge of her thong, lifting it, then trailing down to the fuller, wetter part.

Patrick groans. With his fly open, his hand is doing double-time, pleasuring himself.

"Don't you take away my dessert now," she says, covering the rest of the distance on her hands and knees.

His hand stops immediately, hoping either hers will take over; or does he dare dream—her lips?

His heart pounding in anticipation, he tries to touch her, but she brushes him off, wagging her finger at him.

"Not yet, all in due time."

She was playful and adventurous in the bedroom; however, after the attack, he hasn't pressed; unsure of when—or if ever, she'd feel comfortable again. Now, here she is—he can't believe it. More of a sex kitten than ever.

Taking her time, she slowly crawls up onto the couch and straddles him, grinding her hips down into him—getting comfortable.

The instant he feels her burning bush against his exposed and ready to explode erection sends mini spams throughout his genitals. It's everything he can do to keep it together. Not until he's inside her.

She leans back, playing with the edge of her bra.

A cold sweat rushes through him. The image of Brandy doing almost this exact thing on his birthday, one and half years ago, comes flooding back. The sudden tightness in his chest causes his erection to take a nosedive. He absentmindedly pushes Amber off his lap as he jumps up and beelines to the bathroom, slamming the door behind him. Dinner threatens to make a repeat appearance.

After throwing water on his pale face, it doesn't take him long to realize what he's done. He rushes back out to find Amber sitting on the couch, stunned, wrapped tightly in a blanket—the seductress, long gone.

"Baby, I'm sorry. It's not you. Brandy—when she was my stripper but I thought it was you—she did something like that. It flashed back. I'm sorry. I'm sorry."

He scoops her up in his arms and holds her tight. "I'm so sorry."

Amber wakes and looks at the clock at 3:45 a.m. Patrick's arm is around her waist; he's snuggled up so tight against her, it's like he's trying to merge with her. The heat radiating from his body is like being in a sauna—she's boiling.

Before going to sleep, they put the dishes away in silence, both unable to find the right words to diffuse the situation. Amber has been struggling with her sexuality these past few months, yet determined to get things back to normal; last night, she was hoping it would help break the ice.

She rubs his arm, thinking about how he must have felt the moment she reminded him of Brandy. She's glad he stopped her. It was rather abrupt, yet it proves his disgust at getting pleasure when Brandy was his stripper—before he realized who it was. Amber decides maybe the thin layer of sweat covering her body isn't because of the temperature in the room so she pushes into him. When her backside snuggles into his groin, she feels a pulse against her lower back.

He moans softly.

She reaches behind and strokes him softly, using the tips of her fingers.

He pulses again—two, three times, and snuggles his face into her hair.

Reaching inside the top of his pajamas, she's not disappointed to feel the tip trying to break free. Her finger trails along the tip and the edge of the rim, ever so lightly.

He moans and buries his face deeper into her hair, grinding his hips into her.

She giggles.

His hand moves up from her waist and closes around her breast, gently squeezing her nipple. "Keep that up, and you might get more than you bargained for."

"I'm counting on it," she says as she turns over and slides under him.

He leans on his arms as their legs intertwine. "I'm sorry about tonight. I really am," he says.

She reaches up and puts her finger across his lips. "I'm not. You did the right thing. You have nothing to apologize for. I guess in the back of my mind, I wanted to give you a new— better exotic dancer experience to wipe away hers. I should have known better. Anything other than a stripper you might prefer?"

"You were more of a seductress than Brandy or any other woman last night—WOW! I was so jealous of that door jamb. What would I like to see next? How about a French maid? Or a schoolteacher?"

"French maid I get, but school teacher? Mine were basic— definitely not sexy."

"Oh, Mrs. Robinson," he says playfully.

"You're so bad."

"I can be."

Amber, ready to prove to him, and herself, she's prepared to move on, flips him on his back. "I think I was the one who was rudely interrupted early. I know my sister didn't do this." She straddles him and inserts just the tip inside herself. She teases, inching down with subtle pulses.

"What, no foreplay?" he says with a catch in his breath as his hands go to her hips.

She grabs his hands and puts them up over his head, pulling herself up, so he's barely still inside. "Think you can keep these up here and let me do the work?"

"Oh, I can't make any promises, but I'll try," he says breathlessly.

She puts her hands on his chest and slowly lowers herself, trying hard to stay in control and go slow. Her body is tingling inside, the flames being fanned—begging for her to go faster. She focuses on using her internal muscles to contract and squeeze him as she rises, relaxing as she lowers herself, temporarily keeping the embers glowing without letting the fire burn out of control.

Patrick grabs the bar on the headboard.

As her nerve endings become more and more alive, she loses the battle and the fire roars.

Patrick's hands move to her hips, helping, as her tempo increases.

Her hands find the warm spots on the headboard as her hips now buck front to back, finding the right angle where he rubs against her G-spot. Tiny, fast pulses, back and forth, until the bonfire explodes into the sky, and she screams Patrick's name —several times.

She drops onto his chest—breathless and grinning from ear to ear. Happy, spent, totally satisfied.

"You okay?" he asks.

"More than okay. I'd say—pretty damn terrific."

"Good," he says and flips her in one swift motion. "Remember, I'm bad." He spreads her legs very wide with a sparkle in his eyes and a quirky uptake at the side of his mouth.

He slowly inserts himself, and before she moves her hips, he instructs her to wait. He takes one leg and puts it over the other, twisting her lower half, making it incredibly tight for both of them.

With one hand on the bed and the other one under her top knee, he raises her leg and thrusts until he gets the friction just so. The slipperiness from her orgasm, providing the necessary lubrication to make it possible in such tight quarters.

Her head slowly tosses side to side as he pulls out as far as he dares, then at a slightly quicker pace, pushes every inch of himself back, deep inside, staying to the count of three, as her muscles quiver around him.

His mind blanks as he hears the blood rushing in his ears. He throws open her top leg and slams into her, burying himself as far as he can, thrust after thrust as he feels the familiar tingling rising from his toes, shooting up through his body with the force of a hydrogen bomb.

As he slows to catch his breath, he opens his eyes to find her head tilted back and her hands are holding her knees wide apart—she's close. He drops and immediately sucks on her swollen clit. It doesn't take much—ten seconds before she's screaming again, this time to a higher power. His hands go under her as she lifts her hips high in the air. He slips his finger in and presses, causing her to almost levitate and call-out another octave higher.

They lay side by side, catching their breath, staring at the ceiling.

"Where did you learn to do that?" she asks.

"One of Stewart's books—it always intrigued me. Where did you learn to make yourself come on top like that?"

"I saw it in a movie."

"A movie, huh? What kind of movie—you watching porn?"

"There's a lot about me you don't know."

He pulls her over to him and kisses her. "I'm certainly going to have fun finding out."

CHAPTER FOURTEEN

"Mr. Simpson, nice to see you again, how can I help you?"

"I want to say thank you for everything you did to help get Amber out of prison so quickly. Her video statement and written confession helped me get the judge to fast-track her sentencing and dismiss her case."

"That's great; I'm glad it all worked out."

"I wanted to talk to you about something else."

"Okay, how can I help?"

"Amber has been getting these threatening texts for almost a year now. They assigned a detective to it, but with everyone so busy, I'm sure a stalker isn't a priority, especially since Amber was on trial for murder. This person knows what's going on in her life—as it's happening. It's creepy. We thought someone installed spyware on our devices so we had everything checked—nothing; it has to be someone close. We have a list of potential suspects; Brandy's on top. It's farfetched, I know, but we're checking everyone out. We think there's a connection between Brandy and the guard—the one that helped Amber. She doesn't know her, but she went so far out of her way to help. And then there's the favor and how you said you owed her; it seems like a strange coincidence, and I can't get it out of my head. Did you know Brandy was up in Belle Glade as well?"

"No, I didn't," the detective says, shaking his head. He leans forward at his desk, tilting his head. You can almost see the wheels inside spinning.

"Okay, hypothetically, what if Brandy and the guard are working together with the stalker?" Patrick asks.

"For what purpose?"

"That's the part we're trying to piece together. Brandy has had it out for Amber since they were kids. You listened to her during her confession. She was on a mission."

The detective leans back and clasps his hands behind his head. "She killed that man because he raped Amber. That doesn't sound like someone who's out to get her. Maybe initially, I get that part, but I think he crossed the line and Brandy saw red—literally. Her working with a stalker makes no sense to me."

"Amber says never underestimate Brandy—she's smarter than we realize. I think she had every intention of killing him; it's too elaborate of a plan just for sex. She was hoping we would plead insanity. Amber's life, as we know it, would be over. Mission accomplished. When she found out we weren't, then she was counting on me getting her off so she could implement Plan B. When they found her guilty, the only way to carry out her plan would be if they switched places. Brandy has lived most of her adult life behind bars; it's no sweat off her back to go back there. And if it's the ultimate payback she's after, this would take Amber out for good."

"I think you watch way too many cops and robbers movies," the detective says, chuckling.

Patrick lashes back. "The problem is, I misjudged her before; this is Amber's life we're talking about, I won't make that mistake again."

☯

"Babe, has Cassie called you?" Tina asks.

"No, and court's tomorrow. Doug should have pulled the petition by now. That bastard!"

"Do you think he's going to go through with it? Maybe he's calling your bluff."

"It's not a bluff, I *have* to go through with it."

"Have you talked to Ashanti yet?" Tina asks.

"Don't get mad—no; I was hoping I wouldn't have to. I'll talk to her tonight, I promise. Damn! I was really hoping it wouldn't come to this."

"When I send Nicky a copy of the drive, I don't know how long he'll sit on it. I imagine he'll want his own proof, so he'll inspect Doug's deals. Heck, it might take months. Doug's no dummy; he'll cool it for a while or as long as the Cubans let him. SHIT! I was betting on Doug not taking the chance."

"You know, there's a chance you could win custody? He is a drug dealer."

"I haven't thought that far. I didn't even think tomorrow was a possibility."

Tina pulls Zya into her arms. "No matter what happens, we'll get through this together, all four of us."

"I'm so sorry; you didn't sign up for this shit," Zya says as the steel band across her chest tightens another notch.

"I signed up for the total package. I knew what I was getting into, even our daily shit."

Zya smiles weakly, letting go of the inside of her cheek.

"Listen, you have a show to think about. You're big news. You thought Milan was big. Okay, it was a big deal, but New York—this is the one people are begging for tickets to see."

🔯

"You know I love you; I hate that you're asking me to help you with this."

"I know, but you're my best friend; I can't ask anyone else."

"Are you sure? I mean, one hundred percent positive, I can't talk you out of this, sure?"

"I'm gonna be sixteen soon. All the other girls in school have already done it. You have—what's the big deal?"

"Really? You even have to ask? The boy that wanted to kill you is the one you want to pop your cherry!"

"You need to get over it, Stacey. I don't think he was going to kill me. He loves me—he told me he does."

"Does he? Or is it because you saved his life? They call it a rescue romance."

"What are you talking about?" Ashanti asks as she spins around to face her best friend.

"Are you sure he really loves you, or are you his savior? Remember, he hated you not too long ago."

"That wasn't him; it was his mother talking. You don't think people can change?"

"Of course I do. I just remember changing your bloody bandage the day you"—making finger quotes—"supposedly fell off the bike you don't own."

Ashanti gets up off her bed and throws her door open. "Get out if you don't want to help me. I'll do it by myself. I don't need you."

Ashanti plops down on her bed with her arms crossed. She's watched girls at school lose their best friends over boys, promising it would never happen to her and Stacey—never. She's mad at Stacey, but her mood mellows when she thinks about everything they've been through. She knows Stacey only wants what's best for her. Mitch put her through hell, and Stacey had a ringside seat watching it all transpire.

She slowly walks down the hallway to Stacey's door. Hearing the music bounce off the wood partition, she assumes it's the reason she doesn't answer. After cracking open the door, she finds Stacey on the floor, leaning up against her bed with a magazine in her lap. She glances up at Ashanti and angrily flips a page instead of acknowledging her.

Ashanti sits next to her on the floor and picks at the carpet.

After six or seven minutes of silence, Stacey says, "I just want you to be careful."

"I know, and I appreciate it. You can say your piece; I'll always give you that, just please honor my decision. If you don't want to help me, that's cool, I understand. But in the end, I get to decide. I'd rather have you by my side than not. It's a big step for me, and I need my sister to hold my hand. Well, not during."

Stacey giggles, which builds from laughter into full-on rolling on the floor hysteria.

Tina opens the door and peeks in. "Everything okay here?"

"Yes, Mom—sorry. Ashanti just said something hilarious—and gross."

"Tina, hey, I'm just about to leave to get to the courthouse. You meeting me there?"

"You won't believe this."

"Try me. Nothing surprises me anymore."

"Cassie just called here looking for you; Doug pulled the petition."

"Now? We're due in court in an hour. Can he do that?"

"Apparently, I'm sure there are fines and other hoops he had to jump through, or rather he made his lawyer do, but he caved."

Zya drops her purse and slumps in her chair. She's been running on adrenaline all day, dreading the afternoon when she would have to face him knowing how ugly it was going to be. And that was just the beginning.

"You still there?"

"Yeah, I'm here; that's great news. I'm enjoying feeling suddenly twenty pounds lighter."

"I've been on pins and needles all day too. Are we safe?"

"I think so. He caved. He waited until the last second; he's sending a message."

"Can you take the rest of the day off? I think we need to take some time together. I know just the thing to help release stress, and celebrate this victory. Oh, and I have to choose my trousseau; I'm having a hard time deciding between a few pieces. Think you can help me out?"

"Say no more. I'm out the door."

CHAPTER FIFTEEN

"Six months cancer-free, cheers sweetheart," Tad says as he raises his flute to toast his beautiful wife.

Dominque looks out from the kitchen at the elegant table he set, recreating the night he planned to propose. Plans postponed at the sight of her red-tinged napkin. He never regretted it since here she is, sitting across from him, healthy and as beautiful as ever.

Initially, he borrowed the finest china from his mother, but she has since gifted it as a wedding present, along with a big fat gift card they used to turn their bedroom into a sanctuary. Antique cut crystal wine glasses passed down from his grandmother sit atop a family heirloom hand tatted lace tablecloth from her grandmother. Matching crystal candelabras holding ivory tapers burned one-fourth of the way with drips frozen in time, almost touching the first facet. A dozen long stem red roses sit in the center.

Tad made the quiche she ate through her treatments. It was the only thing that partially hid the metallic taste from chemo.

"Tad, I can't believe you went to all this trouble for me. It smells so wonderful," she says as the delicious aroma of sautéed onions in butter, mixed with whipped eggs and ham fills her nostrils. She can already smell the layers of Swiss cheese she knows he tucked inside; picturing the strings stretching when he pulls out the first slice.

"Are you kidding? I don't want us ever to forget where we've been and what we've overcome. I vote at every milestone, this is precisely what we do," he says, raising his glass in confidence—until he watches as her chin drops to her chest. "Unless you'd rather do something else."

"Actually, for my one-year celebration, I do have something else in mind."

"Anything, what?"

"I'd like to have my feet in stirrups"—Tad's mind immediately jumps to the wrong conclusion—"having our first frozen embryo transfer done."

It takes a second to sink in. He's shaking his head. "The doctor said two years—not one."

"I know, and I promise you, I've given this a lot of thought. Please, just listen to me."

Tad drops his head.

"When I turn forty, the odds of having gestational diabetes, preeclampsia, and other medical problems increase even more so than at thirty-five. We can have the eggs checked for any chromosome issues, so I'm not worried about that. Plus, as I get older, pregnancy itself is harder on my body. I know the doctor said two years—my survival odds are based on five. I'm not waiting five so I don't see why I have to wait two."

Tad can't help himself. "And, he also said, most of those who relapse will most likely have a rapid recurrence within the first two years."

"Baby, I know this is going to be very hard to hear." She swallows as she reaches for his hand. "If cancer takes me away from you, I want to leave a piece of me behind—a living part. A child, preferably two."

Tears sting Tad's eyes. This is not the joyful celebration he planned. "Do I have a say in this?"

"Of course you do. I hope you'll try to at least look at it from my point of view."

"I'm trying—honestly. Dom, if your cancer comes back and you're pregnant, then you're choosing the baby over you. If we face that choice—I choose you."

"I can have treatments during my pregnancy. Not during the first three months, but I can during the second and third trimester, and they won't hurt the baby."

Tad's shoulders slouch. "So, you can have any drug they recommend for you?"

"Not everything; there are some limits, but most. At the very end of the pregnancy, they would stop chemo if I still needed it, because it could lower my red blood cells or potentially cause a premature delivery. No radiation."

"I don't like it; you decide. You've done your homework, and this seems very important to you." Tad says, rubbing his forehead.

"It is. I want us to have a family, something I never had. I want to be here to watch our children go to school, get married, and raise their own families. I want to grow old with you. But, if for any reason, it's not in the cards for me—if it's not fate, then I want you to do that for me. Will you—do that?"

"That's not fair, and you know it. I'd do anything in the world for you. Yes, I'll do it for you, but I still don't like it."

Dominque thinks for a moment, they're stuck. She can understand the position she's putting him in—she's adamant about this. It's too important.

"What if we flip a coin?"

"What?" he says, shaking his head in confusion. "You mean tails I win, and you wait two years? Heads I lose, and you only wait one?"

"No. Tails I win; heads I lose," she says, grabbing both his hands, sending him a brilliant smile, hoping it convinces him she believes this will be okay.

"And you'd honor the toss? You'd let fate decide?"

"I would—I promise."

"Okay, let's flip when the time comes. I have to find a two-headed coin," he says, kissing her neck and then her lips.

"What are you trying to do, make me change my mind?"

"Absolutely not," he says as his kisses trail up behind her ear. "I wouldn't dream of it. Just all this talk about a turkey baster getting you knocked up is making me horny."

Dominque cracks up, laughing at the visual. "Who said anything about a turkey baster?"

"You mean that's not how they do it?" He doesn't wait for an answer, he picks her up and sets her on the edge of the island. With her legs on either side, he continues to place soft kisses on the side of her neck.

"Hmm, what about dinner?"

"It's your six-month anniversary. How about we throw caution to the wind and have dessert first?"

Before she can answer, he puts his arms under her knees and pulls her forward, putting her on the edge.

Her eyes go wide, making her forget what she was about to say.

"You might be more comfortable if you lay back."

She slowly lowers herself as he folds a towel and places it underneath her head.

He puts her feet on his shoulders, then gently teases her through her light blue silk panties. It's so convenient when she's wearing a dress. Since regaining her strength, she's been living in them for when these spontaneous opportunities present themselves.

Panting, she says, "You know dinner is going to burn if you don't hurry."

He leans over and turns the oven off. "Now it can take all the time it—I mean, we—need."

He plants tiny kisses down her leg, starting at her knee, inching his way down until his lips barely brush where his fingertips danced.

Her hips undulate as she moans.

He pulls back, watching her until she stops.

She looks up at him with a wrinkled brow.

He grins then proceeds by trailing kisses from the other knee down until he repeats over the light blue silk, this time adding more pressure.

Her hips undulate more, pushing up, begging for him to stop in the center and move his attention where she's most hungry. Her head gently falls from one side, then to the next, while she moans softly.

He slowly peels the silk away from one side and blows. The sudden burst of hot air sends shivers to her toes, causing her legs to spread wide open.

In one swift motion, his tongue pokes inside. Then one long stroke, slowly, he takes one long lick, as if she's a lollipop and back down, searching inside again.

She gasps and moans; her hips buck and press against him as he repeats this, back and forth, increasing his speed each time, a little faster—and firmer.

Her hips buck wildly, her heels digging into his shoulders. The heatwave surging through her body, causing her skin to take on a rosy hue.

Sensing she's on the verge, he says, "Grab your knees, I'll be right back."

He pulls away and grabs the step stool he conveniently placed nearby earlier. His sweatpants hit the top step one second after his feet do. He tested the height earlier—perfect.

He pulls her panties off as she looks at him through half-slitted eyes, and lips. He watches her cheeks vibrate as she pants in anticipation.

He pushes two fingers inside her, causing a deep-throated moan to escape as her head drops. He uses the juices on his fingertips and rubs the tip of his erection, making sure the entrance is clear of all friction.

As he slowly enters her, she lets out a deeper moan as she throws her legs wide apart, welcoming him in.

"Are you okay? Comfortable?"

She looks up at him and nods as her tongue traces her deep rouge lips. He watches her eyes close, and her head falls back, exposing her long, swan-like neck. From the first time he ever laid eyes on her, she was, and still is, the most beautiful woman he's ever seen. And now, she's his wife. His heart and head crash into each other. Not sure if it's the physical pleasure from the friction or the overwhelming fullness in his heart, their collision sends him into a series of rapid internal explosions, causing his heart and head to explode together.

As he plunges himself deeper into her, feeling his heart and groin both explode in unison, she pushes her hips into him with all her might as she matches his eruption.

Spent and exhausted, he lays his head down on her chest, attempting to catch his breath.

She runs her fingers through his hair, staring up at the ceiling, trying to catch her breath, willing her heart to slow down.

After a few moments, she says, "Is this when they would insert the baster?"

The moans of earlier and current laughter are so loud, they drown out the clicking sounds as the shutter quickly fires off several more photos.

CHAPTER SIXTEEN

Tina comes home early from the studio to find Zya with her head buried into her computer.

"Hey babe, I think you're really going to love the set-up for the show. I played up the romantic Valentine's Day colors as you asked. Stan helped by pulling some deep burgundies and velvety reds in your collection."

"Yeah, sounds good."

"Do you want to keep it mostly reds, or should I add some pinks too? I know your collection is mostly the royal shades. I wasn't sure if soft pinks would clash."

"Uh-huh," Zya says, keeping her eyes fixed on her screen. The mouse zipping left, then right across the pad in front of her.

"I thought we could use some actual blood too, since it's the right shade of red. What do you think?"

"Yeah, sure, you're the master of that domain," Zya says as she squints at thumbnail images.

"How bout we do a Carrie scene and pour a bucket of blood on the wedding dress when it comes out."

"Love it...wait, what?"

"Now I have your attention."

"Sorry. I'm trying to pick a photo to go with this questionnaire. Which one do you like?"

Tina walks over and looks at the images of the family, all four of them. "Wow, I love these. I forgot we took them. It seems like the girls have already aged at least three years."

"Bite your tongue."

Tina laughs. "Sorry, I know they'll forever be our babies. What's this for?"

"An article in *Elle* magazine for their February issue. It's a last-minute request, so I don't have time for us to have a formal shoot."

"Wow! *Elle*, that's big!"

Zya shrugs it off. "Yeah, it's cool. Let me know which one you like best. I've got to pee; I've been holding it forever."

When Zya jumps up, Tina takes her place in the chair and starts scrolling through the images, honored she wants to send one of the entire family.

When she scrolls over to the right, the mouse falls off the table. As she leans over to pick it up, the mouse pad and papers underneath fall to the ground. She picks them up and sees the one with the bold *Elle* letters.

While reading the first paragraph, she quickly nods her head up and down. As she reads on, she pulls back—her eyes bulge. She leans in for a closer look. As she gets to the third and fourth paragraphs, her mouth drops and she gasps.

Zya comes out of the bathroom and heads for the kitchen to open their nightly bottle of wine.

"Zya! This isn't just some interview; you're sending your samples ahead to New York for a photo shoot. They're featuring you on the cover! You don't want a family photo; you want one of your headshots. You had some done last year. Send one of those."

Zya walks over and places two glasses on the desk. She grabs Tina's hands, pulling her up and into her arms and kisses her. "My success is not about me, it's about us—all of us. I'm proud of my family. I wouldn't have this without all of you. It's no coincidence, my shot to stardom has happened since you've come into my life. I want to share us with the world."

"I love you, Zya Monroe."

"I love you too, Tina, almost Monroe."

"Hey, am I taking your name? We haven't talked about it yet."

"No, we haven't. You're free to keep yours; I think changing mine might be difficult. Besides, we have two children to think about. Maybe one of us can hyphenate?"

Tina wrinkles up her nose and says, "We'll see. You shocked me proposing during your show, now you're ready to put it in print in front of the entire world. You know *Elle* is worldwide, right?"

Zya hands Tina her wine glass and, after a long sip, says, "One question they asked is, of all my accolades and achievements, what am I most proud of. I'm sure they mean as it pertains to my designs, and I came up with a few. But Ashanti, you, and Stacey kept popping in my head.

"Before we met, the answer was always Ashanti. And she probably always will be my number one greatest achievement. She was always why I woke up every morning. Then I met you. I almost let society dictate my happiness. When you said your ex wanted to get back with you and you had a job opportunity in Seattle, I couldn't bear the thought of losing you. I realized nobody else mattered except for those under this roof. So, that's how I answered their question. My greatest accomplishment is our family. When they see it, they may decide they don't want me for their feature, and that's okay. I won't change it; it's how I feel. You and the kids are much more important to me than any magazine article."

"Even if it's the February, Valentine's month, and a direct competitor to *Vogue* feature?" Tina asks.

"Even if *Vogue* themselves asked for their December Holiday issue."

Tina and Zya embrace and kiss, tasting the full-bodied 2016 Pinfolds Cabernet, Bin 707, on their tongues.

Stacey comes in the front door, closing it quietly.

"Hey, where's Ashanti?" Zya asks.

Stacey stops at the bottom of the stairs. Without turning around to look at them, she says, "She stayed after school helping Mitch with his presidential campaign."

"That's nice. Why didn't you stay and help too?" Tina asks.

Stacey shrugs her shoulders, still looking at the stairs. "I don't know. They looked all lovey-dovey, like three was a crowd. Plus, I have homework to do, anyway."

Zya walks over to her. "Stacey, that doesn't sound like Ashanti; everything okay?"

Stacey looks up and then quickly darts her eyes away. "Yeah, everything's fine. We're good. Now that they're a thing, I need to give them some space—it's cool. I don't like him, anyway."

Tina joins them. "Honey, it's hard when your best friend gets a boyfriend. It eats into your time. We've all been through it—it's difficult. Ashanti will do her best to balance it out. Talk to her—she's your best friend. Tell her how you feel. She's a smart girl, and I'm sure the last thing she wants to do is hurt your feelings, you know that, right?"

"I know, Mom. I just can't sit around and watch them suck face." Stacey shudders.

Zya does too; but she hides it better. The thought of her baby girl's lips touching someone else's for pleasure—Humph!

where r u?
> *almost home*

your mom is asking ?'s
> *what did u tell her?*

help w/campaign
> *okay thanks*

U okay?
> *think so*

did u?
> *talk later*

CHAPTER SEVENTEEN

"**D**om, Dom, over here." Amber hugs her as she takes the spot next to her in kickboxing class.

"I'm so glad to see you. I wasn't sure anyone else would be here. I was a bit nervous about coming."

"I know what you mean. I've been coming for the last few weeks. All new faces."

"Look, there's Zya!" Dominque says as she waves her over.

Zya quickly sees her above everyone's heads and starts in their direction. "Hey, girls, fancy meeting you here." She hugs them both just as the instructor greets everyone. She nods in their direction, remembering them although it has been over a year since their last class.

As they're pairing up and mentally preparing to destroy the bags hanging in front of them, Debra joins them and asks if their fourth wouldn't mind joining the trio to their left.

"Debra!" Dominque squeals.

"Wow! The four musketeers, back together again," Zya says, holding the bag as the other three take turns gently tapping it with the top of their right foot to warm up.

"I need to lose these twenty pounds of baby fat I gained. Then I can at least be my normal fifteen over I'm always struggling to lose."

They all laugh.

"I could stand to lose twenty myself. This collection has me a little stressed. Everybody talking about me being the next Armani or Versace, has me overthinking my fabrics and designs. I've been living off coffee and fast food."

"And I've heard a bottle of pricey wine every night," Amber adds.

Zya blushes. "Maybe…My little vixen has a thing for fine wine and sexy French lingerie. I refuse to deny her either."

Amber says, "I can understand why you would be nervous, but now is not the time to doubt yourself—it got you this far. Keep doing what you've been doing."

"You're right—I'm not giving up the wine!"

"Or the French lingerie!" Dominque adds.

They switch places, so Debra now holds the bag as the other three throw their elbows into it.

"Amber, you need to gain a few pounds. I know you've been through hell, but you need to eat, girl."

"I have been—nerves, I guess. I haven't heard from my stalker in a while; I think he's just trying to scare me. It's been almost a year since it started; don't you think he would have done something by now?"

"You're not letting your guard down, are you?" Debra asks.

"No. And I'm about to take some serious frustration out on this bag right now. Stand back, ladies."

After class, they head to the juice bar. They look up at the menu board to see the latest crazes. Their usuals are no longer available. The menu now features concoctions, including prickly pears and pitayas, which are dragon fruit, although they look nothing like fire breathing mythological beings. Then there is bergamot orange, yuzu, calamansi, pomelo, and ugli fruit (pronounced ūglee), the peppy girl, and her bouncing ponytail explains from behind the counter. The most significant recent addition is cold brewed coffee or as they call it—Nitro. Not understanding what any of these mixtures are, they opt for bottled waters.

As they watch young girls in tight cotton Lycra cropped pants and sports bras sip their fancy fruit mixtures, giggling and batting their eyes at the muscle-bound jocks standing way inside their personal space, Amber says, "Wasn't that us just last year?"

"That was never me," Debra adds.

"Oh, that was definitely me," Dominque says.

"Dom, what's going on with you? We haven't had a chance to catch up. Married life treating you good?"

"Yeah, Tad's great," she says, grinning so wide even a Cheshire cat would be impressed. She fills them in about flipping the coin in May.

"You prepared to wait two years if Tad wins?" Amber asks.

"Yeah, it's our decision. It wouldn't be fair if I didn't consider his feelings too. We're at a stalemate. How else can we decide?"

"A year and a half?" Debra adds.

"Yeah, maybe, Tad is stuck on what the doctor said—two years. I can't blame him. He puts me first, and I think kids are more important. He has a mom and a dad. And although a bit overly religious, they're very close. I'm a bit envious—I want to have that experience and have an actual family; even if it kills me."

Amber's eyes tear up as she rests her hand on Dom's arm. "I don't have kids, so I can't relate." She looks around at Debra and Zya. "But after loving on their little squirts, I understand what you mean."

Zya says, "There's not a love like it."

Debra nods.

"What about you?" Dominque asks Amber.

"I'd love to have kids someday; I think I still can. I just never thought I'd be where I am right now. I'm grateful to be with the man I love. If kids are in the cards for us; then it shall be. I'm taking it one day at a time."

"He hasn't asked you again, has he?" Debra asks.

"No, and I'm not bringing it up; not yet at least."

Zya asks, "Why do you think that is? He was so gung-ho when he asked you before the trial. It's been three months."

"Guilt. I know it's affected what types of cases he's taking on, passing over the more challenging ones. Stewart told me a few things in confidence. I imagine it will work itself out. It's probably just too soon."

"He got your case dismissed, didn't he?" Zya asks.

Before she can answer, Debra, asks, "And he's looking for your stalker still, right?"

"Yes, and yes. If he can find out who is sending me these texts, that would be great. *That* would be the confidence boost he needs."

"No closer?" Debra asks.

"No, but I'm going to change the subject now." She turns to Zya. "What are we doing for your birthday?"

Zya laughs. "Oh, that, I forgot I have one of those coming up. Can we keep it low key? I plan to celebrate the night before intimately if you know what I mean, so I thought maybe a BBQ at the house in the afternoon? It's a Sunday, so it would be perfect. I hope you all are okay with that."

"You only turn forty once, so if that's what you want, then that's what you'll get. And by we, I mean, we will do everything. Your gorgeous fiancé will take you out of the house in the morning, and when you come back, you will sit back and enjoy—*capisce*?"

Zya waves her hands in the air. "Okay, okay, uncle—I give. But no gifts. Promise me, no presents. I know you're going to say I'm being corny—your friendship is more than I'll ever want. When I met Tina, I was afraid that might change."

"Because you were in love with a woman?" Amber asks, quickly drawing her head back.

"Yeah, you're all women too. We've traveled together, and we've seen each other naked. I don't want any of you to think I'll suddenly look at you differently."

"You can stop me if you think I'm out of line," Amber says. "Women always check each other out, not in a lustful way, with admiration—and sometimes jealousy. We're always eyeing each other's clothes, hair, makeup, shoes, the complete package. Hell, when I see you naked, I wish I had full round boobs like you. I know you bought yours, but still, I'm jealous as hell. I don't want to grab 'em; I'm just admiring them."

"And Dom, those legs of yours. OMG, they go all the way up to your armpits. I don't want them wrapped around me, but you have some gorgeous legs."

"Thank you, Amber," Dominque says, as she bats her eyes, playfully.

"We're your friends. You being in love with Tina will never change that. Just because you found love with her doesn't mean you're suddenly going to want us, and we know that. If you did, you would have a long time ago."

Debra reaches over to Zya. "Any friend whose relationship would change was never a genuine friend, to begin with. And girl, we're not just friends—we're sisters; we're not going anywhere."

"I should have brought this up sooner; it's been weighing on my mind. I love you guys so much; I don't know why I was so nervous. I should have known better. But seriously, no gifts, okay? This here is more precious than anything I could unwrap on my birthday."

"Okay. No wrapped packages, deal?" Amber says, winking at Dominque and Debra.

"Deal!"

CHAPTER EIGHTEEN

"Why don't you come with me this morning?"

"I wouldn't last a block."

"I'll go slow, I promise," Stewart begs.

"I wouldn't even make it up over the bridge. If I pick up jogging, I'll start running up and down the street."

"Okay, how about we go for a nice long walk instead?"

"Why are you so interested in getting me outside?"

"You're as pale as can be. You could use some vitamin D. Now come on, I'm not taking no for an answer. Grab your sneakers."

Patrick reluctantly puts on his trainers and grabs a hat from the closet. "If I need mouth-to-mouth, you better not hesitate."

"Buddy, you're the only man my lips would ever touch."

Patrick pulls back, looking at him surprised.

"Only if you need mouth-to-mouth. Really?" Stewart says with raised eyebrows.

As he grabs his keys from the tray, a stack of papers falls to the ground.

"Oh damn! I forgot to give this to Amber," he says as he holds up a manila envelope. "I'll put it right here," he says as he puts it on the table by the door, "so she'll see it when she gets home."

"Amber's getting her mail here? And did you just say, home?"

"It came last week; I forgot to tell her. And yes, I said home —it's hers as much as it is ours, you know that."

As they head out of their street on the south side of Las Olas Boulevard, Stewart asks, "I'm sorry if I'm prying, you haven't been yourself. Anything you want to get off your chest?"

"This why you want to take a walk?"

"Part of it. You do really need to get some sun, man. You are so white. The Grim Reaper is gonna think you escaped."

"Ha, ha, ha, hilarious. I have no reason to be in the sun."

After several minutes of silence, Stewart asks, "Listen, I know the trial didn't go as planned; it still eating at you?"

"Yes, and…"

"And?"

"Amber's been having these dreams."

After another long silence, Stewart asks, "And?"

"She's killing Brettinger—stabbing him over and over again. She says she can't kill him enough."

"So, what's the big deal?"

"Somehow, in the back of my mind, I began asking myself if she did it—if she could kill him. Would that have satisfied my ego if she had been guilty?"

"But she didn't do it, right?"

"No, detective Ackerman reminded me he was stabbed once in the neck, not repeatedly. Plus, they found the ice pick in the bathroom. She must have just been working through some emotions and recalling part of Brandy's video statement. She says she didn't watch it, and technically—she didn't. She was in the kitchen one night while I was. Anyway, she didn't kill him—it was Brandy. For me to think for even a second, though..."

Patrick hangs his head, beating himself up mentally as they walk in silence the rest of the way to the end of the street. Patrick has plenty of swirling around in his head. *How could I have thought, even for a second, she was capable—even if he deserved it?*

The quietness soon ends as they turn east and head toward the ocean. Cars are already speeding in both directions, and the sun has barely peaked over the horizon.

Runners, walkers, bikers, coming and going on both sides of the streets. Some are out for the exercise. Others are out just to be seen. You could spot them easily by their sports bras two sizes too small and the boy shorts that are—oh boy—not shorts at all; they're more like bathing suit bottoms. Worn so tight you can see the outline of all their curves, including those between their legs.

One guy across the street is sporting a bikini. Yes, you read that right, a man in a woman's two-piece. Hairy chest and his package neatly tucked away, don't ask me how inside a teeny-tiny satin triangle bottom. There have been a few imitators, but this guy is the real deal, full mustache and all.

As they cross the bridge, boats and yachts of all sizes, crisscross underneath with the larger ones waiting on both sides for the designated opening times. At the very top, you can see the blue of the Atlantic and the sculpture that sits on the sand. During the holidays, and since it is Christmas Eve, it's a snowman in a tropical shirt and straw hat.

Once they get to A1A along the ocean, cars creep by at ten miles an hour, mostly occupied by men hoping to catch sight of as much skin as possible. You can always tell the residents from the tourists. The locals are wearing jackets and long pants, as Patrick is today—unless they're running. Then their apparel of choice is wicking tops and shorts. Visitors are enjoying the sixty-five-degree temperatures in their string bikinis, thongs, and speedos. Their skin is tinged a lovely light pink with a thick paste of white across their nose. Even at this hour, just past 7 a.m., the beach is filling up with everyone making sure they find the perfect place. Some choose to be close to the bar by the street, it's always five o'clock somewhere, while others prefer to be by the water's edge to exfoliate their feet during a long walk toward the jetty at Port Everglades or the Angler's Pier in Lauderdale-by-the Sea.

As they weave their way around walkers and joggers, Patrick breaks the silence and asks, "Have you seen Brandy lately?"

"No."

"Why don't you go see her?"

"Amber said she doesn't want me to come."

"That's odd. She cares about you, doesn't she?"

"Oof, I don't know. I wish I did. I know you didn't tell me everything she said on the video; it's probably for the best. It's just hard to believe she played me like that, and it's all an act."

"The player got played, is that it?" Patrick says.

Stewart chuckles. "Yeah, maybe. She's one tough cookie. It could all be a facade—this wall she's put up. Or maybe she's just a world-class bitch."

"Do you want to find out?"

"I think I do. I can't get her out of my head. I don't know if it's the thrill of the chase, or if I really have feelings for her."

Patrick fills him in on Amber's thoughts about Brandy having ulterior motives. If Stewart wants to know, he'll ask Amber to bring him into the loop. Maybe a visit from him wouldn't be a bad thing. Could she keep up the charade with both of them there? If she does care for him, she might crack. And then again, if she doesn't, it could be very painful and break Stewart's heart.

As Patrick finishes his sentence, Stewart's arm goes across his chest to stop him in his place.

Patrick looks up to see a brunette pushing a baby carriage in their direction.

Quickly, Stewart attempts to cross the street. Too many cars —DAMN!

"Stewart! Stewart! Is that you?" The brunette calls after him.

"Oh, hi Isabel," Stewart says, glancing over at Patrick, wearing a forced smile.

Patrick's eyes go wide, hearing her name. He looks at Stewart...then Isabel...then the baby carriage.

Stewart kisses her on the cheek and introduces her. "This is my buddy, Patrick. Patrick, meet Isabel."

"Nice to meet you, *friend*," she says, stretching out the last word in a sultry way. She bats her eyes, holding onto his hand.

Patrick pulls it back quickly as his heart beats in rapid-fire in his chest and ears.

Stewart looks inside the carriage. "Who's this little guy?"

"My son, Eugene. Isn't he handsome?" she says as she lifts him. "Here, want to hold him?" she asks, thrusting him into Patrick's hands before he can answer.

He grabs the baby out of instinct, although honestly, it's the last thing he wants to do. Stewart promised after the late-night, blindfolded, hot tub fiasco, he would take care of it. Now, as he looks down into this bundle of coos in his hands, with a head full of dark ringlets and deep dark brown eyes, the same color as his own, he wonders—*could it be?* Eugene smiles up at him, enhancing the dimple in his chin, and reaches up to touch the replica in Patrick's. *This kid looks exactly like me!*

"Eugene? Isabel, who names their kid Eugene?" Stewart says, reading Patrick's thoughts.

"It was my dad's name. It means noble."

"It means, 'pick on me and kick my ass' in school if you ask me," Stewart says, sarcastically.

Patrick puts Eugene back into the carriage gently yet as quickly as possible. "It was nice meeting you, Isabel and Eugene, but we have to get going," he says and turns, grabbing Stewart by the arm. They're three steps away already when she returns the gesture.

"That kid looks just like me. He has my hair, my eyes...did you see the dimple in the chin? How old is he?"

"Should I go back and find out?" Stewart asks and turns.

"No! No!" Patrick says, turning him back around. "He looked to be about six months. One year and about three months; that's about right...he's my kid. Oh, shit!"

CHAPTER NINETEEN

The holidays have come and gone with little fanfare. Everyone was glad to say goodbye to 2018 and ring in the New Year. They all went through the motions, celebrating Christmas, wishing each other joy, even sneaking kisses under the mistletoe. Stacey gifted Ashanti another weapon this year; this one's made of latex instead of steel. Secretly, they all wanted the last digit of the date to just turn over and start anew.

"When do you think we can pick a wedding date?"

"I'm sorry, you've been so patient," Debra says, just before kissing Brian on the cheek. She grabs her coffee cup with both hands and looks deeply into the light creamy liquid.

"I don't think the date is in there," he says after waiting for a response.

She chuckles. "Sorry, I'm just thinking."

"Should I go turn off the smoke detectors?"

She playfully slaps him. "Funny, you're so hilarious. I thought Patrick would have proposed to Amber at Christmas. She doesn't want to ask him; I guess he has his reasons."

"Is that why you turn your ring around whenever we're with them?"

"You noticed?"

"Yeah, and I think Amber has too. If you don't want to wear it when we're together with them, I understand, it's okay."

"No, that would be too obvious. She wouldn't want me to do that."

"She probably wouldn't want you to hold off planning it either."

"You're right," Debra says. "She's just been through so much. I don't want to add any more heartache."

"Can we make some plans and keep it between us?"

"We can't elope. They would never forgive me."

"I don't mean that. Trust me, I know they would never forgive me if we took off. Even if it was your idea and I didn't change your mind."

"Yeah, they'd never forgive you. They're great like that."

Brian pulls her to him and kisses her with his hand behind her neck. "I only ask because you're turning thirty-eight this year."

"You have to remind me? Didn't your mother teach you anything? You don't talk about a woman's age, or her weight, for that matter. And if you do, you better get it wrong—the other way."

Brian, through bits of chuckling, says, "Yes, my mother taught me how to be a gentleman. Both my parents were also great role models; I'd like that chance too—to be a father."

Debra's eyes pool. She's been so busy taking care of her offspring; she never thought to ask him if he wanted children.

"Don't get me wrong, I love Tracey and Little George as if they're my own—I would do anything for them. What if we had one of our own?"

Debra jumps up into his lap, spilling both cups of coffee across the island. Luckily, they don't fall to the ground. They slide into the wall as a coffee wave splashes up, covering the white linen wallpaper.

Brian's chair almost tips over. He catches it just in time by grabbing the countertop.

"Yes! Yes! Yes! I want to have your baby. Why have we not talked about this before? YES!"

"Debra, can I be your baby daddy?"

She laughs as tears are steadily falling down her cheeks while she nods enthusiastically.

He kisses her then kisses away the tears. "I love you so much, Debra."

"I love you too."

She pulls back and looks deep into his baby blues, thinking how lucky their child would be to have his beautiful cornflower eyes and curly blond locks.

She looks at the clock on the wall. "Fifteen more minutes… scoot your chair back."

"What?"

"Scoot your chair back. It's time for more practice."

"What are you talking about?"

"You've been working out," she says, sticking out her tongue, attempting to flick it rapidly as he does. "I've been practicing too. You're about to find out why those jumbo franks are in the fridge."

☯

"Good morning, sunshine."

"Morning, babe, Happy New Year," Dominque says, stretching like a cat. Her hand touches the wall behind the headboard while her toes touch the footboard.

"I've been thinking…"

"Uh, oh, should we have coffee with a shot of Kahlua first?"

"I think you're going to like this," Tad says, leaning over brushing a strand of hair from her face. Looking deeply into her crystal blue eyes, he says, "Let's go away on a trip."

She jumps up on her elbow so fast, she almost knocks him over. "I love trips. Where do you want to go?"

"Tahiti."

Dominque's eyes sparkle and widen in excitement. "Really? I would love to go to the South Pacific. We can't afford it, can we? We spent so much making sure we could have a family. And we still have to pay for the transfer…it will not be cheap."

"I know, but we deserve it. My mom and dad want to do something special for us. We can get a new car, or fix up the bathroom—and make it the spa retreat you want, or we can splurge and get away. Let's take a second honeymoon. We didn't really have one, anyway. Going to the Bahamas was nice."

Dominque looks at him out of the corner of her eye with a wrinkled brow, causing him to add quickly, "We didn't go anywhere—we stayed in bed the whole time. Not that I'm complaining."

Dominque laughs at the memory, then blushes.

"Before you answer. I know it's impractical, and that's so not me. Every fiber of my being says it makes more sense to invest in the house, but I want to make memories. After helping you through your cancer treatments, I want to see you laugh and that look of wonderment you get when you experience something exciting—I want to see more of that. I know it's on your bucket list, and when we have kids, it will be years before we can take a trip like this. Let's do it now."

"Any part of you thinking I might not have years?"

Tad's eyes cast down, picking at an imaginary thread on the sheet. "Part of it. You deserve to have your dreams come true. I promise you the bathroom will get done bit by bit, each weekend, as soon as we get back. What do you think?"

"When do we leave?" she squeals, rolling on top of him, planting kisses all over his face and neck.

❦

"Think we can keep this tradition up every year?"

"As long as we can get to our car, I don't see why not," Zya says as she rolls Tina over, instantly remembering how hot it was finding her commando when they slipped out to Zya's car to ring in the new year. "You surprised me last night."

"Did I now? I still have several more up my sleeve, you know." Tina playfully plants kisses all over Zya's neck. She stops and pulls back, resting on her elbow. "Maybe it was just me. You seemed hesitant at first. That's not like you; what was on your mind?"

Zya stares up at the ceiling, taking long, controlled breaths before she answers. "The back seat of the car was Doug's favorite place when his New York socialites had actual cash to give him instead of paying in sexual favors. I was just thankful for his company; I didn't think he was using me. Looking back now, I know otherwise."

"Why didn't you say something? We could have found a creative alternative."

"You were so excited about the idea. And once your tongue started playing, all thoughts of Doug completely vanished. He never did those things to me."

"No! You never had oral sex with him?"

"I took care of him. I hated it, but it made him happy. You wouldn't know it by the look on his face." Zya shivers at the memory of his twisted face while he held her head firmly in place and fucked her mouth.

"I'm so sorry—he's such a prick. This is why I'm glad I've only wanted girls."

"Then how do you explain Stacey?"

"I've been waiting for you to ask me about that. Her father is one of the sexiest bartenders in Seattle. I mean, he is HOT! I don't do guys, but this one. His eyes were a bluish-green, like the Caribbean Sea. When he smiled, his eyes lit up. You did everything in your power to keep seeing those pearly whites. I swear, I saw women cream their jeans because of his smile. When he wasn't tending bar, he was working out or at the beach. He wasn't muscle-bound; as a triathlete, he was toned and firm—everywhere. When he mixed his concoctions, you could see the striations ripple across his shoulders like tiny waves coming ashore. His dirty blond hair was always too long, so when he peeked up at you through loose strands, you drowned in his ocean pools. Oh, when he reached up for glasses in the rack, and I swear he planned this, his shirt would rise as his pants lowered to expose that perfect 'V' from his obliques pointing down to…you know where." Tina bites down on her finger as she says the last few words, her eyes fluttering.

"You sure you were never into men? Sure sounds like this one got your juices flowing."

"I've always been able to appreciate a nice looking man; this one was who I compared all others to."

"My ex and I used to hang out at his bar all the time watching the women swoon over him. It was hilarious and embarrassing to watch—especially when they got drunk. I can't tell you how many he took into the back room for a quick blow job. He swears he never screwed them; he wasn't passing up having them wrap their luscious lips around him and suck him dry. If they were smoking hot, he'd finger them until they came hoping they'd *cum* back for more. They always tipped him handsomely. On the weekends, we watched him disappear in the back four or five times. We stayed after closing while he cleaned, and he told us about his escapades. He'd give us every detail, to how big and firm their tits were, and how he sucked their juices off his fingers after he made them scream his name. We'd go home and have mind-blowing sex afterward.

"We talked more and more about having a child, and we weren't getting any younger. We thought of him, but we worried about the ramifications. One night, we were doing shots, so we were nice and toasted; we talked about settling down and having kids. He was dead set against it, so we teased him; what a shame it would be to not replicate himself—he was so gorgeous. How could he deny the world his genes? A few nights later, after closing, he dropped a lab test on the bar in front of us. He had just gotten tested for STDs—he was clean."

Zya sits up and turns to Tina with wide eyes. "You had intercourse him?"

Tina, nodding, says, "That was the deal. He never masturbated because one, he didn't have to, and two, hands never got him excited. If we wanted his sperm, one of us was going to have sex with him. My ex was never going to be the one to carry the child, so I was the lucky participant."

"If he was as hot as you say he was, you had to have enjoyed it."

"The three of us played together; I'll admit, it was a lot of fun. We had some big vibrators, but he was ginormous. He was surprisingly gentle—maybe it was because of the gasp that escaped when I saw the size of it. He took me from behind while I took care of my girl; it was fucking amazing. Since my focus was on pleasing her, and I can't orgasm without being stimulated, it worked out. Luckily, or maybe unluckily, I got pregnant pretty quickly; our ménage à trois only happened three times. He wanted nothing to do with the child. Once I was knocked up, we stopped going to the bar. I'm sure he knew."

"Wow! I always wondered where Stacey got those unusual eyes. Does she know?"

"No way, she thinks, we just picked sperm at a donation bank. Hey, if you want to change our tradition, we can pick a closet or a picnic table…"

Laying back on her pillow Zya says, "No, I'm happy to create a better 'back seat' memory with you."

"By the way, where did you learn that new trick?"

"Which one?"

"You know, where you used the tip to...I mean, you flicked it super fast. And then you licked..."

"Let me just show you," Zya says with a grin and then disappears under the covers.

Tina's giggles quickly turn into low groans as Zya gives her a repeat performance from the night before.

Tina's hips quickly start bucking as Zya's tongue flicks feverishly.

Stopping, Zya suddenly pulls the covers behind her head and says, "I've been thinking about surprises."

"Okay," Tina says, gasping.

"Would you be willing to wear the wedding gown at the end of the show next month?"

"You already asked me to marry you; you're not proposing again, are you?"

"Nope, I have something even better planned."

☯

"You up?"

"I am now," Stacey says, yawning.

"I'm sorry, did I wake you?"

"No, I'm just teasing you. I'm awake. What's on your mind?"

"You're my best friend; never forget that. I know I've been spending a lot of time with Mitch, but I miss you. I know you don't like him. Can the three of us hang out sometime? Would you try for me, please?"

"You know why I don't like him?"

"I know; people can change and he truly has. Please give him a chance."

"You're having sex now, aren't you?"

"We've tried, but we haven't yet."

Stacey leans up on her elbow on the makeshift bed they put together on the floor the night before to watch the ball drop. "Really? I thought you had by now. That's why I gave you condoms for Christmas."

"We will use them when the time comes. We're both just taking it super slow."

"He's a virgin too?"

"I think so."

"I'm shocked. Maybe there's hope for him after all. Can I ask why you haven't, or is it too personal? It's okay if you don't want to share, even with me."

"No, you're my best friend; I don't mind. When he kisses me, my stomach does these flips, and I get all tingly inside. He kisses my neck and my ears, and I swear I think I'm going to come out of my skin."

"Has he touched you? I mean, your boobs, at least?"

"Usually, when we're getting hot and heavy, he stops, and we go for a walk, or he wants to talk. I think he's nervous. It's okay because I know I am; it's nice we're taking it slow."

"You said, usually."

"Two nights ago, we were in the back of his car, and I started kissing his neck like he does mine, sucking on it, I was getting into it. He started moaning and grinding into me. I was lying half on top of him, so he was humping my leg. His hand came up under my blouse and grabbed my breast. It was amazing and terrifying at the same time. I thought I was going to explode, and then he suddenly stopped and pushed me off him. He jumped out of the car and started walking down the street. I chased after him, asking him what was wrong—he kept apologizing."

"He's not a virgin."

"What? What do you mean?"

"I'm pretty sure. In fact, I'd say 99.9 percent he's not. He just doesn't want to take yours away from you," Stacey says as her index finger comes to her lips and her eyes dart across the room.

"You two have talked about having sex, right?"

"Well, not exactly. I mean, we haven't said the words. But it's the natural progression, right?"

"Does he know you're a virgin?"

"Yes."

"And how does he know?"

"My religion."

"Did you ever wonder if maybe that has something to do with it?"

"I told him I've been thinking about becoming Christian."

"Okay, I'm your best friend, so don't get mad at me, I'm gonna be frank with you."

Ashanti nods.

"Changing your religion is not something you do frivolously, and you don't do it for the wrong reasons. You don't stop being Muslim, because you want to sleep with Mitch."

"That's not it; I'm not changing because of him. There are a lot of reasons; I've had my doubts for a while now. My mom and I have had many conversations about this. I'm not doing it for that—that would be stupid."

"Does he know that?"

"You think that's it?"

"Look, I still don't like the guy, but if he's the one who's walking away, then he might have some redeeming qualities after all. If you honestly care about him, talk about it."

"You never told me how you lost yours."

"I'll tell you, but you can never to tell my mom—or yours."

Ashanti nods as she sits up.

"I was thirteen, and looking back now, it was kind of stupid. I thought I was so grown-up; I certainly looked the part with my thirty-six double D's—the joy of going through puberty at twelve. I was at one of those meet-and-greet functions for homeschooled kids. We were at a roller-skating rink, and J.P. was there. He was such a jock, the quarterback for the city North Seattle Titans football team, and he played soccer. We were getting ready to move here, so I knew it would be the last time I would see him. When my mom dropped me off, I had on baggy jeans and a basic T-shirt. She laughed and told me I'd never get a boyfriend, or girlfriend, if I kept dressing like that. Little did she know, I had mini shorts and a little half top and no bra on under my clothes. As soon as I arrived, off they came, and so did J.P. when he saw the bottom of my watermelons when I reached up over my head, which I did several times. I might have accidentally, on purpose, fallen into him a few times on the rink. One time, my hand skimmed his crotch. I swear it was accidental; when I smiled at him, he grabbed my hand and pulled me off the rink.

"The next thing I knew, we were in the boy's bathroom with his tongue down my throat and his hands under my blouse squeezing my boobs so hard, it hurt. He took my hand and slipped it inside his pants, and told me to stroke him, so I did. He was groaning and humping and tonguing me. I swear I was wondering what all the fuss was. Next thing I knew, he came all over my hand. It was hot and sticky and gross. I ran to the sink so fast to get it off me. Next thing I knew, he was behind me, and his thumb went up between my legs with such force. Before I could stop him, he was inside, and he broke my hymen. There was so much blood; you should have seen the look on his face. He ran out of the bathroom and just left me there with this red trail running down my legs.

"I cleaned up, found my baggy jeans, and swore off ever wearing mini shorts ever again."

"You didn't have sex with him?"

"No."

"Have you had sex with anybody?"

"No, no one's been worthy."

"I think you're still a virgin then—technically. I mean, if you haven't had a penis inside you, you're still a virgin."

"You think?"

"Happy New Year."

"Yeah, Happy New Year," Patrick grunts and turns over to get out of bed.

"Can we talk for a minute?"

"Right now? Can it wait?"

"Well, unless you have to run to the bathroom to relieve yourself, no, it can't."

He looks back at her suspiciously. "I'll be right back."

She throws herself back on her pillow. She had worked up the nerve to have the talk, finally. She would not start 2019 on the wrong foot. They needed to clear the air and move forward.

He walks back into the room and sits on the edge of the bed with his back to her, running his fingers through his hair. "What do you want to talk about?"

She gets up and walks around and sits next to him. Grabbing his hand, she says, "I love you, Patrick Simpson. You are one of the most important people in my life. I'm so thankful I get to wake up next to you every morning."

He looks over at her and gives her a half-smile. He pulls her head toward him and kisses the top of it. "I love you too. Now can I get some coffee?"

"What is going on? Today is the start of a new year. Can we start it fresh? New slate? Tell me what's going on with you?"

He gets up and starts pacing the floor, continuing to run his fingers through his hair, causing it to stand up on end. "You almost ended up in jail for a crime you didn't commit. I couldn't protect you, and that's my job."

"It's not your fault. My sister is very conniving. I wish you would stop beating yourself up about it. I'm not in jail—I'm right here beside you—because of you."

He glances over, seeing the pleading in her eyes.

"You didn't want me to plead insanity, although so many people told you I should. If we had, I'd be sitting somewhere in a mental institution."

"If your sister hadn't confessed, you'd be sitting in jail. Where would you rather be?"

"You would have gotten me out on appeal. The hair test sample would have cleared my name."

"It came back negative—it wouldn't help."

"You would have found Brandy and brought her to trial."

"There was still no guarantee I could prove she killed him."

"Who made you God?"

"What do you mean?" he asks, taking two giant steps in her direction.

"If you weren't in love with me, you would have walked away knowing you did everything you could. You wouldn't be feeling the way you do right now." Amber pulls her arms back with her fists balled so tight, they're as white as the sheets on the bed.

"I would have had you plead insanity," Patrick says through clenched teeth. A vein in his forehead and neck throb with his rapid heartbeat.

She takes a deep breath and takes the last two steps toward him. Wrapping her arms around his neck, she says, "I love you more now then ever. And, I've never thought you gave less than one hundred percent for my case. They don't always work in our favor. The fact is it worked out, and here we are—together. Why can't we take advantage of that and just move on? I don't want to waste another day of living in the past, can't we please start planning for our future?"

"How can we talk about the future when we still have so much unfinished business?"

"We'll find my stalker, eventually. He hasn't sent me a text in weeks. If he was spying on me and heard us talking about it, he pulled it—he doesn't know what's happening anymore. I refuse to let him have control over me—he doesn't scare me anymore."

Patrick nods.

"That's not what I mean."

Amber looks at him, perplexed.

"Remember the girl in the hot tub last year? Isabel?"

Chapter Twenty

"I thought I told you I didn't want to see him," Brandy says to Amber.

"I wanted to see you. I needed to know if you honestly have no feelings for me," Stewart says.

"I have no feelings for you—now leave."

"No, make me."

"Guard!"

"Brandy, stop, please," Amber says.

Brandy scowls at her sister; she won't look at Stewart.

The helpful guard steps over to the table and says, "Everything all right here?"

"Just peachy, you can go," Brandy says, glaring at the guard.

Amber catches it, thinking it's strange if they're working together. There's pure hatred in those big brown orbs.

"You know that's the guard who was so nice to me when I was in here, right?"

"Really? Her? I'm shocked! She's the biggest bitch I've ever seen. She was in Belle Glade—and she's even worse here."

"You knew her before?"

"I'm as mean as they come; I'll at least admit it to your face. She'll stab you in the back, smiling the entire time. I don't trust her for one second, and you shouldn't either."

Brandy looks over at Stewart, and for a split second, her face softens.

He smiles, catching the change.

She quickly looks away. "I gotta go; I told you I didn't want to see him. If you want to see me, come alone next time," she says as she rises from the table, pushing the chair back so hard, it falls to the floor.

"Brandy," Stewart says, in a stern voice.

She stops, but doesn't turn around.

"I'm going to come back. You can refuse to see me. You can pretend there's nothing between us, but I know differently. I love you, and I'll keep trying. I won't stop."

Brandy hesitates, her face momentarily softening before quickly returning to her usual scowl.

"Suit yourself."

☯

"Now this is why we live in South Florida," Zya says, stretching her arms out, breathing in the crisp sixty-eight-degree air.

"Here, here, I'll drink to that," Debra says, lifting her drink in a toast.

Long ago they made a pact to meet for dinner once a month and since, have not failed to make it happen. All four determined not to let anything, unless it's a family emergency, come between their monthly female bonding sessions.

Tonight they've chosen an exclusive yet casual restaurant along the water attached to a boutique hotel. You must either be a guest, or a member, to enjoy the mouth-watering delicacies the chef prepares nightly. Zya, becoming one of the town's newest celebrities, has been a longtime member and one of the owner's favorites. When she made the reservation, they reserved the elegant tented gazebo table for her. It usually has eight to ten place settings; however, they've set it tonight for four fortunate diners.

They all pick up their champagne flutes filled to the rim with *Veuve*.

"You guys, look at us! Look at how our lives have changed so much in these last two years. Some good—some bad, yet through it all, we've stuck together—if anything, stronger than ever. I love you guys."

"Love you too, Amber," all three say in unison.

"By the way, those earrings sure are beautiful," Amber says.

"They are, aren't they? You guys shouldn't have. We made a deal—no gifts."

"The deal was no *wrapped* gifts. And if I remember correctly, they were loose in your birthday card," Dominque adds.

"Semantics. You all tricked me with your clever tactics."

"Hey, if you don't want them, we'll take them back. I'm sure between the three of us, we can get great use out of them," Amber says, reaching across the table, playfully attempting to reach for the 10mm peacock Tahitian pearl and diamond earrings hanging from Zya's ears.

"Oh no you don't," Zya says, tapping Amber's hand away. "I love them just fine. I think I've worn them every day. You really shouldn't have—but I'm glad you did," Zya says, touching the dangling dazzlers.

"You are all coming to New York next week for my show. Can I get your men to come with you? It's a Thursday, and it's last minute, but you think they could come up for the evening? It's a three hour nonstop flight. My show is 8:00; if they took a 4:00 plane, I could have a limo pick them up at the airport and in their seats, right next to you, with fifteen minutes to spare."

"Wow, you've thought this through."

"I have. It's Valentine's Day, and you're coming up and spending it with me. I get to have Tina with me; your loves should be with you too. I'd love it if we could all be together on the most romantic night of the year. And to celebrate my show. Please tell me you'll ask them?"

"I think it would be great," Amber says. "It might be precisely what Patrick needs right now."

"Everything okay?" Zya asks.

"I hate to ask this, but we're all wondering—why hasn't he proposed again?" Dominque asks.

"I think he's still beating himself up over my conviction. We're still working through it."

Amber fills them in about Isabel and baby Eugene.

"So Stewart doesn't think it's his? Even though there's a striking resemblance?" Zya asks.

"No, he doesn't. It's driving Patrick nuts."

"Wow! Girl, this could seriously change your life. What if it is his kid?"

"Then we'll deal with it. He wants to do the right thing, and I love him for that. He feels bad. If it is his kid, he hasn't been there from the start. First things first though, we're going to meet with her, and I guess one gets a DNA test done?"

"That's some real CSI shit right there," Dominque says. "Yeah, that's what they do—a DNA test."

"Okay, let's not get carried away; there's still a chance it's not his kid."

"Right. We'll know more after we meet with her. He's going to set it up, and we'll go talk to her together—without Stewart."

"Definitely leave Stewart at home. By the way, I went to see your phone guy at the mall the other day. He's not there anymore." Debra says.

"Really? That's odd, he's been there for years. I thought he was the supervisor. Maybe he got transferred."

"I asked because I'd go to another store, but they said he didn't show up for work one day."

"That is strange. I just saw him a few months ago. Did they say how long he's been gone?"

"Since mid-September."

"That's right about when I was there. Wow, strange. Guess I'll have to find a new tech guy I can bribe with bear claws."

"Deb, what's up with you and Brian? Have you picked a wedding date yet?" Amber asks.

Sheepishly Debra looks up at Amber.

"And please stop turning your ring around when you're around me. I'm happy for you. Patrick will come to his senses."

"You've just been through so much. And Zya, your wedding with Tina is coming up in a few months. I don't want to take away from your excitement. I can wait—it's no big deal."

Zya grabs Debra's hand. "Don't you ever worry about taking away our spotlight. There's plenty of love to go around. You wouldn't be taking anything away—you'd be adding to it."

Debra squeezes back. "Thank you both. I love you guys so much. There's been so much pain lately. I want everyone to bask in whatever joy there is as long as possible."

"Debra, always bending over backward," Amber says.

"While trying to stand on one hand," Zya interrupts.

"So everyone is happy," Dominque says, finishing the sentence.

"We're happy for you. Please don't put your plans on hold. We want to plan another wedding!" Amber says, wiping away silently dropping tears from Debra's eyes.

"Brian wants to have a baby with me."

Zya and Amber jump in their seats with excitement. Dominque gives her a weak smile.

Zya, sitting next to Amber, noticed a large envelope sticking out of her purse. "You getting mail at Patrick's house now? You move in?"

"No, but I might as well. I haven't been back to my place in months other than to shower and change clothes." Amber pulls the envelope out of her purse. "Patrick forgot it was there. It got shuffled around and lost under some piles of mail." She rips into the envelope as Zya and Debra talk more about Brian wanting a baby, while Dominque sits quietly listening.

Amber's eyes bulge out as she lets out a loud, "Oh!" Her hand goes to her mouth, holding back the screams, like the gates at a thoroughbred horse race.

She drops the envelope in front of her; the 8x10 photographs spread out as they slide on the table. The first one is shot through the living room curtain of Ashanti and Stacey sitting in front of an open pizza box. In bold red letters, **THEY ALL MUST DIE!**

Dominque, Zya, and Debra each grab for the photos.

"Amber, how long has Patrick had this envelope?" Zya asks, grabbing Amber's arm.

The squeezing in her chest makes it impossible to answer. She can't breathe. *Not my friends! No, he can't hurt my friends!*

Zya looks over at her, noticing her distress. "Breathe Amber. I'm sure this is just a scare tactic."

Debra says with tears streaming down her cheeks, "Well, it worked. I'm terrified!"

Dominque swallows hard, willing her heart to slow down. "Amber, you've been getting threats for over a year now. I think we all should be cautious, but I honestly don't think they're anything more than as Zya says—he's trying to scare you."

Amber looks over at her three best friends who are all trying hard to hide their fear. Amber nods and picks up the drink in front of her, draining it. She slams the empty glass down on the table, causing a few ice cubes to jump onto the table. "If anything ever happened to any of you, or your family, I couldn't live with myself."

Debra leans across the table and grabs Amber's hand. "You aren't to blame for this—you're a victim. We've all be warned;

we just need to be very careful and take extra precaution. Nothing's going to happen to us." The last sentence she says with authority, hoping to convince Amber and herself.

Chapter Twenty-One

Amber runs backstage to let Zya know the guys have all arrived when she notices three armed guards along the wall. They move toward her when Zya waves them away. "It's okay guys, this is Amber."

"I'm glad to see you are taking the threat seriously. Thank you—makes me feel better. The guys are here; they enjoyed their champagne in the limo. It took their minds off those photos."

"I know it's hard, but you need to live your life. Your stalker is trying to scare you. Be safe, just please stop obsessing."

"How can I? It's one thing to come after me; it's something totally different to go after my friends—and their families. If anything ever happened to any of you..."

"We're fine, and we're taking the appropriate precautions. This is exactly what he wants. You refused to crumble when he was terrorizing only you, so he included us; don't give him that satisfaction. Please."

"The kids are all okay, right?"

"Yes, Ashanti and Stacey are helping Debra's mom and sister with Little George and Tracey; they are all together, and they have police protection 24/7. Please try to relax and have some fun."

"Okay. I'll try—promise." She kisses her on the cheek and wraps her arms around her in a big hug. "Thanks for all this. It's a much-needed distraction."

Stan, Zya's right-hand man, rushes over. "We need you; it's almost time."

Zya kisses Amber on the cheek. "Now go sit and enjoy the show. I'll send a bottle of bubbly out to make sure you do," Zya says and winks as she spins on her heel and out of sight.

Within the ten minutes she's been away, every seat is full and people are still filing in and filling the back walls. Standing room only—again.

The pin lights in one row on each side of the runway light up the shiny white floor, reflecting like a mirror and leaving the gray walls shadowed and muted. All the seats, except those in the very front, are left in the dark. The only hint of a special day celebrating love is from the six reserved throne-like chairs, covered in rich red velvet. Amber's is the only one vacant between Patrick and Debra.

The row of pin lights blink three times as the room suddenly becomes quiet.

The lights go out entirely as the sounds of distant drums beat. A signature part of Zya's show—out of respect for her heritage. The lights blink down the line, alternating in a faint baby pink, filling the floor with a blush softness.

As the drums beat louder and faster, the lights blink quickly — the colors deepening. Then, the lights spin, flooding the patrons in deep red, and the room fills with excitement and anticipation.

It's all a frenzy; everybody is all smiles and laughter as dancing lights cover their faces. Suddenly, everything stops.

The drums come to a halt, and the lights go out. The room is so quiet you can hear a pin drop.

After a pause, the announcer says, "Ladies and gentlemen, welcome to Label Zya's 2019-2020, fall-winter collection."

The lights spin back on in every romantic shade imaginable of pinks, reds, blushes, in deep royals and light pastels, while the speakers boom out a funky beat as models stroll the catwalk, one right after the other. Tall and slender—not too skinny, the women model designs made with satins and silks in rusts, maroons, and fuchsias all accented in gold threads. This season's collection is fashioned in deep royal hues mixed with bold tropical prints. Her signature is combining her African flair with her Florida lifestyle. She has a knack for seamlessly blending the collision of two different worlds.

A casual floor-length sundress is accented with an elegant African shawl in contrasting colors. Another model wears dark orange, raw silk, pencil-thin slacks in a sangria shade chiffon, ruffled, off the shoulder blouse—a perfectly mismatched set.

The men's suits are beautifully tailored in crimson and raspberry with pale pink button-down shirts; never buttoned or worn with ties—that's not the Florida lifestyle. Zya's peers have warned, her designs should reflect the fashion capitals, New York, Paris, Milan. However, she's always been loyal to her hometown roots. She designs for hot, humid temperatures and bodies that like to show skin. Daring, yes—but then again, she is one of the hottest, most sought after designers right now. Following the beat of her own drum is precisely how she's gotten where she is today.

Each design and color combination is as exquisite and unusual as the next. The room is in constant applause, growing louder and louder as each perfectly paired oxymoron walks the length of the runaway.

When the last model exits the runway, the drums die down to a gentle rolling beat, and the lights fade to baby pink as the floor again blushes.

Tina steps out from behind the wall in the last design of the evening. A pastel pink chiffon skirt of ruffles makes her appear to float. The sleeves are waves of the same ruffles resting off her tanned shoulders. The underskirt is a dark fuchsia, only visible as she takes a step and the layers of ruffles part.

Tina was looking over Zya's shoulder one night when she was designing the dress. She loved the rows and rows of curling ruffles, said it looked like a princess's wedding dress, yet it wasn't quite a Label Zya—it lacked that something unexpected. When Zya asked what she meant, she reminded her about the dress in Milan. It looked so proper, Victorian even, until Dominque took a step and a gusset opened, revealing a vibrant color hidden inside. That's when they decided upon the fuchsia underskirt; seen as the layers of ruffles gently parted as the model took each step. Zya wanted Tina to wear it today since it was a collaboration. The excitement on Tina's face when they worked on it together told her it was an extraordinary gown. She had never seen her so animated about any of her designs.

The simple veil is layers of tulle in the same soft pink with a few darker shades mixed in. The headpiece and bouquet are all fresh roses in multiple shades of pinks and reds. A mix-match that somehow looks breathtaking.

Amber turns to Debra and says, "I think that's so romantic having Tina wear the wedding gown again. I hope this isn't the dress she's wearing in June."

"Wouldn't that be bad luck?"

Amber nods.

As Tina passes them, she gives them the pageant wave and smiles. She is beaming from ear to ear. Tina makes her way to the end of the catwalk and back as every patron inside Spring Studios jumps up clapping and whistling. Once she's behind the wall, the announcer says, "Ladies and Gentlemen, I present to you the mastermind behind tonight's stitchery wizardry, Zya Monroe."

Still, on their feet, the loud applause continues as Zya steps out, having changed into a beautiful raw silk floor-length dress in the same fuchsia as the underskirt of Tina's gown. She stops halfway, followed by Tina and the rest of the models.

The applause, if possible, grows even louder with more whistling, hoots, and shouting.

Zya motions for everyone to take their seats and hopefully quiet down as she takes the microphone handed to her.

"Thank you, thank you, please sit down, everyone. This has all been a dream come true for me. Here I am in New York and next year—Paris."

The room erupts again.

"You put me here. It's your support that helps make all this possible."

Zya's success is mostly her incredible talent, but also her humbleness, lack of ego, and always being thankful to her employees and customers. It does not go unnoticed, and as the room continues to erupt and get louder and louder, in praise and congratulations, it's obvious how much they love her. She grabs Tina's hand and smiles—drinking in the affection.

"I believe you all know this beautiful woman, Tina. I proposed to her at my show last summer." The proposal was the talk of the Fashion Industry for months; Tina's official introduction and Zya's coming out. A few wolf-whistles are heard from various parts of the room.

"Yes, she's hot—I know it. We're getting married in June—the twenty-third, to be exact. But then again..." She turns and looks at Tina, tapping her fingers on her lower lip, thinking as a man in a black suit with a pink shirt and tie joins them on the runway.

"No, she isn't!" Amber says as thousands of tiny vellum pale pink hearts float from the ceiling. They are being showered with love.

"Makes sense why she would want us all here," Debra says, dabbing her eyes.

Amber looks around the room for the twentieth time since they've sat. A habit she's gained since the contents of spilled from the envelope. She's constantly on the lookout. Nothing out of the ordinary, except she can't understand why the four seats behind them are now empty. *Why would they leave?*

CHAPTER TWENTY-TWO

Considering the recent photos Amber's stalker presented, Brian works from Debra's more often and today is no exception. Tracey enjoys having him around during the day and can usually persuade him to play school. He caves because she recently dropped the 'Uncle' part; now, he's referred to as just 'Brian.' School day usually lasts an hour or two at the most, but today Tracey is playing strict teacher. After four hours, he is able to review a few files, pleading he has schoolwork to do. Debra needs to run some errands; however, seeing Brian's work dilemma, she opts to take Little George with her and just run to the grocery store; the other stops can wait.

After she checked out, she looked at her text and saw Brian wanted mini marshmallows. Rather than asking questions, she runs back and get them after she drops her groceries in the car. Little George is beside her, buckled up in the cart, waving and smiling at everyone who walks by. His blond curls blowing in the gentle breeze.

"Hi, little man."

Debra freezes, recognizing the voice—the accent.

She spins around, putting her hand on Little George's chest, trying to protect him from Roberto, the other part of last year's love triangle.

"I not hurt him, not to worry," he says, as he unbuckles Little George and picks him up in his arms.

Debra isn't sure if she should scream or stay calm. She opts for the latter.

"What do you want, Roberto?" she says as her fingers wrap around the cold metal canister of pepper spray in her purse.

"I come to see you. I see Little Man. He so big. One year?" Debra nods.

"Can I have him please?" she asks, dropping the canister and reaching out her arms.

"I just get him. You see him all time. Don't be greedy," he says as he turns and walks to the side of her SUV.

"What are you doing here? The police want you, you know. If they see you, they'll arrest you."

"Yes, I know. They try to kill me in Italy when I go home. I get away. I come back—for you."

She's treading carefully, she's seen his temper and how scary he can be, and now, he's holding her son. "Roberto, I'm sorry things didn't work out between us. It's my fault—I was confused. Everything just happened so fast. I needed time to grieve for my husband. I'm sorry I hurt you."

Debra's breath catches as she watches Roberto's eyes turn cold—black.

"It wasn't you; it was that bitch, Amber. She confuse you. You say you marry me, and then you change mind."

"No, it wasn't Amber, it was me. Can I please have my son?" The photo of Tracey and Little George with the words, 'The babies have no future because of you!' in dark red ink flash in her mind.

"We need to go talk somewhere private. Come, let's go." He opens the side door to her car and gets in with Little George in his arms.

"He has to be in his car seat. I can't—I won't drive with him in your arms. Here, I'll do it."

"You think me stupid woman. Get in the car," he says, spitting out the words. His face is red with anger, his lips tight.

Debra does as she's asked. Her phone is in her pocket. As much as she doesn't want to take her eyes off her son, she knows she has to go slow enough to turn the volume all the way down and dial 911.

She gets in the driver's seat but doesn't take out her keys. She turns and faces him. "Okay, this is private, what do you want to talk about it."

"We go to Spain. Me, you, the kids. We go away."

"Roberto, I can't go to Spain with you. I have a life here. We have a life here. My mom, my sister, my friends…I can't leave them."

She watches as his eyes turn even darker. It's as if an internal blackness sweeps through his body, and she can see it through his eyes. Her body shivers; he still has her son in his arms.

"You will come. You have my ring. You say you marry me first. You love me. We will go." His words are short and firm—insistent, and commanding.

She must get Little George to safety. If she can just keep him talking a little longer, the cops will be here. She begins to doubt herself and panic. *Will he hurt Little George when he sees them?*

Debra places her hand on the steering wheel and twists around, looking him in the eye, and says, "Okay, you're right. I still have the ring, let's get it. Please, let me put Little George in his car seat, and we'll go talk about this."

Roberto notices as the sunlight creates a brilliant reflection off her left hand.

Debra spins around to the left to get her son when she hears the back car door closing. Roberto has slipped out after quietly placing Little George on the seat. She quickly darts to the back, gathering him up in her arms. Tears are flowing freely now as she hugs him tightly to her chest, grateful he's safe.

Three patrol cars soon arrive, surrounding her vehicle, yet Roberto is nowhere to be found. He just vanished. She managed to call Brian, however, the only words she could get out were, "Roberto," "Little George," and "so scared," in between her bursts of hysterics.

Brian arrives in ten minutes with Tracey in arms. "Why are all the cops here?" she asks.

"Cause now, we're playing cops and robbers," Brian says, tickling her as they run up to Debra and Little George.

Debra quickly hands a fussy Little George off to Brian and picks up Tracey and twirls her around.

"Mommy, why are you crying?"

"I missed you so much. I was sad. And now, I'm so happy, I'm crying. These are happy tears."

Tracey and Little George are finally fast asleep. This is the first opportunity they've been able to talk since the afternoon scare.

"I think it's time I move in."

"Right now," she says as she walks to him on the couch. "I just need to be in your arms." She throws herself into his embrace and breaks down. She's held back her emotions because of the children. Now, the floodgates are wide open.

Brian holds her tight, smoothing her hair, telling her how much he loves her and how sorry he is. How scared he knows she must have been.

After ten minutes, her sobs quiet down.

Brian pulls a tissue out of the box on the table. Then draws three more, which causes a tiny laugh, and a few snorts.

"I didn't get your marshmallows," she says just before she blows her nose.

"It's time I move in. I'm scared to death something is going to happen to you—or the kids."

"Whether or not you live here, today still would have happened."

"I know. I would feel better if I'm here all the time."

"You gonna go everywhere with me?"

"If I have to until he's caught."

"To the bathroom?"

Brian chuckles. "What are we talking about, a shower? A bath? Something else?"

Debra curls up in his arm. "I'd like it if you were here all the time, but not because of Roberto. Because I'd like us to take the next step."

Brian pulls back, surprised. "Is someone ready to pick a date?"

"I think I am. I didn't want to interfere with Zya and Tina's plans, and well, now that they're married, it's not an issue. And Patrick's going to come around, eventually. She asked me the other day when we are going to pick, so it's time."

Brian takes his phone out of his pocket and pulls up the calendar. "Okay, when are we thinking?"

Debra tilts her head toward him and gives him a sideways smile.

"You already have a date in mind, don't you?"

"February the fifteenth?"

"Really?"

"I wanted Valentine's Day, but I would never do that to Zya and Tina. The fifteenth is on a Saturday. Or we could get married on Sunday the sixteenth?"

"You want to wait that long?"

"It will be just under three years since George's passing; I think it's a respectable amount of time."

"Okay, I'm happy with either day. And when we go out and celebrate our anniversary, we won't spend double and be rushed through dinner because it's Valentine's Day."

He pulls her close and hugs her tight. "I'm so glad nothing happened to you today."

"I don't think he would have hurt me, or Little George. He loves me—I could tell. He's hurt and angry at Amber. He blames her for us not being together. I thought maybe he was her stalker and the one behind the photos; but I don't think he would hurt me or the kids."

"Doesn't matter, please don't go anywhere without me again."

"If you're with me, he may hurt you. You're his enemy. You're the one who should worry."

CHAPTER TWENTY-THREE

Patrick grabs Amber's hand before they get out of the car. "Thanks for coming with me."

"You explained what happened that night. It's okay, if he's your son, we'll get through this—together. If it's important to you, it is to me too."

He gives her a delicate kiss before they exit the car.

Isabel answers on the first knock.

"Hi," she says to Patrick. She pulls his hand into her chest and locks lips with him. When she opens her eyes, she sees a surprised Amber standing behind him.

"Oh, hi," she says to Amber, confused.

Patrick pulls away, cursing himself for not explaining the reasons for his visit.

"Isabel, this is my—um, girlfriend Amber?" he says as a question. As he says the words, it hits him, she's so much more; there's no appropriate label.

Amber walks in between Isabel and Patrick, shaking her hand, pushing her into her home.

"Won't you come in," Isabel says, stumbling backward.

Patrick follows behind Amber, with his head down, thoughts still on the 'girlfriend' description.

"To what do I owe the honor of your visit?"

Amber sits on the couch and pats the cushion next to her for Patrick to sit down. She planned to let him take control of this meeting, however after the greeting, and Patrick's lack of response, the overwhelming flush taking over her body propels her forward.

"Patrick told me he and Stewart ran into you and your son, Eugene, the other day. By the way, where is he?"

Isabel jumps up from her chair before the last words are out of her mouth and asks, "Can I get anyone something to drink? Tea, soda, or tequila?"

Amber laughs. She doesn't want to see Patrick suffer, but watching Isabel fluster is something she just can't pass up. "Wine would be great. Let me help you." She stands up and walks toward the kitchen ahead of Isabel before she can protest.

Patrick sits with his elbows on his knees, running his hands through his hair. He catches Amber's eye as she rounds the corner. She smiles and winks at him.

"So, Isabel, you have a beautiful home. You're fortunate to live this close to the beach."

"Thanks, I am lucky. I love it here."

"What do you do to afford such a luxurious lifestyle?"

"Oh, I don't work; I take care of Eugene."

"I don't mean to pry—how do you pay for all this?" Amber says, pretending to be chummy. As Amber twirls around, she spots a 100-foot yacht tied up to a dock. She runs to the large French doors, with her mouth open. "And that!" she says, pointing at it.

Just then, the front door opens, and a handsome man, in his late seventies, with silver hair and a dark rich tan, bounces in the door with Eugene squealing and laughing.

Isabel comes running around the corner to greet him. "Honey, I didn't expect you back so soon. You told me you would be gone for an hour, at least," she says, her cheeks glowing red.

"Tell him," he says, pointing to the baby. "His bowels had other ideas. He's been through both outfits, and now he needs a third," he says, with a turned head, as he passes him off to Isabel.

The air and odor catch up in the room as she turns and takes him into the nursery.

"Hi, I'm Charles," he says as he reaches out and introduces himself to Patrick.

Amber comes in from the kitchen, putting the pieces of the puzzle together. "Hi, I'm Amber, we're friends of Isabel's. It's so nice to meet you. She's told us so many wonderful things about you." Amber looks up and locks eyes with Isabel as she changes Eugene's diaper.

All those digestive movements must have exhausted Eugene. He was yawning while Isabel cleaned him up, so she laid him in his crib, and within minutes, he was fast asleep. She went straight into the kitchen and grabbed an extra glass, bringing them out into the living room along with the open bottle of wine.

Being a South Florida native, she sees the older wealthy men out with their young arm candy. It's often referred to as generous and loving uncles out with their nieces. Here Amber is sitting in their living room, seeing firsthand how far that generosity extends.

"So tell me about Eugene. I hope I'm not overstepping my boundaries; Charles, you have blue eyes and Isabel, yours are green?"

Charles picks up Isabel's hand and kisses it. You can tell he loves her very much. By the semi-annoyed look on her face, she tolerates it.

"This gorgeous lady can have anything she wants. I had this home built for her."

"And your floating million-dollar condo out back?" Amber says.

"Yeah, anything for my gal. She wanted a baby. We tested my swimmers and they all drown, so we went to a local sperm bank."

Patrick chokes on his wine.

☯

"None of this makes sense. She lives with this man who's what, forty years older than her, while she makes her rounds every night humping every available penis in South Florida she can find?"

"Dude, you're making yourself out to be some whore or something," Patrick says after guzzling down half his draft.

"That's in the past, there's only one woman for me now, whether or not she admits it. But back to Isabel...so this guy built her a multi-million-dollar home in Rio Vista and gave her a 100-foot yacht?"

"Yep."

"And she has your kid."

Patrick leans forward, choking on his beer. The contents in the glass spill when his hand hits it after slamming it down on the table.

"Sorry, I couldn't help myself, dude."

Wiping up the table and apologizing to the table next to them, he says, "You're a dick."

Stewart, cracking up, says, "I have to give it to her, she was out pretty much every night screwing all my buddies. Now that you mention it, it was always late or early morning. I guess old Charles must need some heavy-duty sleeping aids to crash at night so she could slip out and get nasty."

"Isn't it sad, though? He seems like a really nice man. And by the way he looked at her—very much in love."

"Maybe. Look at it the other way. Isabel is a Latino goddess. She's as hot as Sofia Vergara with emerald green eyes. Do you think Charles would stand a chance with her if he wasn't loaded? And, didn't give her everything she wanted?"

"He's a nice man, why wouldn't he stand a chance?"

"Hello…earth to Patrick. In your dream world, women look for what's inside, and I'm not saying there aren't some who still do. Here in South Florida, in this scene, these women are all about what they can get."

"So, she's a prostitute?"

"I guess in a way, she is."

"What do you mean, you guess? If she doesn't love him, what would you call it?"

"An arrangement. Maybe he can't get it up anymore. She was always adamant about me using a condom; maybe he lets her go out and get her kicks."

"Nothing surprises me anymore. I guess it's possible. She told you she was pregnant. Why would she say that if they bought sperm? Was it to trap you? Or was it just matter-of-fact, 'Hey, guess what? I'm pregnant?'"

"She knew there was no condom used the night in the hot tub; she was looking for a daddy."

"Is she fucking nuts? This man gives her everything she could ever want and a baby, and she looks for someone else to raise him."

"Maybe she decided money couldn't buy happiness anymore, and she wanted a young stud like me for a change."

Patrick looks up, not getting sucked in by his boyish grin. "She knew it wasn't you in the hot tub. What did you tell her to make her go away?"

"I told her you were shooting blanks. It couldn't be your kid."

"You weren't kidding! You really said that?"

"I told you I was going to!"

"That kid looks just like me. Don't you think she's put two and two together?"

"Look. You need to calm down. Yes, he looks like you, but he's probably not yours. They bought sperm and made a baby; they're happy—you're happy. You really want to go down that road right now?"

Patrick finishes the rest of his beer and stares into the bottom of his empty glass as if the answer is there. With his eyes still intense inside the empty vessel, Patrick says, "After my dad...killed himself, I needed cash. He had this unrealistic idea since I finished law school, the money would just start coming in. We know it's not the way the world works. So, I sold my sperm."

"How many times?"

"A few."

"How many is a few?"

"I don't know, four, five, maybe twelve."

CHAPTER TWENTY-FOUR

"How are you doing?"

"Peachy. How do you *think* I'm doing?"

"I brought you some books."

"What kind of books?"

"Horror, slasher, and one lovey-dovey romance."

Brandy sits up in her seat and grabs for the pile. "You can keep the romance."

"I know you don't want Stewart to visit, but there will be a text from him by the time I'm out the door asking about you. You could do worse."

Brandy slouches, staring into the stack in front of her. Her tough exterior softens slightly as she opens her mouth to say something. She quickly snaps it shut as her eyes narrow. "Tell him to buzz off, okay. I'm not interested. He can ask all he wants. I used him, and that's all. He needs to get that through his damn thick skull. Playtime's over, tell him to find somebody else."

"I can tell him, but he's stubborn—he won't listen."

"That's his choice—I'm done with him." She says abruptly, twisting to her side in the chair.

"Okay."

After several long uncomfortable moments of silence, Brandy says, "You suing that asshole's estate? You gonna get any money from him?"

Amber stares at Brandy for a second, thinking about her dreams before she answers. "Why did you kill him?"

"What do you mean, why?"

"You said it's because he raped me. But you and I aren't all that close, remember?"

"Yeah—right."

"Why did you really do it?"

Brandy turns around and faces Brandy, looking her square in the eye. "If you must know, I heard some great things about the chicks here in the Broward County Jail. Best pussy lickers in Florida. I wanted to see you sweat through the trial—it was payback. Ultimately, I knew I'd be the one to end up in jail. I'm the muff diver, so let's face it, I belong here—you don't."

"That's bullshit, and you know it. If they found me not guilty, you wouldn't be here. Tell me the truth."

"The truth? I don't think you can handle it. You don't want to hear it."

"Try me."

Brandy turns again and stares across the room. After a long silence, Brandy asks, "You still getting those texts?"

"From my stalker?"

Brandy nods.

"No." Amber is about to mention the photos, then decides against it.

"Those texts were some scary shit."

"How do you know what they said?"

"Stewart, he told me. The guy is nuts, and it's directed at you, personally. You still have your gun?"

"You know about that too?"

Brandy nods, turning her head and meeting Amber's eyes again.

"Watch out, sister; I might confuse this with caring and concern."

"Don't get all mushy on me. I need someone to bring me more slasher books."

"We figured he was spying on me, so we had everything checked. We found nothing so we must have spooked him."

"Who's working on your case in the police department?"

"Why the sudden concern? You were trying to ruin my life not too long ago."

"Like I said, more horror books. You might pick up some Playboy mags for me too. They're a *hot* commodity in here, and I mean the slimy, sticky kind of heat."

"You can't have a normal conversation, can you? Detective Ackerman is working on finding my stalker."

"Oh, please, and tell that hunk of a badge, I said 'hi.' He hasn't been by to see me. I told him I'd let him fuck me good if he did."

"I thought you weren't into men, only women. Gotcha! You *do* have a thing for Stewart, after all?"

"I'd fuck him too. Shit, I'd screw them both at the same time."

"Please come to the movies with us. I haven't seen you all week."

"I've been busy with schoolwork."

"You're lying. Your online college classes take you all of three hours a day, at the most. I've seen how you fly through them. What's up?"

"I forgot I was best friends with the other Floridian prodigy. I don't want to intrude. You've got a good thing with Mitch, and as much as I *have* tried, I don't want to be around him. I can't forgive him the way you did. Every time I see him, I'm reminded of what happened in the park." Pools form in Stacey's lower lids.

Ashanti puts her arms around her shoulders. "I'm sorry, I don't want to have to pick between you and him. But if I do, it's you every time—you're my best friend."

Stacey wipes her eyes. "No, you don't, you love him. If you break up, you'll resent me, and it'll affect our friendship. I'm a big girl; it's okay. Just make some time for us. Tonight, go see your movie."

"Okay. Well, I have a few hours before I'm meeting him. Want to hang out?"

"Sure."

They sit in Stacey's bedroom on the floor, leaning up against the bed, staring at the wall in front of them.

"Have you enjoyed being homeschooled?"

"I haven't had a choice. My mom's job moved us around, so it was easier. Plus, the few times we thought we were going to be in any one place for any length of time, I was frustrated with the schools. I was so far ahead. Even when they tested and placed me in the appropriate grade, they were way too slow for me. I was up helping other kids. I thought I was doing the right thing, but I guess it pissed off the teachers. Homeschooling let me go at my pace. Who else do you know at seventeen doing online junior-level college classes?"

"And you ended up back in Seattle; what a coincidence."

"Not really, my other mom wanted to move back there. Things weren't going so good between them; she thought it would help. It didn't, so we moved here."

"You don't talk about her very much."

"I call her once a week. She's not the domestic type; she never really knew how to raise a kid, so she left it up to my mom. She loves me, but she's also glad she doesn't have to raise me. And it's okay. She's pretty cool otherwise."

"What about friends? Did you make any at those meet and greet outings?"

"Not really. I met a lot of people; I just had nothing in common with any of them. Most of the girls were into makeup and nail polish—even at twelve. I would rather read. They could usually find me sitting somewhere with my book under my nose."

"Wait a minute, what happened at the roller-rink before you left Seattle?"

"I was mad at my mom for moving us again! I guess I was being rebellious. It was stupid."

"You didn't have many friends growing up?"

Stacey shakes her head. "I don't have the patience for stupidity, and lots of kids our age do dumb things."

"Until you met me," Ashanti says, putting her arm back around Stacey's shoulders, pulling her toward her.

"Don't push it; you're not as smart as me," she says, laughing. "But you're damn close. Have you started sending out your college applications yet?"

"University of Miami is a definite. Mom and I are going to visit once school lets out."

"What about John Hopkins? Stanford? Harvard?"

"I'm going to apply to those too," Ashanti says, picking at the carpet.

"Don't want to leave your mom, huh? Or Mitch?"

"Or you! No, I don't want to leave South Florida. If I hadn't missed so much school last year, I would have enough credits to graduate this year. I need a half-credit in English and math. I'm taking Calculus II and English Lit for the first half of the year. I'll still graduate in May with everybody else, and I'll be able to start college in January."

"And eventually find a cure for cancer?"

"That's the plan."

"Pretty cocky of you waiting this long to apply and start in what, nine months."

"I know, my counselor told me the same thing. They're filled out; I just need to talk to mom first."

"Hey, explain something to me. Your mom doesn't talk a whole lot about coming here to the States. I know her dad died the night she left; how did you know your grandmother and watch her die from breast cancer?"

"Actually, she was my great grandmother, my mother's grandmother, Lesedi." Ashanti smiles at the memory.

"Lesedi intercepted one of my mom's letters and saw my picture in it and instantly fell in love. She was very talented, like my grandmother; they both were very artistic. She was also very wealthy and a widow. She put herself on a plane, intending to bring us back. When she saw how talented my mom was, she stayed and help raise me.

"We moved to South Florida within a few months after her arrival when a young Latin designer in Miami hired mom. Lesedi loved the sun and the beach; she was in heaven. Lesedi was in her late sixties and just enjoying life. She fell and hit her head one day while we were playing around outside. It wasn't bad, but mom was worried and wanted to have it checked out. An actor's wife had recently fallen, and although she said she was fine, she passed away the very next day. So, off we went to the hospital.

"They did a medical history because she hadn't had a physical or a well-check exam in years, including a mammogram and pap smear upon my mom's insistence. That's when they found the mass. She was triple-negative just like Aunt Dom, but she was already stage four by then; it had already spread to her lymph nodes and bones. They removed it immediately and recommended an aggressive treatment; she turned it down. She opted to live her life to the fullest with what time she had left.

"It was painful in the end, but she always had a beautiful smile on her face. She wasn't afraid to die; she was grateful for the wonderful life she had and the chance to meet me. I only had a year and a half with her, but she made quite an impression; she was remarkable. I made her a promise on her deathbed, I would work on finding a cure for cancer until my last breath. And that's a promise I plan on keeping."

☯

"Okay, you ready for this?"

Dominque nods.

"And you'll go along with whatever the top of the coin says, right? No two out of three…"

"Wait, let me check and make sure you didn't get a two-headed coin," she says joking.

"Here we go."

Tad flips the coin and lets it fall to the ground. It bounces several times, and then it rolls to the kitchen island. It ricochets off, then wobbles around on its edge a few times before it comes to a complete stop. Tad and Dominque follow it until it no longer moves.

They look at each other before they bend down and look at the top of the coin.

Heads.

Dominque's eyes immediately fill up as she jumps up and grabs her phone. She's unable to meet his gaze, knowing she'll lose it. A deal is a deal.

"I'm so sorry, babe," he says, as he reaches for her to comfort her.

She pulls away and busies herself searching for her calendar. She has to stay in control. She knew there was a 50/50 chance; she prepared herself...or so she thought.

"What are you doing?"

She quickly wipes her eyes, trying desperately to stop them from leaking. "I'm putting today's date on next year's calendar. May 7, 2020, that's a Thursday; make sure you take it off from work. I'll make an appointment with the doctor's office."

"Come here," he says as he grabs her arm.

"I can't. I just need to go on with my day and forget this."

Dominque closes the master bathroom door behind her and slides down to the ground. The tears flow freely now. She grabs the robe from behind the door to muffle the sobs she has no control over.

Tad's tears silently slide down his cheeks as he sits on the bed, listening to the muffled sounds coming from the other side of the door.

CHAPTER TWENTY-FIVE

Busy with a challenging case, Patrick lost all track of time. Partners who owned a local pizza parlor on Sunrise Boulevard are suing each other. One believes his partner's allure with a particular lighter is the reason it burned down. The ongoing dispute of one wanting out, the other refusing to give up, was finally resolved. Patrick is trying to settle as quickly as possible—there's more than enough money for the solo partner to open a pizza food truck. The other attorney is out for blood.

Amber rushes into his office lit with the orange glow of dusk. "What are you doing? We're going to be late?"

"Oh shit! Sorry, babe, I lost track of time. Can we still make it?"

"It's not every day you turn forty. I'm sure they'll be fine. I'll call—you drive."

Amber calls their new favorite restaurant. Since Johnny V's on Las Olas closed, Capital Grille has become their recent splurge. It's also the place where most of Fort Lauderdale's Who's Who is seen enjoying the finest cuts of beef and drinking only the finest of wines. And the truffle fries—Amber's favorite. They are so bad for you, but oh, so good. That's why it's a splurge.

"Our secluded corner, very romantic backroom, table for two, is still available and on hold for their favorite customers. We're all set."

Patrick exhales and stretches out his fingers, allowing blood to flow freely again. Amber asked him where he wanted to go; he knew truffle fries were the way to her heart, and the table is very private.

As they make their way through the dimly lit dining room, Patrick sees a tropical arrangement sitting in the middle of their table. As they sit down, he realizes it's 'Happy Birthday' sprinkles reflecting off the table that also caught his eye. And an added touch, a postcard thanking them for celebrating their special occasion with them. At some point in the evening, they'll be by to take a picture as a souvenir.

"Wow, I've only had flowers sent to me once before."

Amber blushes, remembering those very dry, wet dreams she had when they first met and sending him flowers was her trying to work up the courage to ask him out. It was the first step, even if she sent them as his secret admirer.

"That was you, wasn't it?"

"Maybe."

"What am I going to do with you?"

"It's your birthday—anything you want," she says seductively, grabbing his tie, slowly pulling him toward her until their lips meet.

"Now, now—none of that."

"Stewart; what are you doing here?" Patrick says, reluctantly pulling his lips away from his one and only love.

"Having dinner with a few guys from work, and I saw you walk through. I told them it was your birthday, so they want to say hi. You mind coming over?"

"Dude, I'm having a romantic dinner with this beautiful woman here. And you did just interrupt my first birthday kiss of the evening."

"It's okay. I'm not going anywhere. It would be rude not to go and at least say hi. In the meantime, I'll busy myself with a basket of fries," she says, her eyes bulging and rubbing her hands together. "Don't worry, me and my lips will wait right here."

"Okay, okay, I'm sorry, I'll be right back."

Patrick follows Stewart around to a more private area of the restaurant with his head down in deep thought. Stewart stops, then steps aside, and Patrick hears, "Surprise!"

Amber is right behind and wraps her arms around him. "Happy Birthday, baby."

The staff brings in the tropical arrangement as Patrick comes in and greets all their friends. Zya and Tina are sitting with Debra and Brian while Stacey and Ashanti keep the little ones entertained in the corner with toys and books. Dominque and Tad walk over and hug him. Tad refers to him as 'Old Man' getting laughs from everyone except Patrick. Tad's mom and dad insisted on coming as well; they feel like they are part of the family. It's just as well since Patrick has none of his own left to celebrate with. A few of his attorney friends and their wives are also in attendance. Twenty-four people in all fill the room.

Once he's looped the room, he circles back to Amber. "You planned this, didn't you?"

"I had help."

"And you kept it a secret."

"Didn't you know? I'm a vault—you'll never get it out of me," she says, closing her lips and twists her hand as if she's just locked away the juiciest of details.

"Really, I couldn't even tickle it out of you?" he asks, threatening to do so.

She runs away, giggling. "We have guests," she shouts over her shoulder.

The private room is the perfect place to have an elegant and intimate get-together. Large baskets of truffle fries arrive, filling the air with their distinctive exotic fragrance covered with a layer of freshly grated Parmesan cheese. The vinegar melds with the heat from the peppers in the calamari, creating the perfect amount of heat, acid, and texture for a perfectly balanced dish. They place a two-tiered Grand Plateau in the center of each table, packed with chilled oysters on the half shell, shrimp cocktail, North Atlantic lobster, and jumbo lump crab—a seafood lover's delight. The noise level lowers several decibels as everyone waits impatiently for their turn to attack the plates and baskets. Little George's coos and giggles are the only other sounds heard over the silverware scooping up the delicacies overflowing on small dishes.

Once the guests have finished their appetizers, trays loaded with the night's entrees enter on parade. The guests enjoy sizzling three-inch-thick grilled filet mignon, dry-aged NY strip, and porcini rubbed bone-in ribeye. Amber devours the fries as her appetizer then opts for the double-cut lamb chops for her main meal. She stares at the three thick, mouth-watering cuts, wondering how many she'll have for lunch tomorrow. The servers place plates of lobster mac & cheese, mashed potatoes, and grilled asparagus to share.

Once he's finished all but two bites of his NY strip, Patrick gets up to speak. "Keep eating, everyone." Rubbing his belly, he continues. "I think I've eaten for the next two days—maybe three."

Everyone nods in agreement as their silverware continues in an up and down motion.

"Thanks, everybody, for coming out tonight. I uh...don't give too much thought to birthdays; they're just any other day for me. I usually just work right through them."

Stewart, while chewing his food, says, "I can attest, he's boring."

Laughter erupts in the room. Everyone's eyes, except Amber's, dart between the birthday boy and the delectable fare in front of them. Her eyes never leave his face.

"Thanks, pal. Appreciate the love. Here I am turning forty today..."

"Over the hill..." Stewart says out of the corner of his mouth, making it sound like an echo.

Patrick chuckles, expecting nothing less from his buddy and roommate. "I hope not! I think I'm still in the upward climb. Never set goals or thought much about where I wanted to be at this stage in my life; one thing's for sure, I'm so grateful you're a part of it," he says, turning to Amber, motioning her to stand with him. He grabs her hands and says, "I never thought love would be in the cards for me. It hasn't been perfect," he says, chuckling.

Amber chuckles as well.

"We're perfect for each other. You asked me last month what I wanted. I assumed you meant for my birthday, and I didn't know how to answer you. But then I got to thinking..." Patrick drops on one knee.

☯

Zya comes into Tina's office in a hurry. "Can you come with me?"

"Are you kidding? We're moving locations next week. I think I need to stay right here until then, and I still don't see how we'll get it done. The joys of you suddenly being the 'it' designer," she says, making finger quotes, then heavily exhales as she turns back to the project at hand.

"We'll figure it out, we always do. Come on; it won't take long, I promise."

Reluctantly, Tina shuts down her computer and grabs her purse. "Okay, but when things are not where they're supposed to be when we put Paris together, don't you dare look at me."

"Deal."

Traffic going east on 595 is even better than Zya expected. *It's a sign.* If she can make it to the Seventeenth street bridge before it opens, she will have an extra ten minutes to explain. Luckily, just as she's passing the gate, the light turns red and goes down behind her. *Phew, made it.*

Tina had been talking nonstop the whole way about the Paris show in October. Who moves their operations six months before the biggest show of their career? Label Zya does, that's who. Tina heard it on good authority, Chanel is going to recreate the rooftops of Paris for their theme. Since it's Zya's cruise collection, she wants her thoughts on using the *Canal de l'Ourcq* for her recreation.

Zya nods, unsure what she agrees to, her mind whirling about the opportunity that has recently presented itself.

Tina's nonstop rambling has kept her mind occupied with the show production and off their destination, until they hit the bridge.

"Where are we going?" Tina asks.

"Just wait till we get there. I don't want to say anything until you see it."

"See what?"

Zya takes the first left turn into a guardhouse. The gate lifts without waiting. She makes a sharp left, then a right around the water. They cross several bridges and streets lined with large mansions before she turns down one of them.

Tina stays silent, afraid to ask.

Zya goes to the end of the street and makes a slight right turn, stopping at a guard gate and gives her name. Suddenly, the two large wrought iron gates open, and Zya slowly pulls into the driveway of one of twenty-four homes on this exclusive island.

They pass two garages on either side before they park in the semi-circle in front of massive double wooden doors with floor to ceiling windows on either side and a rectangular one on top.

"Don't you think you're past the time of having to meet clients in their home?" Tina asks.

"Come on," Zya says with a big grin.

As they walk to the front door, they're greeted by a young woman with a friendly smile.

"Mrs. Monroe, so nice to meet you."

"Please, call me Zya. This is my wife, Tina."

"So nice to meet you. Please come on in." The young woman shows them around. She leads them into the kitchen first, with a large, stand-alone, Thermador refrigerator and freezer, and a long marble island with room for eight barstools.

"I'm not sure about the small island in the middle. It looks like it would be in the way. What do you think?" Zya asks.

"The house is a little dated. You might want to do some remodeling."

Tina's mouth drops.

Zya gently closes her mouth and grabs her by the arm, dragging her along.

As they pass two steps leading up and out to a side yard, Zya asks, "Do you think this door and these two windows could be blown out and opened up?"

"I don't see why not. I have a wonderful general contractor I can refer you to. I'll give you his number."

After touring the upstairs and Zya having to close Tina's lower jaw several times, they go outside to explore the backyard.

"Oh, Tina, this is perfect. Can't you see Debra and Brian getting married here?"

Tina nods. She hasn't said over ten words since they entered the property.

"The gazebo, their bride and groom table? The kids can sit there too, and we can cover it in roses. And the pool," Zya says, hurrying down the steps with Tina quietly stepping behind her, "we can cover it in acrylic and make it a dance floor. Think they'll go for it?"

Tina pulls Zya down toward the 120-foot dock, out of earshot. "Zya, are you serious? We can't afford this—can we?"

"I wouldn't be here if I wasn't serious. And yes, we can."

"Well, it's your money, you can do whatever you want to with it, you don't have to ask me," Tina says as she flips her hand in the air before crossing her arms, then turns slightly away.

Zya grabs her arms, facing her, and says, "It's ours—we're married. What's mine is yours; this wouldn't be my home; it will be ours."

The realtor says, "I'm going to make a few phone calls. Take your time and let me know if you have any questions." She walks away with a smile plastered on her face—the same one since she greeted them at the front door.

"I know your label has taken off, but this house must cost millions. We live in a simple home in Pembroke Pines. This is a huge move."

"We've all been living with one eye looking over our shoulder since Amber's stalker as decided everyone in her life is fair game; this gives us more security. Plus, part of my newfound success means there will be more crazies entering our life. I've loved my little house out west; we've made some glorious memories there. We'll make some great ones here too."

"You don't make the same percentages your competitors do. You're so proud of your Made in the USA label, insisting every garment is made here in the States. And I know the lengths you go to make sure they manufacture your fabrics with strict adherence to labor laws abroad. That costs money. Plus, you give a piece of your profits to all your employees. Most of your fellow designers aren't as generous; how can you, or rather we, afford this?"

"I met a client here eight years ago. She fell in love with one of my designs and had me create a wardrobe for her. When I walked through the front doors the very first time, I couldn't concentrate because I loved this house so much. She took me for a tour; she was so proud of every nook and cranny. She and her husband built it together; he had since passed. Every time I visited, I just felt so much at home here. She invited me way more often than necessary; I think she was lonely, and I just loved being within these walls. She promised me when it was her time, I would get first dibs on it. They didn't have any children, and the other family members didn't love it as I did. She died last week; her attorney called me this morning. It's in her will, and the price—ridiculous. She knew I would want it; she made sure I could afford it. The taxes are not exactly cheap; at least half of what the newer ones pay on the island. And the insurance, with the price we're getting this house for, we can more than swing it. And it's very private, very secure, and it too has a history.

"I love this house, and I want us to grow old here. I want Debra and Brian to marry here and eventually, Stacey and Ashanti. But only if you love it too."

"Are you kidding? I'm already moving that island in the kitchen."

CHAPTER TWENTY-SIX

"You are so beautiful, inside and out. You've come through so much, foster families, anorexia, and then cancer. And yet, here you are, still smiling, just as beautiful. I don't know many who could have handled what you have without crumbling. But you —it made stronger. I'm so damn proud of you, baby. I thank God every day you didn't pay your taxes, and we met. I pinch myself all the time—how did I get so lucky to be here with you.

"I get it. I understand why having a family—a legacy is so important to you. You have so much to give and to teach our children. As lucky as I am to have you in my life, I imagine how blessed our children will be to have you as their mother. It's not fair of me to ask you to wait."

Dominque's eyes are open wide as steady streams roll down her cheeks. She can't believe the words she's hearing.

"If you want to try now, and the doctor is willing, I'll be right by your side, cheering you on every step of the way."

Wiping her eyes, she says, "Really, you mean it? Be one hundred percent—don't do this for me."

"I mean it. You deserve it. If it's important to you, it is to me too. I was selfish; I see that now. Thank you for not pressuring and letting me come to this conclusion on my own."

She hugs him, kisses him, then repeats it two more times.

"I can't believe it. We're going to be parents. Tad, we're going to have a family!"

Dominque jumps up and down on the bed in pure delight. Squealing and leaping, her hair almost touches the ceiling on the way down. Her knees are so high they almost reach her armpits. She's had some great days, but this one is at the top of her list. "I'm so happy!" she yells as she takes one giant leap off the bed and runs out of the room.

"Where are you going?"

"I'm calling to make an appointment."

"It's seven o'clock in the morning. I don't think they're in yet."

She comes back into the room with her cell to her ear. "No, but I'll be their first message when they get there."

Zya slept in for the first time in weeks, a lazy Sunday morning. She strolls into the kitchen to put on the coffee and sees Stacey with bags of beans and rice and spices all lined up on the counter. "What's all this?"

"I want to make that yummy butter-bean stew. I even got Halal beef from the butcher yesterday for Ashanti."

"Oh, Stacey, you're such a good friend. You know that's her favorite?"

"I do, that's why I'm making it."

Zya hugs her. "Well, I'll get out of your way and let you work."

"Thanks. Dinner's at six," she shouts just as Zya is out of earshot.

Zya backs up and sticks her head around the corner. "Stace? Today is the first day of Ramadan. Ashanti can't eat until dusk, and the sun doesn't set until about 8:30," Zya says, squinting her face.

"Oops; It's a good thing you told me. Okay, dinner's at 8:30 then. That going to be okay with you and mom?"

"It will be perfect. We can snack if we get hungry."

Ashanti and Mitch enter the house at 8:15 p.m. She spent the day at the library, mostly thinking, away from the mixture of cinnamon, garlic, and cilantro simmering the afternoon away.

Matters of the heart still perplex Ashanti. She's torn between the love of her religion and that of the young man who has stolen it. As she and Mitch have become closer, she's questioning whether she must choose. Interfaith relationships are not unheard of in Islam, but seriously frowned upon.

"Someone is either in deep thought, or prayer," Zya says as they sit at the table.

"Sorry, Mom…just thinking."

"It smells wonderful," Mitch says, as Stacey places the pot in front of him on the table.

"Mitch, I'm so glad you could join us."

"Thank you so much for inviting me, Mrs. Monroe. It smells delicious. I'm not sure I could have stopped myself from nibbling all day." He looks over at Ashanti, who's eyes are looking down at her lap.

Zya, sensing tension, jumps into action, keeping the evening progressing. "Okay, Ashanti, give me your bowl, you get to eat first." Zya puts a layer of rice and then two big ladles full of stew, big chunks of beef, large pieces of tomatoes in a beef broth, and large white beans in her bowl with curls of steam rising toward the ceiling. Once everyone is served, Zya asks, "Is it okay Ashanti if I say grace?"

"Of course, Mom."

"Bless this table's bounties, O' Lord; the food we are about to receive. We give thanks when so many walk in hunger. Let us hold you in our hearts, through Christ our Lord; we pray, Amen."

The only sounds heard within the room are, "hmm," and "yummy," as the food is quickly devoured—the depth of flavor created by allowing the spices to stew for hours, prompting second helpings.

As they finish, the conversations begin again.

"Is it tough to fast all day?"

Ashanti chuckles at the question. In her head, she says, *Like duh!* Instead, she says, "I've learned to deal with it. I get up before the sun and have a big breakfast, and as you can see, when the sun goes down, I pig out. And I eat before I go to bed."

"She's also known to get up in the middle of the night," Zya says, out of the side of her mouth.

If Ashanti's skin tone was a little lighter, you might see her cheeks flush pink.

After the giggling dies down at Ashanti's expense, she asks, "Mom, when Eid comes back around, are you still going to give a portion of your profits to the hungry even though you're not Muslim anymore?"

"Actually, I was going to talk to you about that; I'm glad you brought it up. If you want to go down to the homeless shelter and take food, I'm happy to go with you. Tina and I have discussed it, and we'd both like to go."

"Me too," Stacey adds.

"Mitch and I are working with the Broward Outreach Center and the School Board; we're putting together a food drive and it falls on the last day of Ramadan. We can still deliver food that night; I just won't be able to help make it in the afternoon."

"No, it's okay. You'll be busy and doing your part to help. We can help at Thanksgiving or Christmas."

Ashanti shakes her head, taking the last bite off her plate. "What about the profits of Label Zya?"

"Oh yeah, I want to do something a little different from now on. I still want to give ten percent, and I want each of us to have a say in where it goes. That means you too, Stacey. We'll divide it into fours, and each of us will pick a worthy 501(c)3 charity for our share."

Tina looks over at Zya. "You know how much ten percent is going to be, right?"

"I do—it's what I've always given, even in the leanest of times. We're blessed, and I'm happy to give it—to help. I got help when I needed it—I never forget that."

"Mrs. Monroe, I respect you so much. I know we didn't meet under the most ideal of circumstances. You let me sit at the table with you, means a lot to me."

Under her napkin, Stacey says, "Ass kisser."

Tina's eyes go wide in surprise. "Stacey!"

"No, it's okay." Mitch sits up in his chair and turns toward Stacey. "I know you don't like me, and I get it. I even admire you for it."

This prompts Stacey to lower her napkin and look at him with a, 'You're an idiot' look on her face.

"If it were my best friend, I wouldn't trust me either. You know what they say...keep your friends close; keep your enemies closer." He winks at Stacey and stands up and begins clearing the table.

He picks up Stacey's bowl as her mouth hangs slightly open, the wheels turning in her mind, and he says, "Thanks for not putting razor blades or poison in my food."

As he turns away, Stacey jumps up and says, "Mitch, let me get dessert for you."

Chapter Twenty-Seven

"Are you excited about Tahiti?" Zya asks.

"I am. I'm so looking forward to getting away. I can't believe we're going to the South Pacific, and on a cruise."

"I'm so jealous. I wish I could take time off and go away," Zya says.

"You should, you know. You're going to burn yourself out," Debra interjects, dunking a piece of bread in the olive oil mixture on their table.

"Too late. I know eventually, things will level out, and I'll get some time. For now, I need to keep riding the wave."

"Any backlash from Doug?" Dominque asks.

"No, and I'm kind of worried. It was too easy."

"You don't think making you sweat it out until the last possible moment wasn't payback in his eyes?" Dominque asks.

"Maybe, for someone normal, we know he's not. So no, I'm waiting for the other shoe to drop."

"Maybe that is his payback, making you think there's more coming," Debra says.

"Shit! You know, you may be right. Now *that* I wouldn't put past him."

Zya calls the waiter over to order drinks. When they get to Dominque, she orders club soda with a splash of cranberry.

"Spill," Zya says, stopping in mid-motion.

Dominque looks down at her stomach and rubs it.

All eyes and mouth open wide, as their hands stop in midair.

"Dom, you're pregnant!" Debra squeals.

Rapidly, she nods her head as her friends all congratulate her and take turns getting up and hugging her.

It's still early, so Cafe Vico is quiet. Within the next thirty minutes, it will make a complete transformation as every table and the bar and will be full, once the live music begins. Marco, the owner, sat them at their favorite table, in the corner by the window. The few diners clap and congratulate from afar, although they don't know what they're celebrating.

"We're not telling anyone else; it's still really early. But I have to tell you guys."

"Okay. We'll keep the celebration to a minimum—for now. How far along are you?" Amber asks.

"We just found out yesterday. I had the transfer done on the seventh, so about three weeks."

Zya squeezes Dominque's hand. "I'm so happy for you, girl. You deserve everything. I feel good about this."

"Your doctor says it's okay for you to travel?" Debra asks, with her forehead wrinkled in concern.

"Yeah, no problem; she said it might do me some good. No stress," she responds, laughing. "I'm so looking forward to sleeping late. No cooking, chef prepared meals whenever I want, and the water...oh I can't wait to get into the beautiful blue ocean."

"You're allowed to go swimming?" Debra asks, as her eyes wrinkle, matching her forehead.

"Where we're going, to the pearl beds, is the cleanest water around—no boats allowed. The clams, which are one of the most sensitive marine life, live there by the thousands. I can't wait! The doctor said, no small bodies of water—clean ocean, fine. Okay, Mom?"

Debra, blushing, says, "I'm just worried about you. You've been through so much. Sorry, I'll shut up now."

Dominque hugs her and says, "No need to apologize. I know you say it out of love for me and"—looking down at her belly—"little Emily."

"You're having a girl?" Amber asks.

"I don't know! I just like the name. And I've had dreams every night about a little girl. Tommy, if it's a boy."

"Enough about me, Amber, what's going on in your life?" Dominque quickly changes the subject. "You've been so quiet tonight."

"I'm going ahead with the lawsuit. I'm not excited about rehashing it, but I want to help Mary Ann and anyone else who might suffer because of that man. Patrick is drawing up the paperwork. I want nothing from him; I just want to set a precedent so they can follow behind and get what they're due. Mary Ann's son deserves to be taken care of."

"And Brandy?" Zya asks.

"I'm still not sure. I keep trying to trip her up, but she hasn't fallen for it yet. I still don't know why."

"Any chance you two can patch up your differences?" Debra asks.

"I don't know, I doubt it. Too much has happened. Although, I might be seeing her tough-guy act starting to peel away. We've talked more these last few months, then we have our entire lives. Might be Stewart's doing, or me trying to find out if she's involved in more than Brettinger's murder. Somehow, we're actually conversing."

Zya giggles, which grows into chuckles, then escalates into hysterical laughter. "I'm sorry! I'm sorry!" she says, putting a hand up in front of her face, trying to hide her laughter. "Anyone listening in on our conversation would have a heart attack. 'Involved in more than someone's murder…' I'm sorry. It's just so surreal to be talking like this. I know it's not funny, but it kind of is."

Dominque chuckles, followed by Debra, and quickly Amber jumps in. Soon the entire table is filled with laughter.

Once they catch their breath, Amber says while holding her stomach, "It is funny, kind of, thanks for making me laugh. That felt good."

"I hate to bring this up, any news on your stalker?" Debra, mother hen, asks.

Amber's smile fades, replaced with a more severe and somber look. "No. I'm so sorry. I know you all have just as much invested in this now as I do. I've pestered Detective Ackerman to the point he won't accept my calls anymore. I feel so damn helpless. Brandy even asked me about it. I didn't tell her about the pictures; she asked about the texts. She told me not to let my guard down. They were too personal. He might intentionally be waiting for me to slip up."

"A shiver just ran down my spine," Debra says as her body visibly shakes. "I can't imagine. You still have your gun?"

"I do. I carry it with me all the time. I've thought about taking it out of my purse, then something stops me. So, for now"—she pats her bag gently—"she's always with me."

Zya's eyes dart from side to side.

"What's up, Zya?" Amber asks.

"It's probably nothing; I'm sure I'm just scaring myself. I swear I keep seeing Cuban gangster men everywhere I look."

"You mean as in the ones Doug might or might not be working with on the side dealing drugs?" Amber asks.

"Our lives are some messed up shit, ladies. We have our very own soap opera, As South Florida turns."

"Be careful—all of you. If anything ever happened to any of you, I'd never forgive myself."

Zya reaches across, putting her hand over Amber's. "My mind is probably just working overtime. We live in Florida— Hello! There are Cubans everywhere. I'm just stressed. We're careful, the kids too. Let's all try to not stress over this—while being on the lookout," Zya says, trying to convince herself more than anyone else.

"How was the move?" Amber asks Zya, wiping her eyes.

"Chaotic." Zya looks up at the ceiling and exhales loudly. "Why did I move?"

"Because you are a famous designer now, and you needed the space."

"Keep reminding me please. Four months before Paris and I can't find half of my sample fabrics. I know I have them, I just don't know what box they're in. Tina is at the studio tonight trying to find them for me. She said she can't take one more night of being kicked in the shins and yelling in my sleep."

"Other than your show being in turmoil, life is great otherwise? Oh and, when do you move into your fabulous new house?"

Zya lets out an enormous sigh. "I hope this contractor is as good as my realtor said he is because I haven't checked on him. He could be robbing me blind for all I know. He should be done in August—maybe September—before we leave for Paris, for sure. And then, Ashanti needs to decide on a college. There's a lot on my plate right now. Where are those drinks?"

"Debra, how about you? How many packages of Hebrew Nationals have you been through?" Dominque asks.

Debra blushes and quickly responds, "Only one. I've been practicing on the real thing now."

"Oh!" Dominque says. "Good for you girl. I'm sure Brian isn't complaining."

"Practice makes perfect!" Zya exclaims as she reaches for her drink just as the waiter arrives.

"And that tongue of his," Zya says, sticking her tongue out as far as she can, making the tip wiggle fast. "I've been practicing too."

Everybody laughs.

"So, I have a question for you all, and don't you go embarrassing me for having the courage to ask," Debra says, looking directly at Dominque, who quickly does a 'Who Me' bit. "How much sex is normal for a couple?"

Zya quickly picks up her drink, after having just put it down, and says before the rim hits her lips, "Don't ask me that question; you won't like my answer."

They all turn and look at her as she drains her vodka tonic.

"My life is upside down right now. I don't know up from down, left from right. When I get home, I can barely make it into the bedroom before I collapse. I know there will be time once I get past Paris. I'm counting the days."

"I'm sure Tina is too," Dominque says.

Zya squints her eyes at Dominque.

"You're newlyweds, you're supposed to be having sex every day," Dominque adds.

"Are you? You're not quite one year yet." Zya asks.

Dominque looks down at her hands, then sits up straight and looks directly into Zya's eyes. "We're going to fuck like rabbits on our trip."

Zya locks her stare, then smiles a wide grin and chuckles. "I'm so damn jealous, girl. Fucking my girl like a rabbit is exactly what I'd like to be doing every day for twelve days straight. I'm booking us a two-week cruise for October twenty-fifth, the day after my show."

Amber grabs Zya's hand and says, "And you're here with us tonight. You should be with Tina if you've been so busy. You know we'd understand."

Zya covers Amber's hand with hers. "I wouldn't miss this. We agreed—once a month. We are family too. I love Tina, and I love all of you. She sees me every night. I might be snoring and drooling, but I only get this once a month. We have sex, it's just not nearly as often as we'd like. She's so damn sexy. And that French lingerie is killing me." Zya says as she puts her index knuckle in her mouth and bites down.

Once the chuckling dies down, Amber looks across the table at Debra. "Can I ask how much sex you and Brian are having? You are the one who started this conversation."

"Now, it's more oral. We can't keep our hands off each other. With two little kids running around, it's tough to get any real quality time."

"What time does Tracey go to bed?"

"Around 8:30-9:00. I help her get into her nightgown, we read a book together, and then I must stay until she falls asleep. By then, it's 9:30-10:00, and Brian is sawing logs on the couch or in the chair."

"Naps?" Dominque asks.

"She's eight, she claims she's too old, and school is out for the summer. I asked her if she wanted to go to camp; the shelter has a great one for a week. I may have persuaded her; she loves animals so much. Now I'm just trying to find a slot for her; they fill up so quickly."

"How about your mom? Wouldn't she take her for a few hours? And Little George too, to give you guys some time?" Dominque asks.

"And Megan, I bet she would help," Amber adds.

"And they have; they've been great. I just can't ask them to do it for me every week." She says, looking at everyone, wondering if it's the correct answer to her original question.

"Oh, I get it now," Amber says. "Patrick and I have sex two or three times a week. Of course, we don't have kids." She looks around to Dominque and Zya, and adds, "All of our lives are different. There's no right or wrong answer."

"Deb, with kids it makes it more difficult to find the time and the energy. The fact that you two are enjoying each other at every opportunity is great. If you can get your mom one week, and Megan the next, perfect. Maybe you'll find another time during the week when Brian isn't snoring after you've put Tracey to bed."

"I think there's a book called *101 Great Quickies*. If you've only got a few minutes, why not give it a shot? Or find an interesting way to wake him up." Dominque says and winks at her.

Debra blushes. "So, it's okay if we can only make love once a week?"

Zya says, "Honey, there are happily married couples that can't have sex at all for whatever reason, but they keep on loving each other. Sex isn't everything. A connection between two people doesn't always happen between their legs; intimacy is much more important. Do what's right for you. Don't go comparing yourself to anyone else. You do what makes you happy. Damn girl, you're not even married yet; stop worrying and just enjoy."

Outside the window, two cars down, he's sitting, watching. *Laugh, Little Miss Perfect, laugh now while you can. I'm getting everything ready for you. I've thought of everything— it's going to be perfect.*

CHAPTER TWENTY-EIGHT

"I'm so happy we're here, but I'm exhausted."

"I know me too. Bummer, our room isn't ready yet," Tad says.

"Look at that water. I can't wait to jump in it and swim. First, I think I need a nap."

"Go ahead. I'll stay awake in case they buzz us," Tad says, stretching out in one of the poolside lounge chairs.

He researched everything about this trip, wanting it to be perfect. And already, they've had a few hiccups. They flew into LAX airport from Miami, where they had a four-hour layover until their Papeete Tahiti flight. They were starving, so Dominque picked a restaurant they would return to in Terminal 7 as they headed over to check in for their Tahiti flight.

Because it was an international flight, they had to claim their luggage and check it in with them. Luckily for Tad, Dom's overstuffed bag was a roller so he could just push all sixty-eight pounds of it. He would find out later, at least forty pounds of it were shoes.

They had to go outside to access Terminal 8; however, they found the Air Tahiti station closed. The sign said they would open at 11:15 p.m., forty-five minutes before boarding. No problem. They would go back into Terminal 7, have dinner, and come back later.

Murphy was at again...the airport is only open to travelers with valid boarding passes. Because it was an international flight, they couldn't check in via their mobile device; they had to do it in person with picture ID. No amount of explanation gained them access to the terminal or the restaurant his ravenous and pregnant wife urgently needed at that moment. Tad suggested taking a taxi to get something to eat. She didn't need to say a word; the defeated look on her face as she glanced between their four suitcases surrounding them took that option off the table.

She pretended it was okay as they wheeled their suitcases back to Terminal 8, where at least there was a bench they could wait on. Dominque munched on a bag of almonds she found at the bottom of her purse. After brushing off the few loose hairs and wads of lint, you could convince yourself they were fresh.

Tad regularly checked his watch, willing time to pass by quicker, creating the opposite effect—making it crawl.

Dominque's eyes lit up when she saw the seats turn into beds. She squealed and hugged him tightly. He managed to keep this little tidbit a surprise. A nice luxury his parents surprised him with at the last minute. All was forgiven— PHEW!

The stewardess came over as soon as they sat down and asked if she could bring them something to drink. Tad explained the dinner fiasco and the other situation. After asking a few questions, she told them she'd be right back.

Within minutes she brought Dominque a cold Caesar salad, assuring her they made the dressing with pasteurized eggs and a sliced chicken breast on top accompanied with a bottle of seltzer water. She brought Tad a beer without him asking.

Dominque fell asleep shortly after she took the last bite of her salad. The plane was still at the gate when she curled up on her side and zonked after a few seconds. She stayed in that exact position for seven hours and thirty-six minutes. Tad knows because he didn't sleep a wink. He ate his meal and had a few more beers, hoping they would put him to sleep. He even caught up on the latest flicks he'd been eager to see. His eyes were still wide open when the lights came on and the attendants began serving breakfast.

Dominque stretches, knocking over a water bottle at the crack of dawn. "How d'you sleep?" she asks, yawning at him.

"Not bad," he lies. "I'll have time to catch up."

"Not on this trip, you won't," she says and winks at him.

The cruise line offered a one-night stay at the Continental Hotel at a reduced rate. They splurged and upgraded to stay in a bungalow; another of Dominque's bucket list items. They had already decided they would take a nap after an afternoon swim off their back porch.

Everything was right in the world again until they arrived at 8 a.m., seven hours before check-in. Not used to traveling, he didn't think about this part. It wouldn't have been so bad if they had packed their poolside essentials in their carry-on. If they wanted to get at them, they would have to unpack half their suitcases.

The hotel customer service attendant promised them housekeeping would go to the first bungalow checking out to help accommodate them.

"You comfortable enough? Dom?" Tad looks over and sees her mouth hanging slightly open and her arm hanging down. Here she is, the woman of his dreams, fast asleep in her jeans and blouse with temperatures hovering in the upper seventies. It could be worse.

His vibrating phone wakes him; it's 9:23 a.m., they've both been dozing for an hour and a half. As Tad rubs his eyes, he realizes they are surrounded by other hotel guests showing much more skin.

Their room attendant takes them down a long wooden walkway, past several other bungalows, until they get to the very last one. The thatched roof is made of woven fronds, with windows everywhere. When the door opens, they are pleasantly surprised to see all the latest luxuries. The outside appears as if it hasn't been touched in decades, yet the inside has all the latest in modern amenities. Tad's eyes go directly to the king-size bed for some immediate reasons, and then later, for more satisfying ones. Tad rearranges himself thinking about the latter. The bathroom is very luxurious with a large whirlpool for two, and double bowl sinks with the finest toiletries and plush robes.

Dominque lies across the bed as the attendant opens the sliders to the back patio area. Tad steps out and instantly feels his blood pressure drop as the ocean breeze rustles his hair. He breathes in the salty air, letting his eyes drown in the turquoise waters. Being the last bungalow has its advantages.

The attendant lets himself out as Tad stands at the railing, feeling every ounce of stress leave his body. Remembering Dominque wanted to reserve the luau, he rushes inside to find her stretched out across the bed with her mouth slightly open, taking long slow deep breaths—the sounds of slumber. He pulls off her sandals and gently lays a robe across her shoulders.

Their dinner was everything they had hoped for, and more. The fish was so fresh, Tad joked they had fishermen catching them as customers ordered them. The most delicious part was the rice with vanilla and raisins; and some sort of South Pacific magic. It was like no rice either of them had ever had before. They didn't order dessert; they wanted more rice. Dominque even asked if they could have it for breakfast.

Waiting for the show, Tad watches as Dominque rests her head on her hand and catches a little shut-eye. He snaps a few pictures for their album. Hopefully, she'll laugh about them. Tad should be exhausted; yet he's wide awake. Must be the time difference; 8 p.m. here is 2 p.m. in Florida.

A male Polynesian singer introduces himself and the musicians dressed in tropical shirts and khakis in a hut behind him. He begins the first ballad as four female dancers sway their hips back and forth. Their arms create a wave up toward the stars, then down, flowing at their feet.

Two more dancers join the stage as the music changes to a fast, exhilarating beat. All six sets of hips are now jerking side to side quickly, the tassels hung along their hips, beating wildly. Their hands roll in front of them to a beat of their own —a combination of belly dancing and hula.

From the corner of their eyes, they notice water splashes on either side of the stage. Six men, three on each side, are in the shallow parts of the pool, their feet slapping the surface in tempo with the drums.

Dominque's eyes flutter as the beat gets louder. Seeing the men jump on stage is all the motivation she needs to keep them lifted.

Tad smiles. She always says, 'Married, not dead. When I stop looking—you better worry.'

The music takes on a bolder, more aggressive beat as decorative rings of fronds on the men's biceps and calves fly when their elbows and knees flare out in opposite directions, their thigh muscles tensing under their weight. Their chests push out in sync as they pull back their elbows, causing their biceps to bulge. Three of the men out front begin twirling sticks with both ends on fire. They're spun so quickly, a bright orange circle forms in front of them while their knees continue to thrust out in opposite directions.

The women in the audience give their full attention, watching the finely tuned athletic forms glisten with sweat as they hop around to the rhythm of the beat.

Watching as Dominque licks her lips, her eyes glued to the scantily clad men on stage, Tad is hopeful the night will go better than the afternoon. He jumps over to her side of the table, pulling her as near as the chunky arms on the big round chairs will allow. Tad reaches over, enduring the pain the carved wooden end causes jabbing into his abdomen—better him than her and begins the night's festivities up her neck, causing an immediate tightness in his khakis. He takes her hand in his as his lips reach her earlobe, gently sucking and nibbling. He places her hand on his crotch. "Do you see what you do to me? You drive me wild, woman," he whispers in her ear.

She moans and says, "Oh baby, as much as I love the effect we have on each other, I can barely keep my eyes open. I'm just too tired. Can we try in the morning?"

Tad pulls back, kissing the hand causing his heat to rise. "Sure, babe, I understand." At that point, his mind goes into battle. A cold shower or the fancy lotion in the bathroom?

The next morning Tad bounces out of bed and gets the coffee maker going. He's packed his few clothes he used yesterday and jumps in the shower, super excited to board their ship today.

Suddenly, as he's singing and thinking about chasing after his beautiful wife on the sands of the South Pacific, Dominque rushes into the bathroom, barely making it to the toilet, vomiting everything she ate the night before. And, it appears, from the previous few days.

Tad quickly jumps out, still dripping, and grabs her hair. Memories flood back as this was his role after her first round of chemo; before her long locks fell out. Her hair has regrown to where it's just touching her shoulders, long enough to get in the way as she thrusts her head forward again and heaves. Nothing comes out as her body convulses, again and again.

Eventually, she turns and sits against the wall with her arms resting on her knees.

"Babe, something you ate?"

"The smell of the coffee, it woke me up and instantly…" At the thought of the smell, she jumps back toward the toilet.

Tad, stark naked, runs into the other room and grabs the coffee pot and the filter with the grinds, and puts them outside on the patio, closing the sliders behind him. He runs to the front door, opening and closing it rapidly, fanning the room with fresh air.

Dominque slowly walks out, dropping on to the bed.

"Morning sickness?"

"Yeah, I think so."

"What can I get do to help?"

"Dry toast or crackers?"

233

Tad calls for room service, then opts to go himself when he's told it takes an hour. As he runs down the wooden walkway, he curses the fact they have the very last bungalow. And of course, the restaurant is on the opposite end of the property.

Out of breath, he can barely place his order. "That's it? Just plain, dry toast, sir?" the waitress asks.

"Yep, that's it. If you could please hurry as quickly as possible, I would really appreciate it. My wife has morning sickness. She's not feeling very well."

"Ah," the woman says, spinning on her heel.

Within minutes, she's back with two bags. Tad looks at her questionably as he peeks inside.

"Ginger ale is good for her—one cold, one room temperature, whichever she prefers. Toast for now; crackers and rice cakes to keep with her. She should snack often. It will help."

Tad hugs the woman, so appreciative of her unexpected kindness and for making him feel less helpless.

He runs back, faster this time, and finds Dominque slowly packing her bag.

"Here, babe, I'll take care of that. Sit down."

He lays out the goodies, explaining precisely as they were to him.

She smiles at him. "I'm so sorry. This certainly hasn't gone according to plan."

"Please don't apologize. You're carrying my child. You can do no wrong."

She chuckles.

"Do you want to go home? I can see if we change our flights and just go back if you're not feeling well?" Tad asks.

"Are you serious? We didn't get insurance. We'll lose every penny if we don't get on that boat today. I will not let morning sickness stop us from checking this off my bucket list."

"Well, you could officially check the South Pacific off, because we are in Tahiti. We could just stay here for the week?"

"We can't afford it. And I don't want to lose the money your parents paid for our beautiful cruise. Never tell me how much it cost; I don't want to know." After several seconds of silence, she adds, "I want to go if you do."

"Yes! Of course, I do." He grabs her suitcase, forgetting how heavy it is, immediately regretting his memory as he feels a pull in his left shoulder. If only he had used his right hand, he might have gotten away with it. The suitcase drops the ten inches back to the ground and bounces.

"Tad, are you okay? Did you hurt yourself?"

"Nope, I'm okay," he says as he rubs the top of his left arm, hoping she didn't see the look of pain on his face.

Using his right arm, he gently lowers it to the ground and opens it. He carefully gathers her items around the room and puts them on the bed, wondering how he's going to fold them. His left shoulder is throbbing—he's sure he pulled something.

He knows she's watching him closely as he crisscrosses in front of her.

When she's finished her toast, she grabs the ice bucket and heads for the door.

"Where are you going?"

"You have to ice it for the first forty-eight hours. I have some zip-lock bags; I'll be back."

"I can go, you stay here."

"You went to my rescue already; it's my turn. It would be good for me to get some fresh air. Just please don't hurt yourself—again."

A two-week supply of sunscreen, pain relievers, rice cakes, and ginger soda, and they somehow manage to make some beautiful memories.

The ship is decked out with Lalique crystal chandeliers, lamps, even tables. Velvet upholstery, marble counters, top-notch décor is everywhere, including in their Owner's Suite. The suite features a vast king-size bed, a sitting room, and two bathrooms—one with a large tub Dominque drooled over more so than any other luxury feature. Tad staked claim on the second bathroom. A bottle of champagne was on ice from his parents, wishing them a wonderful trip. A beautiful touch, even though Dominque couldn't have any. Chocolate covered strawberries from their travel agent were delivered later that day. Dominque would usually have devoured the outer covering, leaving the fruit, however since her little being inside joined her, she couldn't even look at anything starting with the letters *choco*.

The plans of getting back into a normal newlywed sex life after cancer treatments get thrown out the window as they deal with these unexpected events; their new motto is quality, not quantity. They recently added Tad's stubbed toe from running into the room after a failed attempt on the balcony. They were both so excited she was awake and feeling okay...they didn't think about how close to shore they were until a passing boat shined their spotlight on them.

Aside from everything else, Dominque enjoys snorkeling at the pearl farms after Tad cakes on the SPF 80 to protect her ivory skin. The colorful clams do not disappoint with their bright turquoise mantle lips making Mick Jagger jealous. Tad stays on dry land, unable to rotate his left arm without excruciating pain, and limping on his right leg. However, he enjoys watching how quickly they nucleate the oysters with mantle and beads to create new pearls. Some specimens they show are magnificent, and to think an animal made them. He has a newfound appreciation for the earrings the girls picked out for Zya. He promises Dom will have some as well.

They walked along the black rock beaches in Nuku Hiva until they found a calm beach where they waded, holding hands, just enjoying the beautiful water and sun. Tad was able to catch on video the two stingrays that floated by, later finding out, it was the shuffling of their feet which brought them close to shore.

Boarding the tender to take them to their ship later in the afternoon, a local man greeted them in a grass skirt with matching adornments on his calves and arms. His body was painted like a canvas with traditional inks, telling a story of his heritage. Tad caught Dominque giggling as she caught sight of his bare rear when the wind lifted a few strands of dried grass while he was blowing into a shell—a traditional horn. Tad knows already what's going through her mind...*what happens if the wind blows up front?*

As they settle into their first-class seats on the flight to the mainland, Dominque says, "I had a blast. What an amazing adventure, even if I was a little sick. Oh, Tad, I've never seen water so clear and coral, fish and those clams—I'll never forget this trip for the rest of my life. I'm so happy we got to do this before our little one gets here. Thank you for making it happen."

"It has been an amazing trip. I'd change a few things," he says, chuckling. "You're right, I'll never forget it either. I'm glad we got to do this before our little legacy arrives." Tad settles back, watching his soul mate. The smile plastered on her face is worth every pulled muscle, stubbed toe, and cold shower.

CHAPTER TWENTY-NINE

"I brought you two slasher books and two romantic thrillers this time."

"I know what you're trying to do, and it will never work. And why the hell did you bring him with you?"

"I have a name, you know. You used to have no problem remembering it when you screamed it out before," Stewart says.

"I don't think your name is God," Brandy retorts.

"You've never believed in God a day in your life," Amber says, without skipping a beat.

Brandy looks at her, then busts out laughing. "Damn, girl, there's hope for you yet."

Amber smiles and asks, "Do I dare think you might be rubbing off on me?"

Brandy stops laughing suddenly. Looking Amber straight in the eyes, she says, "Don't even joke about that. You've got a good thing going, and a man who loves you, don't be like me."

This tender moment takes Amber by surprise. She wants to believe there's some good in there, but it's too convenient. Amber shakes her head, her thoughts a tumbleweed of confusion. "Don't be going and get all sappy on me now," she says to Brandy. "I'm not sure I know how to handle that."

Brandy slides down in her seat and looks over at Stewart, her face contorting back to the bad girl they've all known and expected. "You here for a conjugal visit? The ladies here have some talented tongues, but if my memory serves me, your big dick really makes me scream." Brandy licks her lips and then puts her index finger in her mouth and sucks on it, causing an immediate physical reaction in Stewart's jeans.

"If you want all eight inches of my hard cock, I'll see what I can do," he says and jumps up from his seat because now that she's opened the door, he'll be damned if he's going to let her slam it shut.

Amber sits quietly at the table. In the past, a conversation such as this might have caused her cheeks to blush. Now she expects nothing less; it doesn't faze her anymore. "If I ask you how you're doing, will you give me an honest answer, or put on your tough girl image like you always do, and say you're hunky-dory?"

"I'm hunky-dory. You shouldn't even bother to ask."

"Brandy, can you be serious for just a minute? We have a chance to start over, you and me. We're going to be thirty-eight soon, don't you think it's time we try to have a relationship?"

Brandy says nothing; she sits staring at the wall, shifting in her seat. You can almost see the wheels turning.

Amber stays quiet. She was taught long ago, the first one who speaks—loses.

Finally, Brandy sits up and looks her in the eye. "I don't see how we can—too much bad blood between us. We'll never have your version of a fairy tale. You know that, right?"

Amber smiles and nods; Brandy lost.

Brandy stares at the shit-eating grin on her face. "What? Why are you smiling like that?"

"Look, we don't have the greatest past, but it doesn't mean we can't have a better future."

"Don't push it."

"We can't go back and undo what's happened; I want to move forward and have some sort of relationship with you. I want you in my life. You killed him because he raped me. And then you turned yourself in, knowing I would never survive in prison. After all, we've been through, you couldn't stand it that that man forced himself on me, and it made you angry. The thought of me sitting in prison made you even more nuts."

"No man should ever force themselves on a woman. No means, no! I would have killed him even if it was someone else he had raped."

The wind gets knocked out of Amber's gut at Brandy's words. She takes a deep breath deciding the wall is going to be harder to break down than she thought. "Zya's daughter Ashanti has taught us all about forgiveness. I hated you so much, and now—I forgive you. Brandy, I don't know what tomorrow will bring, I just know I want you to be a part of it."

Amber watches as Brandy's eyes fill with tears. She wipes them away as quickly as they come.

Brian grabs the last box from his cottage-style office and home and walks around to the front parking lot. He's wanted to add a child therapist to the practice, but he needed space for their office and a playroom. Now, moving in with Debra, he has the room.

He makes a mental note to have his secretary make plans for the expansion as he puts the box in his trunk with the rest of his belongings. The few remaining pieces of furniture Goodwill will pick up the first of the week.

As he closes the trunk, he looks up and sees a cold hard face staring at him from the intersection, across the street.

Brian slams the trunk and jumps in his car as fast as he can. His haste only makes it harder to get the keys in the ignition. He curses himself for not getting a newer car with a push-button start. Finally, the car roars to life, and he jerks it into reverse, barely touching the brakes. A car horn blares when he almost backs into it, temporarily forgetting his office is on a busy boulevard.

By the time Brian can safely back out and turn right, in the direction the car he's following went, all he can see is a line of brake lights in front of him waiting for the Las Olas Boulevard light to change. He hits his steering wheel in frustration. Roberto could have turned down any of these side streets.

❧

The windows have a film of condensation making it impossible to see out or in, either from the high humidity or the heat coming from the back seat.

Mitch lays Ashanti down and puts his leg between hers. *It's time,* she thinks.

She can feel his erection throbbing through his jeans on her thigh. *Is it supposed to excite or terrify you?* Right now, she's shaking—trembling.

When they first started working on the No Tolerance Bully Program together, Mitch was a little chubby, barely five feet, five inches tall, and his face still wore the telltale signs of a teenager. Now, two years later, he's grown three inches in height, and his daily gym routines have taken him from pudgy to pumped. One afternoon, having to run from football to a rally as class President, Ashanti stopped by the locker-room to give him his speech notes. He called her in as he was alone; he wanted to know what she thought. He left her by his locker as he took a shower, reciting his words over the sound of running water.

Staring at the wall, she listened, trying to drown out the background noise so she could concentrate on his speech. The water stopped, and his words became much clearer as he came around the corner, wearing a towel low around his hips.

She no longer heard him. His lips were moving, but her eyes could only concentrate on his ripped body traveling from his broad, defined chest down to his chiseled six-pack abs.

"What do you think? Sound good? Ashanti?"

"Sounds great," she said, as she ran out the door.

Ashanti already had all the curves of a beautiful woman at fourteen when they met. Now, at almost seventeen, she is more beautiful than ever. Something everyone noticed, including Mitch.

Ashanti pulls Mitch's shirt out from his jeans, running her fingertips in the crevice between his abs.

Mitch grabs her hand and pulls it to his lips. "I want you so bad; I have dreamed about this moment—but I can't."

"Because I'm not eighteen?"

"Actually, I checked. Once you turn seventeen, you can legally consent, and I can't get into trouble. I'm not too worried."

"I'm not seventeen yet."

"If I hadn't stopped you just now, what would you have done?"

Ashanti's cheeks burn; her caramel kissed skin hides it perfectly. "I guess you'll have to wait to find out," she says, trying to sound confident when inside, she's cringing.

"Look, you and I didn't start out like normal people. I don't want to screw this up. I really like you."

"I like you too. You're going away to college soon, and I want you to be my first."

He sucks in air and says, "Hear me out before you throw anything at me. Better yet..." He takes her purse and slips it to the front seat as they sit up. "I never deserved your kindness and forgiveness; somehow you gave it to me anyway. And now you want to give me something so precious and rare—I'm not worthy."

"Wait—what? So, you don't want to have sex with me?"

"Seriously? You have no idea how much I do."

"Well, then..." she begins to take her shirt off, but he stops her.

"I'm probably going to regret this, and I hope you don't hate me but rather thank me one day; I can't. You're going to fall madly in love with someone, and that's who you'll give yourself to. That person isn't me. I really care about you, and I hope we can still be friends, at least until I leave next month."

Tears sting the back of her eyes as she jumps into the front passenger seat. "Take me home—now."

Mitch gets in the driver's seat. "Ashanti," he says and places his hand over hers.

She pulls away, willing the tears to stay back.

He quietly drives with his face turned to the left.

Confused, hurt, and ashamed, she glances over, seeing a single tear slide down his cheek in his reflection in the window.

CHAPTER THIRTY

"Tad, I'm bleeding."

"Did you call the doctor?"

"I did. He said it was normal, but something came out. I think I just lost the baby," Dominque says between gut-wrenching sobs.

"I'm on my way. Call the doctor back and tell him we're heading to the hospital."

A few hours later, the high-risk OB-GYN joins them in the emergency room.

"We've looked at the tissue you brought in, and I'm so sorry, it was the fetus."

Dominque brings her legs up, pulling her arms in to form a tight ball. The sounds coming from the table are a mixture of moaning and wailing, like an injured animal.

Tad nods to the doctor as his eyes turn glassy.

"I'll sign her release papers so she can go home whenever she's ready. Please just watch out for a fever. She'll continue to bleed for the next few days, heavier than usual. I'll see you two in my office next week, and we'll plan for the next transfer."

He squeezes Dominque's shoulder. "I'm truly sorry."

Dominque reaches up and grabs for Tad, pulling him down, clinging to him as if her life depended upon it. She had so much hope for the love she would give their child. The future they already started planning. She already picked out the white crib with a matching changing table and dresser; pink sheets with ballerina slippers for a girl, boats and planes in shades of blue if it was a boy. She had wardrobes picked out for both sexes' sizes from newborn to twelve months.

"Babe, we'll try again. These things happen. I'm so sorry. Please don't give up hope."

"We should have just put the money into the house," she says between sobs, with her face still buried in his chest.

"What do you mean?"

"The trip—it was too much. I hurt our baby; I lost our baby," she moaned.

She continued to sob as Tad crawled up on the bed with her, cradling her in his arms, reassuring her she did nothing to cause this.

She can hear his voice, yet the words don't get through. Her heart is so heavy—it aches. It was a girl, she knew it. The image in her mind of a little girl in a floral dress looking back, laughing, disintegrates into the grains of sand on the beach they're running on.

She was so excited when she found out she was pregnant, so eager to pick out names and start the nursery. Tad asked her to hold off and wait at least until she was twelve weeks. She always brushed him off—so certain everything was going to be *just fine*.

She didn't tell him she had already started a baby registry and picked out eighty percent of the items. Now she wishes she hadn't. Her due date looms on the first page—February 24, 2020.

☯

Zya's arms flail wildly in the air as she fills Tina in on the request from *Vogue*.

Tina quietly sits and listens.

"Well, aren't you gonna say something? This is it—this is the dream, baby! This is what we've been working for."

"I thought Paris was the dream?"

"It is honey—everything is just happening at once. I didn't expect *Vogue* to invite me to present at the Forces of Fashion at the same time as Paris." Zya sits down on the chair opposite Tina at the table in the kitchen, slightly deflated. "I know—it's impossible. How do we make it work?"

"I don't want to burst your bubble." Tina looks down at the ground and takes a deep breath. After several moments of contemplation, she slowly shakes her head and says, "We'll figure it out."

"Thank you so much, Tina."

"You said yes without talking to me first. You didn't ask me what I thought, and you knew you'd need me to do double-duty."

Zya's eyes bulge with a dazed look. "Oh honey, you're right, I was so excited—this is an opportunity of a lifetime. I should have asked you. I don't take you for granted; I hope you know I appreciate everything you do for me. If I turned it down, I doubt they would ever invite me back. You don't turn down *Vogue*. I didn't think. We *are* a team. I'm so sorry."

Tina stands up and hugs her. "I know you are, but it hurts you didn't ask. In the future, include me in a decision that's going to turn our already loony world, more upside down."

Zya places Tina's hand over her heart. "I love you, Tina Monroe. You are my everything. We are a team, and I promise I won't make that mistake again."

"Okay, but since you already did, let's deal with this right now. Because wife, I'm horny as hell, and the faster we get these details over to them, you get to make it up to me."

Zya opens her mouth to say something, and Tina puts her finger to Zya's mouth. "No excuses, you owe me. You can lay back, and I'll do all the work. Don't worry—you won't fall asleep." Tina leans over and gives Zya a deep tongue thrashing she feels from the tips of her toes to the top of her spinning head.

The front door bursts open as Ashanti barges in, slamming it behind her and racing up the stairs with a scowl on her face.

"Ashanti honey, is that you? I have some great news," Zya calls out.

When she doesn't get a reply, she says to Tina, "*Vogue* can wait."

Zya finds Ashanti face down on her bed, sobbing into her pillow. "Oh, honey, come here. What's wrong?" she asks, pulling Ashanti into her arms.

Ashanti doesn't reply. She puts her head on her mom's lap and continues to wail as Zya smooths her hair.

Ashanti's bedroom door opens, and Stacey rushes in, not realizing she wasn't alone. "Oh, sorry, I'll come back."

"No, you come on in. I have a feeling you know what's going on here. You know we don't keep secrets from each other, right?"

Stacey nods; her eyes are on Ashanti, who's looking up pleading at her with tear-stained cheeks.

"Mrs. Monroe, I'm your daughter's best friend, and I'd like to keep it that way. It's her place to talk to you, not mine." Stacey backs out of the room, slowly closing the door behind her.

Ashanti sits up, wiping her eyes.

"Honey, why don't you go wash your face. I'll wait here."

The Jack-and-Jill bathroom adjoins Ashanti's and Stacey's sleeping quarters. Convenient when she's trying to sneak more time with her BFF, but not when all she wants to do is escape.

While she washes up, she tells her mother everything. She may get mad, but they agreed. The few times they've swayed, it's only caused pain.

When she finishes, she meets her mother's eyes and is surprised to find a loving smile. She expects the wrath of Medusa after mentioning Mitch and sex in the same sentence.

"I'm proud of Mitch. Most teenage boys allowed to take something so precious from a beautiful young woman wouldn't think twice about it. Don't be mad at him—respect him. I think that boy has it bad for you."

"What do you mean?"

"He loves you, sweetheart."

"I love him too, Mom. Shouldn't he be the one?"

"I know you don't want to hear this. I certainly didn't when I left home. You have strong feelings for him, and it might be love. Honey, you're gonna experience all kinds of emotions in your life, from lovers—and friends. He's right. Giving your virginity is a gift and not something to give just because the other girls at school have. In fact, I bet, most of them are all talk—they're still virgins."

"You think?"

"I know," Zya says, chuckling, remembering some of the lies the girls in her dorm spread. She was quiet and didn't say much...those are the ones you should beware of. They don't miss anything.

"And since when do you care what anyone else thinks anyway? This doesn't sound like my daughter."

"I know. I just hate being the good girl all the time. Didn't you want to do something bad when you were my age?"

Zya is lifting one eyebrow. She was only sixteen when she gave herself to Doug, thinking he was the one. Her baby girl is turning seventeen in a few days and is still pure. Almost gave it away—but not yet.

"We're not talking about me. I've come to like Mitch, and I can see why you're so fond of him. He's earned my respect. If you two are meant to be together, you will be. Have you heard the saying, if you love something, let it go?"

Ashanti says the last verse with her. "If it comes back to you, it's yours to keep. If it doesn't, it never was."

"There's a lot of truth in that. Mitch is going where to college?"

"Stanford."

"I can't believe I'm saying this because it's as far away as you can get from South Florida."

"Actually, Seattle is, Mom."

"Smart Aleck. What I was going to say is, you have a full ride to any school you want, and you applied to Stanford. If they accept you and allow you to start in January, would you consider it?"

Tears begin to pool again in Ashanti's eyes, filling her lower lids. "I don't know. I thought I'd go to the University of Miami because I want to stay close to you, and Stacey and Tina

—and everyone else. Yet, part of me wants to go where he'll be."

Zya's eyes copy Ashanti's as she hugs her close. "Honey, you go where it's best for you. Go to the school which gives you the best opportunity for your future. I understand part of that also means you have to be happy. Whether having family close, or Mitch, defines that for you, is your choice. Just make sure part you make part of the decision with your brain, and not all heart."

"You'd be okay if I go to California?"

"We'd make it work. I'd probably have to look into fractional plane ownership because my butt would be on campus visiting you at least three, maybe four times a month."

"Promise?"

Zya's heart swells, knowing her daughter would want to see her that often rather than cringing at the thought.

"Promise and pinky swear."

CHAPTER THIRTY-ONE

"Babe, how are you doing today?"

Dominque shrugs her shoulders. She really doesn't know how she feels. Amber told her to take a few weeks off, but Dominque was adamant; work is exactly what she needed. Keeping busy was the best thing to distract her. She's done pretty well these past three weeks—now she's only breaking down in hysterics three times a day… morning, noon, and night.

"How's the bleeding? Has it stopped?" Tad asks.

"Just spotting now."

Their conversations lately have been pretty much one-sided. Dominque has the one to three word responses down to a T. She knows it's frustrating for Tad, and he's tried to get her to open up; she doesn't feel much like conversing. He's been very patient and loving—even a bit smothering at times. She knows he means well, but sometimes she wants to be left alone. Sleep is a good a distraction…except when she's dreaming about the beach, a floral dress and ribbon.

"Are you ready to make the appointment for the next transfer?"

Dominque turns and looks at him. Confused and afraid, she takes a deep breath and decides it's time to talk about it. "Yes, and no. Part of me is ready to take the next step; my heart keeps reeling me back in."

"It's your decision and I'll go along with whatever you want to do. Am I allowed to give my opinion?"

She smiles as him and grabs his hand. "Of course—I want to know what you're thinking."

"I don't know the totality of what you're going through, but *we* both lost the baby. I may not be the one who was carrying it, yet my heart has been crushed just the same."

"Oh Tad! I'm so sorry, I haven't been there for you." The never-ending tears start again.

"I'm not telling you this to make you feel bad; I'm sharing because I want you to know we're in this together. You told me starting our family early was what you wanted more than anything. You said putting your life on the line was a gamble you were willing to take to ensure your legacy. There's no guarantee; you might lose the next one. And yet, there's a good chance you won't. This sucks, but I think we need to take the chance. No matter what happens, I'm with you every step of the way. I'm ready if you are."

Dominque feels as if she's fallen in love with this beautiful man all over again. She jumps up and throws herself into his arms. She can't talk—the sobs come continuously; she can barely catch her breath.

Tad holds on tight, wiping away the stray tears escaping his eyes. Once her sobs turn down in volume and frequency, he grabs a tissue from the box next to them and hands it to her.

Pulling away, she wipes her eyes and then blows her nose. It's so loud and horn-like, they both crack up laughing. Just what they needed to lighten the mood.

"Can we afford to do another transfer right now?" she asks.

"Yes, we can."

While Tad stayed strong for Dominque, it was his dad who gave him strength. Their nightly phone calls, once Dominque was asleep, had become a ritual. At ten o'clock, his dad was waiting by the phone to help ease his son's helplessness. Tad and his father had always been very close, at times more of a best friend than a parent—his mom got that role. Tad shed many tears over the years to the man who would always be his hero—his idol. As a child while the kids at school would laugh and make fun of him when his eyes leaked, his dad always told him—a real man is not afraid to show his emotions. Crying is healing; it would him get through the pain quicker to let it all out. Then he could deal with the really hard stuff.

His parents have always been very generous. He dared one day to look up what their cruise cost them. He nearly had a heart attack when he saw the five digit figure. They cruise all the time so they probably got a break—yet their generosity to help make Dominque's dream come true is something he'll never forget. They love her just as much as he does. Tad mentioned it one night on the phone; his dad just chuckled and said, "We'd rather be alive and see you kids enjoy it now rather than after we're gone." His dad assured him, they were there for him and Dominque, no matter the cost. He also mentioned they would be more than willing to help cover the transfer costs if it helped get them grandchildren. The feeling of family —unwavering love and support—is what Dominque never had until now. If he had any doubts about the chance she was taking, getting pregnant before her two-year anniversary, it was that call which took the last bit of uncertainty away.

After putting the kids to bed, Debra tiredly drags her feet into the kitchen and finds Brian's head leaning over a file with stacks. Towers of books are piled on both sides. He's taken over half of the dining room table. They've been eating on the kitchen island every night, which is quite a feat with a seven-year-old in those high chairs.

"Babe, come with me." She holds her hand out and begs him to take a walk with her.

"I'd love to, you know I would, but this file is on a new client I see in the morning. I need to get through it before I see her. You understand, right?"

She leans down and kisses him sweetly on the lips. "I do, but come anyway—it won't take long."

Brian follows her down the hall to the last door on the left. He's never been in there because it's never open when he's in the house. She quickly turns the knob and pushes it open, following behind its path. Brian peeks his head in first and looks around.

The smell of wood and leather instantly hits his nose. It's a man's room—this was George's office.

"You need an office, and I want my dining room back. George would want you to have this room. Come all the way in," she says, grabbing his hand, gently tugging.

"I don't know about this. Why don't we turn it into a bedroom, and I can take another room?" he says, making a full 360-degree turn, then stopping directly in front of her.

"That's silly, this room doesn't have a closet. It's an office —yours now."

Brian walks over to the desk running his fingertips across the mahogany top. He slowly walks behind it, taking in every curve of the hand-carved legs and sides, finally stopping to rest his hands on top of the black leather tufted executive swivel chair. He looks out into the room, taking in the custom bookcases along the wall made of the same fine wood as the desk, and the arms and legs of the chair. The shelves are lined with classics like *Don Quixote, The Mayor of Casterbridge, War of the Worlds, Tales from 1,001 Nights,* and *Pride and Prejudice.* There are even first editions of F. Scott Fitzgerald's *The Beautiful and Damned,* and Doyle's *Sherlock Holmes.* Brian rushes over as he recognizes the words on the spines and gently picks up a few. His mouth hangs open as his fingers glide over the embossed lettering. "These books are amazing. I would love to read some of these one day, if it's okay with you?"

"George would love for them to be read. You can have them if you want them."

"Oh no, I can't take these—they're treasures. You need to keep these for the kids. Pass them down through generations. These are priceless."

"Okay, I'll tell you what. You have now been dubbed the protector of these priceless treasures until these children, and our future kids, understand their value, deal?"

With hungry eyes, like a kid in a candy store, he replies, "Deal. Wow, I can't wait to find the time to go through these. I don't know which one I'll start with first."

"Well, how about, *first* thing tomorrow, you move your files and your books in here?"

"Sorry," Brian blushes and says. "Yeah, I did take over the table, sorry. I promise I'll move everything in the morning. I do have to get back to that file, though."

He stops and hugs her tight. "Thank you for this. I really appreciate it. This means a lot."

As they walk out, Debra grabs a canvas from behind a cabinet.

Brian catches a glimpse of it and catches up with her snatching it from her hand.

"Hey, what are you doing?" she says, spinning around.

He puts it out in front of him, admiring it. "You painted this, didn't you? It's the yellow daisies from your dreams when George passed. You said you were going to paint them on your anniversary, and you did. These were the flowers you imagined Tracey was holding on the other side of the hole."

Debra looking down at the floor, hesitates before answering. Finally, in a tiny voice, she says, "Yes, those are the flowers."

"Why isn't it hanging? It's beautiful!"

"I put it up in his office on the first anniversary of his death. I sat for hours that night talking to him and telling him all about the dream—all about you. I felt at peace afterwards. Then, it was Tad and Dom's wedding, and I was ready for us to be together. When I came in here the other day, I just knew George wanted you to have his office. I could feel it—he's happy for us. I was going to put it in Tracey's room since she was the one holding them in my dream."

When Debra looks up at Brian, she notices the glassy reflection in his eyes. He's been very upfront with never being a replacement to George, he's his own man, and their love will be different.

Brian walks back into the office with the painting in his hands. He sees the hook on the wall where it must have been hanging and puts it back up. "If it's okay with you, I'd like to hang it in here so George and I can enjoy it."

Today she would have been nine weeks pregnant, three weeks away before she could tell the world. She had already told her friends, and Tad's parents, but upon his insistence no one else knew. She tried to be positive and excited about today's appointment—eager to try again. Yet each time she went to the bathroom and saw red; it was like ripping the scab off every time.

Although she had a bright smile on her face, inside she was dreading being there. The last time they were here, it was not a happy ending. Being back makes it all so real again.

She doesn't flinch when the cold gel hits her abdomen; she just wants to move forward. The life they lost will always be a part of her; yet today she wants to look toward a future.

"That's odd," the doctor says.

Tad jumps over to the screen. As he looks at the different shades of gray on the monitor, his eyes get big; his smile even bigger. He looks at the doctor, then at Dominque.

The doctor turns the screen so she can see what the sudden giddiness is all about.

She can't believe it. In the middle of the screen is a tiny heartbeat. Its fast rhythmic pulse is a magical sight—a miracle.

Tad runs over and hugs her; her eyes stay glued to the screen. "I don't understand."

"It's possible you ovulated around the same time we performed the transfer. Your cancer treatments most likely damaged the egg your body naturally released, so your body rejected it. But this little one right here, looks perfect."

CHAPTER THIRTY-TWO

"Are you going to marry my mommy?"

"I am in six months," Brian says, picking up Tracey and twirling her around the room as she squeals in delight.

Debra's mind immediately focuses on the six months part. "Wow, it's coming fast."

"Not fast enough if you ask me. I'd marry you tomorrow at the courthouse if you'd go along with it."

"Really? Should we?"

"You're joking, right?" Brian asks, gently lowering Tracey.

"Well, Roberto is back. If he thinks I'll run away with him, if we're married, then I can't, right?"

"Your friends are planning this beautiful elaborate wedding at their home, of which they've already spent thousands of dollars on, and you want to ditch it and get married by a judge?"

"I'm not saying skip the ceremony in February; we can always renew our vows. Do you think it would be a deterrent if we were already married?" Debra says, standing up pacing across the room.

"I doubt it. Do *you* need one?"

"What do you mean? You think I want to run away with him?"

"You were in love with him once. And you did say yes to him before me."

"I love *you*. I want to spend the rest of my life with you—not him."

"Then why do you still have the engagement ring he gave you hidden in your closet?"

Debra stops in front of him as the color in her face drains.

"You asked me to get something from there last week, remember?"

She nods.

"I saw the Louis Vuitton box, and curiosity got the best of me. You don't strike me as the high fashion designer kind of gal, so I wanted to see what treasure you had..."—Brian pauses for a moment, then continues—"tucked away inside."

Debra turns and walks away, stopping to look out the window. "I don't know what to do with it. I gave it back to him when he took me to the hospital—the same day he gave it to me. I have no idea how it ended up back in my nightstand. I found it there after Amber marched him off. What do I do with it?"

"I wish you had told me about it. It would have been better than me finding it."

"You're right, I'm sorry. I wasn't hiding it from you, I just didn't want to be reminded about it, and I don't know what I'm supposed to do with it now. It was a family heirloom, so I know I have to give it back to him."

A sly smile spreads across Brian's face as he rubs his chin. "Hmm, smart guy, after all."

"What do you mean?"

"If it is a family treasure, he knows you'll want to give it back—you'll have to see him. He made sure you got it after you chose me on purpose."

"You really think so?"

"I know so. The first thing we're going to do is make sure it really is this priceless treasure. Let's go see the jeweler today."

☯

"I'll call you when I get off the plane. I'm excited you're coming out to Cali. Whether it's to be with me, or because it's the school you really want to be at, I don't care, I'm just glad I'll get to be near you. As friends, or more—whatever you want."

"We'll answer that when I get there. You'll be six months ahead of me; I'm sure the ladies will peg you the first day they see you on campus."

Mitch cups Ashanti's chin and pulls it up toward him. "There's no one else in this world for me, except you—no one as smart, as loving, or as beautiful. If you'll have me, I'm all yours. The ball is in your court. I'll be waiting for you." He kisses her sweetly on the lips. They quickly forget they're not alone as the spark turns to flames. Out of respect, Zya turns her head. She wanted to come and say goodbye to this young man who may one day be carving the holiday turkey.

After several seconds, Zya, feeling a bit uncomfortable, clears her throat. "Ahem."

"Sorry, Mom," Ashanti says, wiping the edge of her lips.

"No disrespect Mrs. Monroe. I know it's going to be a few months before I get to taste them again."

"Okay then—Mitch, have a nice trip. I want you to know I am very proud of everything you've accomplished. You've done a total transformation. You could have taken a very dangerous path, but you turned it around and look at what you've made of yourself. Political Science suits you. I hope to be voting for you one day."

"Yes, ma'am—that's the plan."

"Hey babe, whatcha working on?" Amber says, leaning over the back of Patrick's chair, seductively running her hand down his chest.

"This new case I took on today. I'm sorry I can't discuss it with you—it's pretty touchy," he replies, never looking up. He doesn't notice she's wearing a micro-mini maroon silk nightie —commando.

She walks in front of him, pulling the dress up high enough so the light from the TV behind her silhouettes the curves between her legs. "It looks interesting. You seem very intrigued."

"It's tricky, that's all," he replies, motioning her to move to the side so he can see the headlines.

Standing beside him, and picks up his hand and examines his fingernails. "You need a manicure," she exclaims.

"I don't do those—you know that," he answers, his eyes darting between the file and the television.

"The first step is moisturizer, and I've heard natural oils are the best." She props her foot on the ottoman and puts one of his fingers inside herself.

His eyes go wide as his head snaps up at her.

He throws the papers to the left and pulls her down on the ottoman. His finger is now lubricating on its own.

She's moaning as he doesn't start slow. He jumps in with sudden abandonment and surprise as she did him.

He slides her hips to the edge as he drops to his knees and gently pushes her back.

Her head hangs on the side; there's barely enough room for her to fit while his head dips between her legs.

A wide smile crosses his face as he lowers himself into position. The tip of his tongue gently glides between her engorged lips, causing her to writhe beneath him. His tongue continues its exploration, round and round it goes, stopping to flick across her most sensitive part, causing a throaty moan to escape her lips. Every time he touches her there, it's as if a pair of cymbals slam together. The unexpected crash, sending vibrations up and down her body.

His tongue and finger begin to work in tandem, teasing then together, creating instant pleasure as they apply pressure where her nerve endings are most sensitive. He brings her to the very edge, then pulls back too many times to count.

In the throes of wild abandonment, her knees go up to her shoulders, spread wide apart. She soon finds his rhythm, pushing herself into him, willing him to suck harder—flick faster, his finger to plunge deeper, while the vibrations surge throughout her body. Every nerve ending is alive and throbbing; she's bucking like a bronco, the crescendo building —she's so close—when suddenly, he stops.

Out of breath, she looks up at him, confused.

He slowly unzips his pants, relieving his swollen member from its imprisonment. He doesn't take his eyes off her, grinning as he slowly puts just the tip inside. The height is perfect. Placing his hands on her thighs, inch by inch, he sinks into her.

"Hold on to your knees for me, baby. I want you to feel every bit of me slowly sliding in and out." As he pulls out, he says, "Squeeze me as tight as you can. Yes! Yes! Like that. Don't let me go."

He's never talked to her like this before. It's hot as hell, and she does precisely as instructed.

He moves his hands to her butt cheeks, lifting her hips slightly, the angle allowing him to sink deeper. He goes slowly, making sure not to hurt her.

She writhes underneath him, now relaxing her muscles letting go so he can come back, slowly sinking in. *I'm so glad I've been doing my Kegels.*

He grabs her hips, and he plunges again, this time, pulling her hips toward him at the same time.

She gasps. "Oh!"

"Can you feel every inch of me?"

"Yes," she says, in barely a whisper.

"Tell me what you want."

"What?"

"What do you want? Fast or slow?"

"Fast," she says, looking up at him, locking eyes.

"Okay, I'll go slow," he says, licking his lips with a suggestive gaze.

She drops her head back, chuckling as he continues to pull out slowly, then thrusts quickly, causing a low moan to escape. Each time, she gets louder as the tip quickly presses down over her already amply teased and pleasured G-spot.

With their eyes locked, he slowly puts his thumb in his mouth, making sure it's nice and lubricated. He pulls it out, showing its slick surface to her, and asks, "What do you want me to do with this? Tell me." The last two words escape as barely a whisper, causing her to take a deep breath.

Her cheeks glow as she says in a tiny voice, "Press it against my clit."

"Like this," he says as he pushes it into and up against her.

"Oh!" she says and exhales as she squirms, her head thrashing side to side.

"Would you like me to do it again?"

"Yes," she says in a whisper.

"I can't hear you."

She lifts her head, looks him straight in the eye and says, "Yes, I want you to play with my clit until I scream your name, or God's, and explode all over your thick, hot cock you've buried deep inside me."

Patrick's eyes grow wide. "That's better. Your wish is my command."

The only sounds are moans, groans, and lots of 'Oh Gods' as he continues to thrust while rubbing his thumb as she demanded.

She pulls herself up, her hands still locked onto her knees as the volcano erupts, sending wave after wave of ecstasy through her body. He grabs her hips pulling and pumping, meeting somewhere in the middle until he grunts out every bit of his eruption, between the sound of his name from her lips.

He pulls her into his arms as he sits back in his chair, both gasping for air. It had been several weeks since they were last intimate. A habit Amber was determined to break tonight.

"Are you going back to work on your case?"

"I would, but you've been a very naughty girl interrupting my work. I think I need to take you into my bedroom and punish you. Would you like that bad girl?"

She looks up at him with a sweet and innocent look. "I'd like that very much."

Outside the large picture window, the bushes move. They are so exhausted and wrapped in each other's arms, they don't notice. He's been very patient—it's wearing thin now. He's taken dozens of pictures with Amber's head hung down, her face full of ecstasy. He's imagining how he's going to get the ottoman from the house so he can tie her up on it and take these same shots, but with a very different expression.

CHAPTER THIRTY-THREE

"You're not going to believe this."

"What?"

"They don't want to fight—they want to settle."

"Really? Brettinger's estate?"

"Yeah, the attorney handling the probate is inundated with complaints from women saying he abused them. Several women even claim they have his children—ones he knew about and supported so long as they never went public. Sound familiar?" Patrick asks.

Amber's mouth drops open. The more they dig into the case, the more dirt they find and horror that would shock Lucifer himself. He's definitely rotting in Hell, that's for sure. "Just when I think it can't get any worse, it does."

"You mean, he's worse than the excrement from pond scum."

She can't help but smile at the memory of when they met, and playfully told him how some people refer to attorneys.

"No, he's not even the amoebas that live on the excrement of pond scum."

"Can amoebas live on pond scum?" Patrick asks.

"I don't know; I just can't think of anything more disgusting."

"Pedophile?"

"Oh, God, let's hope not."

Patrick cringes at the thought. "You're right—that would be the final straw."

Amber doesn't respond; her mind is ticking away. "I'm going to uncover every last one. I don't care how long it takes."

"What are you talking about?"

"He had zero respect for women. They were just a thing for him—something to conquer. I'm going to uncover every last dirty secret of his. Let it be a lesson to all men who think women are just *things*," she says with narrowed eyes.

"Whoa—let's think about this first. His estate is willing to help the women who come forward with a valid DNA report, proving their child is his."

Amber turns and looks at Patrick, her face softening a little, encouraging him to continue. "They have agreed to pay child support based on the cost of living expenses and set up a four-year Florida college education fund for each one."

"What about the women he abused but didn't impregnate?"

"Well, that's where an attorney, namely me, comes in. But I wanted to talk to you about it first. If you go off and start causing trouble, you might make them rethink this whole deal. They'll have to honor helping the kids; I can make it happen quickly. The other women, those will be on a case by case basis. I'm not going to charge them, so I'll have to do it on the side, one at a time. I do have bills to pay. Oh, and by the way, I was hoping you would help me since you are an investigative reporter, on top of your other writing duties."

Amber gets up and begins pacing around the room. Her fingertips unconsciously seek the inside of her lips. An internal struggle is raging inside. Does she dig into his past, bringing up all his dirty little secrets and try to deter future predators in the making? Or, does she help those he's already hurt? She knows all too well how being a rape victim affects your life. You don't sleep. You're afraid of your shadows. You start to mistrust those you're closest to…especially those of the opposite sex. It affects your job, and therefore your future. How a few short minutes of a man proving his masculinity, or lack thereof, can change your life forever.

"Can we make a deal?"

"Why do I think I'm going to regret this? Okay."

"Let's help as many women as possible. What if I write a book—as a victim? If I need to keep his name out of it, I will begrudgingly. Maybe the women we help will want their own chapter. I want to tell the victim's emotional side and demoralize the rapists who do these heinous acts."

"You're going to piss off a lot of people."

"So. Maybe I'll get through to some too. How many times do we hear about young college girls getting raped at frat parties? One guy leads the pack and takes advantage of the girl who drank too much. 'Oh, she was asking for it,' they say. His buddies don't want to be singled out as pussies, so they go along with it. We've seen it on video. They're banging her and hiding their faces at the same time."

Patrick nods in agreement.

"*Those* are the ones I want to get through to before it's too late—before they become a Brettinger. If they see what damage they do to these women, maybe they'll think twice."

Amber gets quiet and turns away, fighting away the tears burning the back of her lids and the tightness in her chest.

Patrick gets up and takes her in his arms. "What else is on your mind?"

"Ashanti is leaving for college in a few months. I get sick to my stomach at the thought of her ending up in one of those situations."

Patrick draws his head back quickly as Amber fills him in on how she almost succumbed to having sex with Mitch. His eyes grow wide several times, as she explains.

"I'm shocked. After everything she's been through. I would have thought peer pressure was the last thing that would get to her."

"Teenagers can be very cruel. Ashanti is smart, sometimes too much for her own good; it makes her an easy target. Jealousy is usually a motivating factor. Have you seen her lately? She's becoming quite a beautiful woman."

"Um, that's not how I see her, and I'm going to plead the fifth on answering that question. She's like a niece to me."

Amber rests her head on his shoulder. "I know—sorry. She's gorgeous. I watch as men and women of all ages admire her when she walks by."

Patrick pulls back, holding Amber at arms distance. "Okay, now you really have to stop; I don't want to hear anymore."

Amber playfully slaps him on the arm and walks into the kitchen to open a bottle of wine for the much-needed glass before dinner. "Women admire other women, all the time—and not like that. Get your mind out of the gutter. We admire hair, clothes, shoes…"

"And I know you admire breasts, legs, and butts too. I've heard you all talking trash."

Amber cracks up. "Yeah, because we're jealous. We want perfect tits, asses, and legs that go all the way up to here," she says, pointing to her armpits.

Patrick comes up behind her while she struggles with the corkscrew. His hand slips inside the front of her dress, gently squeezing one of her breasts. "I love your tits," he says as his other hand reaches under her skirt and pinches her butt cheek. "And your ass is just perfect. And your legs…" His hand goes immediately between her legs, causing her to gasp. "I love right where they lead."

The case, future book, and the bottle of wine, temporarily forgotten, as Patrick shows Amber why other women have nothing on her.

CHAPTER THIRTY-FOUR

"So, how was it?"

"Exciting, exhausting, exhilarating...I can't think of any other E words to explain it."

Tina laughs. "It was worth it, huh?"

"Only if we're okay, and we make it through Paris intact."

"We're okay, and we'll be even better when we pack everything up after the show, send everyone home, and we head off to London for a week of R&R."

"We're doing that?"

"Yes, *please*, we are."

"If it's what you want, then that's what we'll do. I thought you wanted to go somewhere more exotic?"

"I want to spend time with you and explore a fun city where they speak English."

"And the French lingerie shops? You do plan on shopping before we leave Paris, right?"

"While you help Stan get everything packed up, I will be visiting *Chantelle, Maison Lejaby, Aubade, Simone Pérèle,* and *Galeries Lafayette.* I have a full day planned."

"Sounds like lots of work. You sure you'll be able to handle it on your own? You don't want someone to help you in the dressing room?"

Tina laughs and puts her arms around her sexy wife. "I've missed you. I know you were only gone for two days, and I've worked my ass off, but I really did miss you."

"I missed you too. I'm looking forward to when all this craziness is behind us, and we can have newlywed time."

Tina laughing even harder, grabs a bottle of water from the fridge and says, "You know that's come and gone. And, once we have little ones again, there won't be time for anything."

"We're having kids?" Zya asks, her eyebrows raised to the ceiling.

"We talked about this last year."

"You said you thought you *might* want to have more kids, but we never talked about *actually* doing it."

"You know it's something I want. Don't play me like that."

"Can we talk about this later? I just got in, and we've still got so much to do." Zya walks away, rubbing her forehead.

"No—we're having this discussion now. You've known I want more kids; we haven't talked about it because you've been busy crushing the fashion market. I haven't complained; I've been nothing but supportive. At some point, we have to talk about it. Ashanti is off to college in January, and I'm sure once she's gone, Stacey is gonna start looking to make her way into the world as well. She's only holding back because they're best friends."

"Exactly, why would we want more kids, once we have our lives back?"

Tina's eyes bulge out. "I'm going to pretend I didn't hear you just now and give you an opportunity to rethink your sentence." She crosses her arms and begins tapping her foot.

Zya walks over and grabs her elbows. "We'll be able to run around the house naked and go off on trips whenever we like.

We've done our jobs as moms, and damn good ones at that. It's our time," Zya says, carefully thinking about each word before they come out.

"You're only going to get busier, and maybe eventually, you'll hire more people. As far as taking off for vacation on the spur of the moment, we both know that's a fantasy. I want more kids, Zya—not babies; I want to give a kid a chance who's lost in the system. Especially after hearing Dominque's horrible foster home experience. I want to help a kid in need. We're moving into that big beautiful house next month. We have such an incredible life, thanks to you."

"And you too, don't sell yourself short. You're a big part of Label Zya's success—especially this year."

"Thanks, but that's not what I mean. You have so much to give. There's more here than either of us will ever need or want. You loved that part of being Muslim—helping. Let's really make a difference, you and I, together."

"A pet won't do it, huh?"

"I'd love a pet, but no, let's make a kid's dream come true."

"Can we get through Paris and discuss it more? I'm not saying no, I do like the idea of helping kids. I think about what Dominque went through all the time. Let's get through Paris first. We'll talk about it while you're modeling all your sexy French lingerie you're going to buy."

Zya walks behind Tina and tucks her hands down the front of her low rider, denim shorts.

Tina abruptly pulls them out. "Oh no, you don't. You got two days of catching up to do. Pull your hair back missy, time to get moving." Tina turns to walk away then stops abruptly. Looking over her shoulder, she puts her finger in her mouth and slowly pulls it out. "If you get busy—maybe later, so will we."

Zya grabs the counter, catching herself as her knees buckle.

CHAPTER THIRTY-FIVE

A mber, Debra, and Dominque are the first to board for their Miami to Paris flight. Zya arranged everything and left nothing to spare for her sisters, as usual. In La Premiére class, their seats turn into beds with mattresses made of memory foam and their pillows filled with down feathers.

Dominque is starving and exhausted, both at the same time. Once she gets settled, she can barely keep her eyes open. The flight attendant greets them shortly after they are seated to see about cocktails while they wait for the plane to fill. Amber and Debra order champagne. She turns to Dominque to find she's already sawing logs. The attendant switches off her light as she passes by. When she returns, Amber explains Dominque's delicate situation and lets her know she will be eating dinner— she's just napping. As she walks away, she says to Debra, "I certainly hope that's what she wants. I've seen those hormones in action."

"She needs to eat. Even if she's grumpy tonight, she'll thank you in the morning."

Amber has her recorder out and attempts to put her emotions into words about life after rape as the plane taxis, lifts off, and eventually reaches cruising altitude. She hits rewind and record several times, attempting to find the right combination of syllables. Once the seatbelt sign signals it's safe to move about the cabin, she abruptly lifts the top of her buckle and bolts toward the bathroom wearing a scowl. After several minutes, and splashing her face with cold water, she returns to find a fresh glass of bubbles, a warm washcloth, and a small hot dish of mixed nuts waiting for her.

Debra smiles as she passes and raises her glass.

Amber picks up her glass, touching Debra's. "Cheers. We're going to have a great trip. Paris!"

"You okay? You looked a little miffed."

"Yeah, trying to find the right words has never been a problem. I guess it's because it was other people's—not mine. I'm baring my soul—it's tough. The champagne helps."

The attendant comes back with dinner menus and the bottle to top off their flutes. They choose all three entrees. Dominque will surely like something.

The finest chefs prepare the food for the world's top French airline. When the plates arrive, their noses fill with an earthy mushroom sauce combined with shallots, thyme, and rosemary, the perfect complement to the thick filet mignon hidden beneath. The lemon from the Chicken Francese is so fragrant, it fills the cabin once the cover is lifted. Under the final dome is the Provençal Cod. The thick tomato sauce is still bubbling. Debra can't help herself; she touches one of the fillets with her fork and watches as it flakes apart. They both look at each other with hungry eyes and drooling mouths.

"Which one do you think Dominque will want?"

"I'm trying to decide which one I don't want," Amber says.

"I want them all," Dominque says as she raises her seat and reaches for her tray table. "It smells heavenly. What did you order for me?"

Debra and Amber look at each other and then back at the plates.

"Dom, I think we're going to share—we can't decide."

Amber has the seat between Debra and Dominque, so she passes the plates back and forth. As they devour their dinners, they catch up on each other's lives. Luckily, for this trip Dom is past the morning sickness phase. She suffered during the first, losing a few pounds, so she's making up for it.

After they've practically licked their dinner plates clean, the attendant brings a tray of cheese and crackers, macaroons, two bowls of sorbet—*fromage blanc*, and champagne flavors. She figured they would want one of each again.

Dominque eats two macaroons and empties one of the bowls of sorbet and then calls it a night. Within five minutes, she's lightly snoring, wearing her, 'I enjoy bacon periodically' eye mask. Tad found it and had to get it for her when she was undergoing chemo treatments. The word bacon is spelled out Ba C O N, as in the elements on the periodic table. Reminding them of the bacon quiche; the only thing she could eat that didn't taste like metal.

Debra, with a fresh glass of bubbles, pulls out a book and tries to focus on the story. Her eyes are heavy, either from the excitement from the day, the heavy meal, or the champagne—most likely the combination. Before long, sleep wins and the book falls across her chest.

Amber smiles, hearing the book drop. She picks it up and tucks it away. Pulls the blanket over Debra's shoulders and turns out her light.

With the dishes cleared, she's now able to work on her laptop, so she pulls it out, intending on making a dent on her manuscript while she's on this flight. To do this, she must put herself back into *that* place. Physically would be so much easier; emotionally it means feeling utterly powerless and hopeless. Struggling did nothing but sink her deeper underneath him, trapping her further. The moment she stopped fighting, knowing it was futile, was the worst. She's never given up—she's always been a fighter. Yet she knew if she continued to fight him, she would only be hurt more, and the abuse would last longer. By then, she just wanted him to finish and get off her. That feeling right there, that's the part she's had the hardest getting past. Will she give up again when the going gets tough? Will it be easier? What will it cost her in the end?

It could have been worse. Many women she's interviewed feared for their lives; she knew he wouldn't kill her, so there's that. A silver lining—disgusting, but true.

The right words form in her mind, and she starts typing away, only to press and hold the delete key after reading it back. She does this several times. Her eyes get heavy after several attempts during the next few hours. Finally, her lids win as they drop one last time.

He slides over to her side of the couch, his hand accidentally brushing against her thigh. No, it wasn't an accident; he did it on purpose. Her fight or flight instinct kicks in. Once she's on her feet, he stands up in front of her putting his hand over her mouth. In one swift move, he puts his other arm around her waist, picks her up, then pushes her down on the sofa with his body crashing down on top of her.

She tries to wiggle free—she can't! She tries to scream—nothing comes out! She can't move, he's too heavy—too strong.

Her dress is up around her hips from all the squirming. He rips her panties off and thrusts into her. It's happening so fast! The pain is excruciating! He's going to rip her in two. She tries to scream again, but his hand is tight across her mouth. His arm across her chest is pinning her down. He's so heavy…she can't breathe.

As if in slow motion, she sees his red face contort as his lips pucker out. He squeezes his eyes while he slams into her, over and over again, as his hair slowly bounces up and down. His voice deep, his mouth moving at a snail's pace, "You like that, don't you, you little vixen? See, before I can let you interview me, I have to know what you're really like. You play the shy little girl, then come in here with your four-inch stiletto heels and your boobs begging me to grab them. I know your type. You want me to throw you down and fuck your brains out. Damn, you're so tight; you feel so good. I'm going to fuck you so hard. You're going to beg me to fuck you every time you see me." She hears the last sentence spoken as if someone just flipped the record player off, letting the record continue to spin, slowly coming to a stop.

Amber stops fighting and just stares at the ceiling. It's no use; she's helpless.

She can't feel anything—she goes numb.

Amber wakes with a start; a layer of sweat rests on the top of her skin. The sensation of him holding her down—penetrating her—invading her, as if it just happened. She jumps up from her seat, hitting her head on the overhead compartment, creating a loud THUD.

The attendant comes rushing over to make sure everything is okay. The lights are dim; only a faint blue strip illuminates the floor, and pin lights glow overhead. How long has she been asleep?

"I'm okay. I'm sorry, I had a bad dream. I just need to use the restroom."

She hurries into the small toilet area and flips the lever behind her, brightening up the room. She doesn't recognize the woman staring back at her in the mirror. Her face looks drawn and pale with dark circles under her eyes. Her hands go to her face; she's shocked by her clammy touch and the shaking in her hands.

Her clothes, hair, and skin are still damp from the adrenaline pumping through her body. Staring at her reflection, she wills herself to calm the fuck down. *Breathe, girl, take a breath. Stop letting this asshole inside your head.*

After several deep cleansing breaths, the effect becomes genuine. She can feel her heart slowing down and watches as the color returns to her cheeks. She slaps water on her face and decides, it's now or never. It's not going to be any fresher than if it had just happened. She trots back to her seat and fires up her laptop. This time, she doesn't think about it, she just types. She doesn't go back and read the words, or even check if anything makes sense, she gets it all down. Tears constantly stream as her hands fly feverishly across the keyboard. Amber catches sight of the flight attendant passing by several times— she never looks up, afraid to break her focus.

Not sure how much time has passed, she jumps as a hand gently touches her shoulder.

"I'm sorry, I didn't mean to startle you," Debra says. "I read a few lines—it's raw—it's deep—it's perfect."

Amber looks up and sees her friend's shiny eyes. "Thanks, Deb. I had to get it down."

"I had no idea; I'm so sorry."

"You have nothing to apologize for. I didn't share with anybody. Hell, I don't even think I knew how I felt until now.

It's actually healing. I'm exhausted, but I'm so glad I did this. I'll wait at least until we get back home to edit it."

"Honestly, if you ask my opinion—and I know you didn't, but I'm going to give it to you anyway—I wouldn't edit it. It's your honest words and it should stay that way. When other victims read it, they'll understand; they're who you're writing it for, right?"

Suddenly the cabin fills with the wonderful aroma of coffee. Amber's face breaks into one of the broadest—most genuine—smiles she's had in a very long time. It wasn't until just then, she realizes she hasn't dealt with the attack—not wholly. She thought she was, but she admits it was all a facade. With newfound energy and determination, she puts away her laptop, fixes her hair, and checks her reflection. The face looking back is not the same from a few hours before. Her eyes are bright and shining; her skin is fresh—dewy, with rosy cheeks and lips.

She looks over at Dominque, who is stretching and waking. The flight attendant is already beside her with orange juice and a small bowl of fruit ready to take her breakfast order.

After a smooth landing and quickly getting through customs, the car provided by the airline whisks them away to Aloha - Hostel, where they will be staying and the location of Zya's show that evening.

The guys were not able to join them this trip. Overseas on a Wednesday was something they couldn't swing, Tad having just gone to Tahiti, and Brian, saving his vacation time for when he whisks Debra away for their honeymoon.

It's Paris Fashion Week, however, it's Zya's first time. Her show is on the first night and the last time slot at 9 p.m. She doesn't care—she's here, it's all that matters.

Zya left most of the details to Tina, her production coordinator. Zya is not a control freak—well, not mostly. Her attention to detail is one of the reasons she is so successful. She sees things others don't. And little things others think aren't necessary, are for Zya. It's one of the reasons she and Stan get along so well, he's just as meticulous. Tina is determined to blow this show out of the water—literally. Everyone is going to talk about it.

The buzz about Chanel's Paris rooftops is today; tomorrow, it will be Label Zya's *Canal de l'Ourcq*. It's perfect for Zya's cruise collection with the sophisticated shades of green and natural hues.

Zya is very busy backstage pairing the outfits with the proper accessories, shoes, handbags, sunglasses, hats, scarves. Everything seems to be just a little off. Zya blames it on being so busy and not paying enough attention the weeks before the show. While she curses herself under her breath, Stan is making sure Zya is nowhere near the stage so Tina can add the finishing touches.

Paris Fashion Week is held at several locations. Most of the designers will show at the *Carrousel du Louvre*, the underground mall below the Louvre museum featuring the inverted pyramid. Several other designers will also be showcasing at the Aloha - Hostel; however, tonight, Label Zya has it exclusively, allowing for some creativity.

Tina had a runway explicitly built for tonight. It extends the length of the room as you would expect; however, it forms a wide T at the end.

While Zya is busy in the back, a rolling green grass is brought in and placed in front of each row of chairs, allowing the spectators to sit easily; however, their feet will be hidden.

Weeping willow trees line one wall perpendicular to the runway. Once all the trees and grass are in place, a large wooden arched bridge is perched against the wall where the models will come out along with another large weeping willow tree to one side of it. Its branches drape behind the bridge covering most of the wall. It looks more like the French countryside than a runway. That is, until the music starts.

After freshening up, and Dominque's nap, the girls hurry downstairs hoping to slip in and see Zya before the show. The buzz with everyone moving about so quickly is contagious; you can't help but get caught up in the excitement.

They find the location where Label Zya will be showing, with the doors closed and guarded. Amber tries to sweet-talk her way in, but even batting her eyes and Dominque showing her long legs, although he much appreciated it, doesn't gain them entrance.

Tina thought she heard Amber's voice and peeks her head out. "Amber!" she yells as they turn and walk away.

They hurry back and are allowed entrance in to see the wonderland Tina has created, the doors closing before Amber hears her name called out from the hotel elevators.

"Wow, Tina, this is beautiful. I feel like I'm standing in a meadow," Amber says.

"Just wait; it gets even better."

"Really? Do tell."

"It's a surprise. Zya has no idea. Don't say anything about what you saw out here. She's been franticly running around in the back." Tina looks around the room, trying not to look guilty. "She can be mad at me later. Go back and see her, but don't be surprised if she shoos you away."

Exactly as predicted, Zya is so happy to see them, and she's super busy—the doors open in just fifteen minutes; the show starts in thirty.

"You need me to do anything? You look a bit stressed."

Trying to stay focused by not looking at her, Zya says, "No, I'm good, a few things are a bit out of order, but we'll get it together. I appreciate the offer, though. There should be some champagne out there for you, and sparkling water for Dom, go help yourself."

"You need me to videotape anything? Planning any extravagant surprises or announcements, I should know about? Proposal at one, married at the last one…you do have a history, you know."

Zya chuckles and stops what she's doing. "No surprises, no videos, it's all covered. I need you to find your seat and sit back and enjoy the show. Okay?"

Amber grins and hugs Zya, not letting go. Finally, breaking the hug, she says, "I'm so proud of you, go get 'em, girl." Amber turns and walks away, chuckling. At least she gave Tina a few more minutes.

Once the doors open, the room fills up quickly. The seats are set up on both sides of the runway and around the T at the end. Once every chair is filled, and the back walls lined with standing patrons, Zya peeks her head in. Her eyes open wide in amazement as she drinks it all in. A soft mist begins to gently roll across the floor, filling the room with a morning dew crispness.

Zya runs around to the back just in time as a low gentle rolling of the drum, along with tingling bells, duplicates the sound of gentle rain falling. It's beautiful; Zya's heart fills with pride—and love.

Tina sees her. She runs and kisses her on the cheek. "Just wait, you haven't seen the best part yet. And this is all for you."

Zya stands back and lets Tina and Stan run the show.

The top of the runway splits in half, revealing a pool of water. Each side slides across to the edge, then pops up and slides down along the sides. The underside of the rolling top has a green grass edge duplicating what's on the floor, continuing the grassy meadow effect. The water is a deep green like the canal the scene replicates, with lights shimmering underneath. The attendees gasp as the French countryside unfolds before them.

The original partition with Zya's logo on it slides across the far wall with the help of a few sexy male models. As soon as there is room, the first boat gently glides down the waterway. A male model outfitted in beige slacks and an emerald green tropical print shirt, propels the canal boat by way of a pole, the length of the catwalk. The female model, dressed in a beige and green linen short jumpsuit with a wide emerald green belt and big floppy hat, is gesturing at him, pointing at her watch. He's smiling at the crowd and waving, taking his time. The performance is witty and funny, not your typical high fashion show. When they get to the wide T, the next boat is slowly propelling down the canal. The female model is wearing a chiffon ruffled dress with a matching umbrella and hat; an outfit fit for high tea. The gentleman is wearing a suit, smiling at the guests, and tipping his hat. As the second boat reaches the T, the first boat is now being propelled by the woman, who has decided she can do it faster, while the male model lies back lounging, blowing kisses at the ladies as they pass.

The boats continue to take turns, two passing each other somewhere along the long stretch. The performances include some flirting amongst each other, causing splashing, and some boat hopping. If you didn't know there were wheels underneath to keep them from capsizing, you'd swear they were going over. The wheels don't make the boats sit completely flat; some rocking is allowed—as planned.

Once all the designs make their waterway appearance, the runway top closes, allowing the models to do their final lap on foot. They are laughing, flirting, and still playing as they take those last steps, another strange occurrence during Fashion Week.

A standing ovation and thunderous applause deafen the room. It doesn't stop. Zya is announced, and it gets even louder. She walks to the end of the T, holding her hands over her ears, unable to contain the smile on her face. She says into a microphone, "Wow, thank you all; I think I need my hearing checked. Is this what it sounds like when you go to a rock concert?" she asks. Her answer comes as the patrons get even louder.

"Thank you all so much. It's such an honor to be here in this beautiful city—Paris. I knew I'd be here one day, and not just as a visitor."

More applause, whistles, and shouts come from every corner of the room.

Zya holds her hands over her ears, then suddenly spins around with her arms up above her head, causing more of the same from the crowd.

Stan comes out from behind the willow tree and runs up along the stage and grabs the microphone from her hand.

"Keep it coming, everyone. She's worked her ass off to get here. Show her the love!"

Another standing ovation and applause so loud, the room vibrates.

Zya's eyes water as she hugs Stan. "I love you, man. Thank you so much for everything." They embrace again.

"I was blown away by this show tonight. I designed the outfits, but I had nothing to do with the production. Ladies and gentlemen, my wife, Tina Monroe, did all this," she says, motioning around to the decor of the room. "Tina baby, would you please come out here?"

As Tina walks on stage, the patrons again are on their feet, as some even dare to stand on their chairs. Their hands surely should be red and sore by now, yet they continue clapping as Tina makes her way to Zya's side.

"I said I wasn't going to make any announcements or have any surprises planned tonight, and honestly, I didn't. But after seeing all this..."—she turns to Tina—"you did all this for me?"

Tina nods as tears silently stream down her face.

"I can't believe how lucky I am to have you, and you put up with me. You let me have this year to make my dream come true. It's your turn—let's go get us some kids."

☯

The next morning as the girls are heading out for a day of shopping and sightseeing, Dominque realizes she forgot her emergency bag of rice cakes.

"I'll run up and get it. Check with the concierge and see if there's anything else we should add to the agenda. I'll be right back."

As Amber waits for the elevator, she begins to scroll through her email. She's received lots of stories from women all over the country, detailed accounts of their attacks. One woman, in particular, stood out while Amber was doing her research. She has been gently coaxing her to tell her story. Her rapist has yet to be caught, and the local authorities have all but given up. Amber is sure her attacker is a serial rapist, and getting her story out might help other precincts connect the dots. Amber's eyes stay glued, recognizing her name in her inbox. As the elevator doors open, she absentmindedly steps inside, continuing to read as the writer is still hesitant to come forward.

As if the conductor of the Philharmonic Orchestra himself were there, the next few events could not have happened in more perfect timing.

As Amber steps inside, a tray of plates come crashing down around the corner. Someone yells Amber's name, but the noise drowns it out. The sound takes Amber's attention away, until her mind realizes what the noise is. Not enough for her to lift her head.

The person calling to her runs to reach her while his foot catches the one-quarter inch lip of the elevator floor, causing him to lose his balance. He trips forward, his hands shoving Amber into the corner.

Amber sees a shadow out of the corner of her eye, blocking the light overhead as he falls into her. The next thing she knows, she's being pushed—trapped. Pure instinct kicks in and her knee comes up square in his groin, causing him to buckle. She shoves him away—hard.

The elevator doors open again, as another rider has pushed the up button before the car has a chance to move.

He flies backward out the doors and into the button pusher who is stepping forward. They both go crashing back and down; luckily, neither hits their head on the glossy white marble floor.

Amber recognizes her attacker—it's Christoph, the Frenchman who's been in and out of her life since she met him on the French Riviera in the summer of 2017. Amber runs to their aid. The gentleman rambles French words at Christoph she knows must not be very nice by the color quickly appearing on his face.

Christoph, still doubled-over, shuffles over to a nearby couch. He grabs a pillow and puts it immediately in his lap. He sits, leaning forward with a look of sheer pain across his pale face. His breaths are quick puffs of air, making his cheeks pop out.

"Stay here, I'll be right back," Amber says as she runs off toward where the dish cleanup is taking place. She runs into the kitchen, not caring she's not supposed to be there. In two minutes, she's running out with a massive bag of frozen peas and hands them to Christoph. "They didn't have anything smaller."

Christoph smiles and gladly accepts the bag, placing it under the pillow. "You say no surprises. I don't plan this time. An accident. I'm sorry," he says in his beautiful thick accent.

"Christoph, it's me who should be sorry. You caught me off guard. I was reading an email from a woman who was raped. Remembering how it felt for me, and…"

"Ma chéri, what do you mean, you?" he asks. His eyes are wide in surprise, his mouth wide open.

"Let me go tell my friends where I am. I'll be right back."

"What do you mean Christoph is here and you're ditching us to go be with him? You're engaged to Patrick, or have you forgotten?" Dominque says, wagging her finger at Amber.

"No, I haven't forgotten. I just hurt the guy, and I owe him an explanation. All I'm asking is for you to give me an hour, that's all. I'll meet you back here." Amber turns on her heel without waiting for an answer. Angry at Dominque for even suggesting she would ruin one of the best things that's ever happened to her.

In exactly an hour, Debra, Zya, and Dominque enter the hotel lobby. They search everywhere, but Amber is nowhere to be seen.

After fifteen minutes of searching, they decide to go up to the room and see if she left a message. As the elevator doors open, out steps Christoph tucking his shirt into his trousers, and a flushed Amber beside him.

"Hi, you two," Zya says, her eyebrows raising the same octaves as her voice.

"Ladies, nice to see you. Amber has told me of your successes. I'm happy for you. Zya, I knew your show would be big success. I was there to see. I will be sure to be there every time you are here in Paris. I will leave you to enjoy your day."

He turns to Amber and puts his hand behind her head and pulls her toward him. He kisses both her cheeks. "*Mon amour ma chérie*, I wish you well. I'll always be here for you."

Debra and Zya are standing with Amber while Dominque stands off to the side. All heads turn and watch as the gorgeous billboard physique saunters away. They watch as every woman's head snaps as he passes by. He smiles at them, making several swoon.

Zya says, "Mmm, mmm, mmm, now he is one sexy piece of manhood. One day girl, you're gonna have to spill the beans on what it was like to roll in the sheets with him."

Amber watches him too. Not with lust or longing, more with cherishing memories.

"Why were you coming out of the elevator?" Dominque asks, challenging Amber.

"If you must know, the frozen peas made the crotch of his pants wet. I told him he could use the hairdryer in our room. Plus, when the accident happened, I blurted out I'd been raped —he asked, so I explained."

"How does one just blurt that out? You didn't sleep with him, did you?" Dominque snaps.

Amber's temper starts to flare, but she tamps it down before it's unleashed. "I was reading an email from one of the rape victims for my book. In my haste to explain why I didn't recognize him, it slipped out. I'm going to say your hormones are on overdrive because I don't believe for one second my friend would question my love or my loyalty to Patrick. Even with a stud like him."

Debra jumps to Dominque's side, putting her arm around her. "She doesn't mean anything by it, Amber; she's just trying to protect you. We all know the past you have with him. You almost lost Patrick once because of his sneakiness. And although you say it was innocent, maybe it was a little too convenient."

"Look, ladies, I skipped out of packing away all my shit today and let my luscious lady go lingerie shopping without me so we could spend some quality time eating crepes and seeing the sights. So, no men, or significant other talk, it's just us today, like it used to be, okay?"

"Okay," Amber says, jerking her body toward the doors in anger.

As they all head out, Amber slows down until she's walking beside Dominque. "I would never do anything to jeopardize my relationship with Patrick. Thank you for looking out for me. I know you don't trust Christoph—but you can trust me."

Dominque stops and hugs her tight. Her hormones are haywire and her emotions all over the place. She has no control, and now tears are streaming down her cheeks. "I'm so sorry for being so mean. I don't know what came over me. Of course, I know you wouldn't do anything to hurt Patrick. I'm sorry."

"It's okay. Now I want to go see the *Quartier Pigalle*," she says as she drags them out and onto the street.

"What's that?" Debra asks.

"The Red Light District," Zya answers for Amber, while her eyebrows dance up and down. "Oh yeah, you get your lingerie baby, momma getting us some new toys."

Chapter Thirty-Six

"Wow, Zya, the house is amazing."

"Thanks, girl. A month past due, yet it was worth it. Come on, I want to show you something."

Zya takes Amber's hand and pulls her down a long hallway and opens two double doors to the last room. She steps aside, letting Amber walk in first. Zya has put her studio here, allowing her to spend more time at home instead of at the atelier. Several dressmakers' mannequins are draped with next season's fabrics and designs. Two sewing machines and tables are set up, one across from the other, with one chair between them. A large standing drafting table is off to the side, next to a large picture window.

Amber walks over to the table, in awe of the workspace. "This is perfect. Heck, you're only using half the room; Stan can come here and get even more done."

"Actually, the other half of the room is for you."

"What? What are you talking about?" Amber asks as she whirls around, looking at the space.

"I picked this room because it faces north. When I had it designed, I thought maybe my best friend who hasn't picked up a paintbrush in months, might want to share it with me."

"I don't know what to say."

"Look, I know you don't feel safe at your place, and Patrick's house is still his; you haven't moved in yet. I know how much you love to paint; it's always been your escape. I want you to have a place to come and de-stress. And get back to creating your masterpieces. I have a lot of wall space in this house. I'm counting on you filling some of it. And..." Zya opens the closest doors and steps back. "It's too damn heavy for me to move, so you'll have to come over here to look at it."

Amber walks over, admiring the solid wood easel. She's speechless. Her eyes dart back and forth between Zya and the wood framework able to hold the largest canvas. Finally, she touches it, and it reminds her of the smell of turpentine and varnish. As her fingertips explore the knobs and curves, her eyes fill up. This is one of the most thoughtful gifts she could receive. Painting has been the one thing that's always helped ground her. She's missed it; she didn't realize how much until right now.

"Oh Zya, I don't know what to say," she says, as her arms wrap around Zya with such force, she almost knocks her over.

"I just want you to be happy. Now, if you bring your man over here to paint him nude, give me a heads up first, okay? That's something I won't be able to unsee."

Grinning from ear to ear, she's already planning what her first painting is going to be. She's been saving pictures on her phone's photo app. Her favorite is one of an owl with its head cocked sideways as if it's saying, 'Huh?' It always makes her smile.

"Come on—we got to go. Everyone else should be here by now."

As they walk into the family room, Patrick hands Amber a flute of champagne and kisses her on the cheek. "Why are we all smiley?"

"I'll tell you later."

Tina walks forward and hands, Zya a filled flute and asks everyone to gather around.

"I'd like to make a toast. Two years ago, my daughter found her BFF, Ashanti, at the pool down in the Keys. Their chance encounter led to another when I met Zya. The woman of my dreams—the one I needed. She had no idea, but I knew one day she would realize I was exactly what she needed too. We're soul mates. What an incredible journey we have been through and an amazing family we have with all of you. On this day of thanks, as we celebrate in this magnificent home, I want you all to know how truly blessed we are to have each other. For this, I am truly thankful. Happy Thanksgiving."

"Mrs. Monroe, do you want me to carve the turkey?" Mitch asks.

CHAPTER THIRTY-SEVEN

"Oh, Mom, don't cry. At least I'm only going to be a three-hour flight instead of eight."

"I know! I know! I'm so proud of you. Harvard—WOW!"

Tina comes up and hugs her. "Are you sure we can't go with you?"

"You guys helped me get everything set up two weeks ago. I want time with Stacey—you understand, right? Plus, I'll see you next month at the wedding."

"And we'll be up to see you in March," Zya adds.

"See, it will be like I haven't even left."

"Oh baby, I'll know you're gone; I'll miss you terribly, but I know you're going to do great things, so I'll deal with it."

Stacey steps forward and hugs her mom and Zya. "I've looked at Ashanti's class schedule. It's pretty scary—even for me. I promised her when I get back, we'll sit down and work out times we can visit that won't disrupt her labs, classes, etc., okay?"

"Look at you playing Mother Hen," Zya says, arching an eyebrow. "I sure am glad you two are besties," she adds, chuckling.

Zya waves as she watches the future cancer-curing doctor and scientist walk into the next stage of her life. One of the hardest parts of being a parent is letting them fly and hope you've taught them how to use their wings.

On the ride home, Zya asks Tina to drive. Zya has somehow remained calm, yet she feels she could lose it at any moment.

"You okay?" Tina asks.

"Somehow, I am."

"You never told me how Mitch took it. Her going to Harvard."

"He talked her into it," Zya responds.

"What?"

"I know, surprising, huh? They've been FaceTiming every day. It was a little sickening at first, but then I think I fell in love with that boy myself.

"A fraternity tried to recruit him; he told them he was too busy. I might have overhead and yelled at him from across the room; he was making a big mistake. Freshmen don't get asked. Anyway, he's got his nose in the books—he's got big dreams.

"Ashanti asked him about the girls on campus. He laughed about it and told her there are lots of them there, and he's not sure how they got in. They're mostly into partying and boys—classes are not part of their schedule. But there's no one like her. He's playing football too. Now that, I don't understand. I would think he'd want to protect his precious brain.

"Anyway, Ashanti told him she got accepted to the undergraduate Harvard Medical School program. He told her it would be foolish if she didn't go—it was Harvard. She was hurt at first, thinking he was trying to break it off, and that was his opportunity. Then they had this very mature conversation about their future and made plans. He asked her if she could be

First Lady and do her research in Washington D.C. at the same time."

Tina snaps her head around and presses the brake a bit too firmly, causing a loud sound from the car behind her. "I think I love him too."

"They have these plans, and they're laser-focused. I've never heard of anything like it, especially at their age."

"Really—I have," Tina says, smiling at the very person she's referring to.

"Me? I don't think I was that focused."

"From what you've told me you were, and still are. Look at everything you've achieved just this year alone, married the love of your life, and a feature in *Elle* magazine in February. *Vogue* Forces of Fashion conference just two-and-a-half weeks before your Paris show—Hello! Anything ringing a bell?"

"I guess I am pretty amazing, aren't I?" Zya says, laughing, raising her chin in the air.

"I know you're not saying that seriously, but you are."

"Thank you. All those achievements came at a price, and you've stuck by my side. You sure about this?"

Amber leaves her office enjoying the nice crisp January air. She's hopeful for the start of a new year—2020. Her phone rings as she gets in her car to visit her sister.

"John, hi, how are you?"

"Miss Fiore, I'm so sorry to bother you, I know how busy you are; however, you've just received an urgent package. I thought you'd like to know."

"John, you're not bothering me, and please call me Amber. Um, I wasn't expecting anything." Amber thinks for a moment, then decides it must have something to do with the book. But then again… "Who's it from?"

"Staten Ferry Publishing in New York. It's a large white envelope. Want me to open it for you?"

"No, it's fine. It's from my publisher. Yay! I need to pack up a few things—"

"Pack up?"

"Patrick and I got engaged; we're getting married in a few months."

"Oh, wow, congratulations. I'm so happy for you."

"Thank you. You've been wonderful. I'm going to miss you."

"Likewise. You want me to put it upstairs in your unit?" John says, his voice taking on a cold, hurt tone.

"I'm on my way to see Brandy. I can get Patrick to come by when he gets off work. You know what, on second thought, I think we'll have a pleasant night at my place this evening. I'll pick it up then. Will you be there?"

"Oh, for sure, I'll be here. I'm looking forward to seeing you, Miss—Amber."

"Me too. Thanks for always looking out for me."

☯

"It's too bad it's taken us this long to have a relationship."

"I guess I have to kill someone for you to get you to notice me."

"Bad—that was so bad on so many levels. I'm glad we can joke about it now. Patrick said he could start asking about parole for you in ten years. The judge was very lenient, only giving you fifteen even though you've got priors."

"I know. We could celebrate our fiftieth together."

"That would be great," Amber says.

"You don't really mean that."

"Yes, I do. We have a lot to make up for. Oh, there's that guard, I have to ask a favor."

"What favor? Please don't ask her anything. I'm telling you, she's bad news."

Amber brushes her off and runs to catch her before she gets through the locked door.

Brandy sees a lot of nodding between them. The guard looks over at Brandy and nods again at Amber. Amber hugs her and runs back to her sister.

"I'm afraid to ask," Brandy says.

"It's still a few months off, however, I was hoping since you can't be there in person, maybe they would let you FaceTime when Patrick and I get married in April."

"And what did the bitch say?"

"You should try to be nicer to her; she's been nothing but kind to me."

"That's what scares me. She's not all sweet and nice; she's hell on wheels—takes no prisoners. She's someone completely different when you're not around."

"Maybe she just likes me."

"Ewww, that's even worse. That's one pussy these lips will never touch," Brandy says, as her body visibly shivers.

"Brandy, come on, that's just crude."

"Yeah, and?"

"Well, she seemed okay with the idea and said she'd see what she could do. I believe her."

"That's your biggest mistake."

"What's going on with you and Stewart?" Amber says, changing the subject.

Brandy's tough facade fades as her eyes soften. A sweet smile attempts to turn up the corners of her mouth. "We're back to having phone sex."

"What? How does *that* work?"

"I get 300 minutes a month. I don't call you; I use them on him—literally. The warden loves those trashy romance novels you give me, so I trade her. She lets me get him off over the phone so keep them coming. I think she secretly listens in and plays with herself at the same time."

"I don't think I want to hear this," Amber says, turning in the chair. She quickly turns back, leaning forward and says, "Wait, he can't get you off."

"He has…"

"No way. Over the phone? With other people standing in line?" Amber says, leaning forward.

"Use your imagination, dear sister. He wants to marry me."

"He proposed?"

"Not exactly. He wants conjugal visits. I've tried to tell him we don't get 'em in Florida. I told him about the novels I'm handing off to the warden, and he thinks he might be able to work out a deal with her once a month. Especially if we're married."

"He's got it bad for you. He doesn't want to marry you just to have sex, Brandy, he loves you. Ten years is not *that* long to wait."

Brandy is quiet for a while, just looking down with her shoulders slouched. The tough-girl image completely ripped off. "I'm sorry, you know," she says, eyes glued to her hands in her lap.

"I know."

"I don't think you do. I was so jealous of you. I still am a bit, but you didn't deserve it. You did nothing for karma to bite you so hard; you didn't ask that fuck-wad to rape you. I always thought I hated you, and my anger clouded so much I didn't allow myself to feel anything else. Until the day when I knew he hurt you. The rage was different; I wasn't mad *at* you, it was *for* you, and it was tenfold. We have a tarnished past, and I know we don't just wave a wand, and it all goes away, but I promise I'll try. I can't swear I'll be perfect, but I will put in the effort. I know I must earn your trust. I get it, it's okay. For the next ten, or however many years I'll be in here, that's my goal."

Amber reaches across, going totally against protocol, and hugs Brandy. The guard standing along the wall moves to intervene when the one Amber likes grabs her arm. "Let them be. Who knows when they'll get this chance again."

CHAPTER THIRTY-EIGHT

"Hey, Stewart, I gotta let you go. I'm heading into Amber's building. I'll call you back in a bit."

"John, so nice to see you," Patrick says, with a poor attempt at a smile. "Is Amber here yet?"

"No, Patrick, she isn't. I'll be happy to let you up to her apartment if you don't have a key," John says, intensely staring at him with a clenched jaw.

The hair on the back of Patrick's neck stands up. *How does he know I don't have a key?* "No, I'll just wait down here, but thanks anyway. You have an urgent package for her?"

"Already upstairs," John says in a clipped tone.

"Oh—okay."

Patrick paces, looking outside the glass doors, watching as the traffic passes by on A1A. You can't see the ocean from here because of the high rise across the street. Amber's unit sits on the eleventh floor, with floor-to-ceiling windows facing east, framing the ever-changing Atlantic seascape.

"You know what, screw it. The view is better upstairs. If you wouldn't mind, John, I'll wait up there."

"Of course, Mr. Simpson."

Patrick does a double take. The sinister grin on John's face causing all the hairs on Patrick's body now to stand on end.

No words are spoken as they ride in the elevator; however, Patrick's mind is screaming; something's not right. Not one to be bothered by small spaces, his body flushes at the close quarters, longing for the doors to open. He breathes a sigh of relief when they part and he's in the hallway.

Patrick stays several steps back as they walk to Amber's unit, taking deep breaths calming and berating himself for being paranoid; he just doesn't like John—and the feeling is mutual.

Once they reach Amber's door, John unlocks it, walks in, and disarms her alarm.

Patrick stands inside the door staring at him, stunned. "You know her alarm code?"

"How else do I get her mail up to her? Or let building maintenance in?"

"I don't live in a condo, so I guess it makes sense," he says, shaking his head and proceeding inside. He removes his jacket and makes a beeline to open the blinds and enjoy the deep blue Atlantic Ocean. She bought this place because of the view.

He gets two steps past John when he hears him say, "She shouldn't be so trusting."

"Excuse me," Patrick says, turning around.

John thrusts his right hand forward, sinking a four-inch blade into Patrick's abdomen.

Patrick's eyes bulge in disbelief as his hands go to the shaft of the knife impaling him. He doubles over as a crimson stain quickly spreads across his shirt. "No! No!"

He falls the rest of the way down to the floor with his hands still on the handle. The color is quickly draining from his face as he fights to keep his eyes locked on John's.

John stoops down over him and says, "She's mine now. You'll bleed out in about, hmm, I'd say ten minutes, at the most. It's too bad; I had hoped to take you two together so she could watch you die. I know that would be the ultimate torture for her. But, I'll just have to show her this instead." He pulls out his phone and takes a picture of Patrick. His pale blue shirt quickly changing colors, "It will have to suffice. You recall those texts I sent to her? As you take your last breaths, remember you failed her again. You can't rescue her. I plan to do everything I promised—and so much more."

John calmly goes into the kitchen and washes the blood off his hands.

Patrick watches, willing himself to stay alive—for her. The room slowly fades as John's whistling becomes fainter. His eyes get heavier and heavier until finally, they close.

☯

Amber's phone rings as she's checking out at the grocery store. It's the Broward County Jail. She answers it, thinking it's odd—Brandy never calls. "Hello."

The supervising guard on duty introduces himself quickly and says, "I'm calling about your sister, Brandy. She's been stabbed."

"What? How does she get stabbed in prison?"

"Someone made a shiv. Anyway, it's bad; she's on her way across the street to Broward General Hospital. I wanted you to know."

"Thank you…I'm on my way."

Amber leaves the line and her cart and frantically runs through the double doors.

"Hey, Amber. How's it going?" The guard from the prison is entering the grocery store as Amber is leaving.

"I can't talk! It's Brandy! Someone stabbed her!"

The guard from the prison who greeted Amber turned to run with her. "My car's right here. Let's go."

"He got her! My stalker—that bastard hurt my sister!"

The guard's van is in the first space, the one marked with the blue sign. The guard's arm goes around Amber's seat as she looks behind her to back out. Her hand stops along the way, injecting Amber in the neck.

Amber looks at her with wide eyes as her hand goes to her neck. The guard continues to back calmly out of the space, wearing a satisfied grin. It's the last thing she sees until she wakes up with her wrists and ankles tightly secured with plastic cable ties.

She's thankful she still has her coat on, and it's buttoned-up because it's freezing in this cold, dark, empty warehouse. She's in a fog and nauseous as slowly the reality of her situation becomes clearer. Then she remembers—Brandy.

Her eyes pop wide, and the first thing she sees is the guard. The one she thought was her friend. Brandy warned her.

"Did you hurt Brandy? Did you have her stabbed?"

"All in due time, my pretty. My brother is on his way. He had some other business to attend to first. I think he said his name was—Patrick?"

"No! No! No!" The flood gates open wide. "Please don't hurt Patrick, please," she begs.

"Oh, look at those tears. Sorry, but we plan on hurting everyone in your life, as you did ours."

"I don't understand what you're talking about." She sobs, thinking about Patrick. "Oh, God, please protect him. Don't let any harm come to him. Please, I beg of you."

"God won't save you now, honey. Or Patrick, or Brandy, or any of your other friends."

She's still drowsy from the drugs; however, the adrenaline pumping through her system is helping her become more alert. She doesn't care what happens to herself; she doesn't want anyone else hurt.

Suddenly, the door opens at the far end of the room and slams shut.

"Just in time."

It surprises the guard and Amber to see Roberto dragging in a bloody and a barely moving Christoph.

"Christoph…" Amber says, in barely a whisper.

Christoph lifts his head barely off the floor and looks at her with the slit of his left eye. His right eye is purple and swollen shut—his left not far behind.

"Where's Bill?" Roberto asks with red smeared fists and a sweat-stained shirt.

"He'll be here."

Amber shakes her head. "This doesn't make any sense."

"Not tough now, huh bitch?" Roberto says as he walks over and backhands her, causing her head to snap to the right, mixing Christoph's with the blood trickling from her nose.

The door opens again.

"Who got blood on Amber?" a male voice shouts.

He grabs a tissue from his pocket and gently wipes away the blood.

"Oh John, thank God you're here. I don't know what's going on; you've got to get me out of here, please," she whispers to him.

He continues to clean her face. Once he removes the blood, he turns to Roberto. John's face turns a deep red as he yells, "Who drew the first blood? Was it you? You know I was supposed to get that pleasure—not anyone else."

Amber cries again, realizing John is her stalker.

John spins on his heel. "Yes, my dear Amber, I'm sorry to tell you, I can't help you get away, honey, because I'm the one who brought you here."

"Why?" she pleads through tears.

"Why? Why, you ask? You were so eager to make a name for yourself; you didn't care whose lives you ruined along the way. You see, there are always two sides to every story. You chose to tell only one.

"Fourteen years ago, you told the world about a simple plumber who might have charged a little extra on a few jobs to make a bit more money. Do you remember the story?"

Amber nods. "He wasn't making a little money; he was tacking on thousands of dollars. He was gouging," the reporter in her answers, rather than the prisoner, angering him.

With clenched fists and jaw, he says, "They were rich. Those multi-millionaire bastards had money to spare. You have no idea the bullshit they put him through. Made him come in the middle of the night just to shut off the water because they couldn't be bothered to find the valve or bend down and shut off the toilet. You know how many Thanksgivings and Christmases he missed because their spoiled brats flooded the bathroom, shoving their new toys down the toilets?

"You're damn right my dad added an inconvenience tax to their bills; he should have charged more. And then you, this do-gooder, fresh out of school—green behind the ears reporter, decide to come to the rescue of South Florida's wealthy and uncover the lowly plumber scam."

"It was my job. Someone brought me the tip, and I followed through with it. If your dad wasn't so greedy, he might have gotten away with it," Amber says, defending herself.

John backhands her the opposite way Roberto hit her, only harder this time, toppling the chair.

She falls hard. Her purse is still across her shoulder, underneath her jacket. It was between her and the floor; the contents are not warm and fuzzy, but cold and made of steel.

Roberto comes over and picks her up by the cable ties on her wrists, pulling her up so her feet are dangling while John uprights her seat. Roberto's sweat-soaked face is close to hers as he dangles her wrists high in the air. Part of her wants to kick him in the shins, but she knows better. The ties are digging into her wrists, yet her weight is also stretching them slightly—maybe just enough.

"John, I was just doing my job," she says after Roberto unceremoniously drops her back on the cold metal seat.

He gets in her face, yelling and spitting his words, "My name is not John—it's Bill."

Bill paces back and forth in front of her while she slowly works the ties back and forth on her wrists, pretending to be rubbing them.

Bill stops abruptly. "If you would have just waited six months, that's all I needed. They buried us in medical bills because of our mother's desire for drugs and his need to save her; they ate up our savings. Finally, she overdosed—with a little help." Bill looks over at his sister and winks, prompting a wicked smile to appear on her face. The corners of Bill's mouth turn upwards, matching that of his sister's.

"It was her or us. I had a plan, and it was all coming together. I just needed a little more time, and I would have enough money for us to get away. All of us, to disappear and live out our lives in luxury. But no, you had to go and ruin it for us. My dad committed suicide after your article; did you know that?"

Amber shakes her head. Her eyes now diverted downward.

"Yep, you killed our dad. And because I wasn't quite sixteen and Janice here was only thirteen, we got sent to Child Services. You know they don't keep siblings together, right? It wasn't too bad for me, I'm a boy, but for my sister here, why don't you ask her how it was for her. Go ahead—ask her."

Amber keeps working on her wrists. She needs to be able to rotate them just enough…

"Ask her!" he yells.

Amber looks at Janice, who's staring at the far wall with her hands between her thighs. She's rocking back and forth with her lower lip quivering, suddenly looking fifteen years younger.

"Janice, I'm so sorry. Child Services are doing the best they can…"

SLUG! Bill punches Amber in the stomach, knocking the wind out of her, knocking the chair backward. Amber's head snaps forward from the punch, then back when it hits the floor, both making loud thuds. The weight inside her purse, pulls it further behind, under her coat.

Bill paces back and forth as Amber tries to catch her breath. She's rolled onto her side on the floor, trying to keep the bile down her throat.

"That's not asking her! I'll tell you what happened to my sweet, innocent sister. She found a home quickly with one of those families who take in as many kids as they can for the money. I'm sure you've heard about those. She was the perfect age to make into a slave. Clean the house, do the laundry, cook the meals. And the boys in the house…oh yeah, it was her job to satisfy them too, including dear old dad. The mom couldn't be bothered. She was busy spending all the money on those shopping channels. And when she needed more cash, she made the boys build another wall, making their closet-sized rooms even smaller to meet the criteria and bring in another teenage boy to cut lawns, clean gutters, or whatever odd job they could demand. And for my sweet sister to satisfy," he says, crouched down beside her.

Bill picks up Amber's chair then grabs her by the wrists and pushes her into it, causing it to rock on its two back legs.

Amber quickly lunges forward, bringing all four legs to the ground, swallowing down the vomit shooting up from the jarring motion. She focuses on Janice's sobs to clear the ringing in her head.

"That's the life you gave her for three years until I rescued her. I never found a family, which was fine. I used the computers at the Children's Village to find her, rebuild our future, and plan our revenge.

"Because your little story said good old dad stole over two hundred and fifty thousand dollars, they confiscated all the computers; mine included, even though there was nothing of dad's business on it. They came in while I was at school and took everything. They even found my backup I hid under my box spring. They took my plan away from me. Do you have any idea how long it took me to put it together? It was a beautiful thing. Every month, minor charges adding up to over thirty thousand dollars, dropped into my bank, then quickly spread out to my other financial holdings. They thought our dad was the mastermind behind it all. Right! As if! He was so dumb!"

Amber cocks her head, trying to understand what his plan could be.

"Curious, aren't you? It's the investigative reporter in you. Well, since you won't live long enough to talk about it, I'll tell you." His back straightens, and he puffs out his chest as he brags. "People never question minor charges of $2.95 or $3.95. If you don't get greedy and only charge them twice a year, you'll have a steady income. All you need is a few cards, and it becomes a ripple effect. One hacked card's charge history leads to many small retail shops with minimal credit card security. I steal the numbers and set up a recurring subscription charge. Cards are never present for those, and most people can't remember what they subscribe to anyway, so they ignore those small charges. For every card I hack, I get a new charge history which leads to new retail stores, leading me to more cards, and so on. If you take your time and do it right, before you know it, you're charging thousands of cards every month, all across the country. We've just reached my magic number of fifteen thousand charges this month, earning us over fifty thousand dollars."

Amber can't help herself—she has so many questions. "Doesn't your merchant ask questions when you transfer the money?"

"Come on. You must know I'm smarter than that. It gets processed through several businesses we own whose losses"—he winks at her—"are discreetly sent overseas. I'd really love to go into even more details, but time's a wastin'."

He walks over to Christoph, who's barely moving, and kicks him.

Christoph grunts so softly, you can barely make out any sound at all.

"This one here was an unexpected bonus. Had you not run into him—literally, while in Paris, he wouldn't be here right now. I thought he was completely out of your life. He came running when you sent him a text saying you needed him right away. And here he is."

Bill takes a gun out from the back of his waistband and slowly screws on a silencer, looking up at Amber.

Tears pool as Amber shakes her head violently. "Please don't kill him. He didn't do anything, kill me—not him. He's innocent; he did nothing."

"Oh, not to worry, I plan on killing you. We were innocent too. You need to take responsibility for your actions. What is it they say? Oh yeah—payback's a bitch." He turns around and, without pausing, aims the gun at Christoph's chest and shoots, causing his body to jump on impact.

Janice and Amber's bodies jump as well.

"Enough talk. I need papers, so I get Debra. You kill Brian, yes?" Roberto asks Bill.

"No!" Amber screams. "Leave Debra alone. She doesn't love you. Leave her alone!"

Roberto turns and takes two steps toward Amber when Bill grabs his arm. "Don't you dare lay another hand on her, or it's you I'll be killing."

Roberto continues, anyway.

"She love me, you interfere. When Brian gone, she love me again. We live in Spain. Don't worry, she be happy." Roberto spits in Amber's face as he turns and walks back toward Bill, who hands him a manila envelope.

"Your passports, all four of them—including the kids, and everything you need to start your new life."

They shake hands as Amber continues to sob. *This must be a dream; it can't be happening.*

Amber watches as Roberto leaves, paralyzed by the feeling of helplessness. She must fight this feeling of defeat; it's not only herself this time—she can't give up.

Swallowing the fear, and with newfound determination, she works her purse back toward the front of her jacket.

"Now, where do I start with you?" Bill asks, cracking his knuckles, walking back toward Amber.

"Is Brandy somehow involved in this?" Amber asks, addressing Janice, trying to buy time.

Janice turns and looks at Amber. She jumps down from the table, walking toward Amber. "Oh no, she was a pawn."

"I don't understand," Amber says, she must keep them talking.

Bill won't give up the spotlight so easily. "I swore I would get even with you, so I started following you fourteen years ago. I knew all about your family and your rebellious sister. I decided Janice was going to get into the penal system. I figured your sister wasn't going to reform herself anytime soon, and I was right. And then again—I always am.

"If you haven't figured it out already, I'm a hacker. Not just any hacker, I'm the best. I created this beautiful spyware—just for you. I just needed someone to install it for me." He spins around and stops in front of her. "Your friend at the mall, he had a price—just about everybody does. It was a little inconvenient every time you got a new phone, so I had to give it a problem making you see him. I paid him handsomely. Too bad you figured it out, though. He removed it when you questioned him. He got spooked and told me he wanted out...so I killed him."

Amber is trying so hard to stay in control; too many lives depend on it. She's always been an excellent judge of character, or so she thought. First John, now the tech guy she brought bear claws to—who else has she trusted too easily? Her thoughts and eyes turn to Christoph on the ground. She can see his chest is barely moving; okay, he's still alive. *Patrick, oh Patrick! Please be okay!*

"Lucky for me, you left your phone everywhere you went so I could hear everything. When you screwed your Frenchman in New York, did you even realize you dropped it on the floor? And positioned perfectly, I might add. I propped up so I could see every way you fucked. I watched you suck him off, and I jacked off watching him take you from behind. I pretended it was me ramming my cock inside you, only you were screaming for me to stop because I was splitting you in two. I couldn't listen to you and Patrick—you loved him. But Christoph here, now that's made for some great jacking off sessions. I've watched your New York hotel stay several times."

Amber cringes at the thought of him pleasuring himself, watching her and Christoph. Bile rises again in her throat and projects outwards, popping a button on her coat.

"Clean that up!" he orders Janice, who jumps down and quickly obeys.

"That bastard Brettinger ruined one of my plans with you. I wanted to be the one to violate you. See the terror in your eyes when I plunged my cock into you, over and over and over again." He thrusts his hips at her as he says those words, causing her to pull back, almost tipping the chair.

"Unfortunately, I couldn't see the look on your face—but I heard you. I was pissed it wasn't me, yet I took pleasure in hearing how hard you tried to scream. I heard your muffled cries for help, and then you just went mute. How hard it must have been for you to just—give up."

He turns away then spins back quickly, putting his hands on the arms on her chair, causing her to tilt her head to the side, his face inches from hers. "And then your damn sister goes and kills him! That was unexpected. She must really hate you to set you up like that. It was perfect; your identical twin sister commits murder and pins it on you. It certainly looked like you were guilty; I thought for sure Patrick wouldn't let you go to jail. What a loser he is; he couldn't keep you out of the slammer, and you didn't even do it! It's a damn good thing Brandy confessed, I was already planning on how to break you out." He spins back around and walks away toward his sister.

"The rest I'm sure you can piece together. The very jail where your loving sister was serving her sentence, employed Janice. A few clicks on my keyboard, and I made sure she got an early release. The job at your building, your security manager needed to take an early—permanent leave, and I was the best person for the job. Or rather, John was. The rest came together rather nicely—tied with a bow."

He puts one of his massive hands around her neck and squeezes. Spittle covers her from his maniacal laughter, increasing in intensity as he watches the color drain from her face.

She can't breathe. It's now or never.

Finally, her purse is within reach. Her hand plunges inside and clutches the coldest, hardest item she can find. She pulls it out, praying it's in the correct position—it is. She pulls back the hammer and squeezes both the trigger and her eyes as tight as possible.

She hears two shots. How is it possible?

When she opens her eyes, she sees a perfect round red hole between Bill's eyes as he stumbles backward; a sulfur smell fills the air.

Janice, with wide eyes focused over Amber's head, is standing behind him with her arms up in the air.

"And you keep them up!" she yells, trying to control the gun and her emotions.

A hand comes behind her and gently lowers her hands into her lap.

She jumps at the touch and spins her head around. The scream dies in her throat when she sees the dark blue uniforms, bullet-proof vests, and badges.

She drops the gun on the floor as her body joins it, suddenly drained.

Detective Ackerman catches her in the nick of time. "Amber, you're okay."

She looks up at him, her voice breaking. "Patrick. He killed Patrick."

"No, he's in the hospital—in surgery. It's serious, but I think he's going to make it."

"How? He said he killed him?"

"He never hung up from Stewart. When Stewart went to make another call, he heard what was happening and called 911. He saved Patrick's life."

"How did you know to come here?"

"I guess they didn't think anybody would look for you right away. Where's your phone?"

Amber thinks about it—her phone, of course. She giggles, which quickly turns into laughter from the stress or relief. Or because if she doesn't, she'll lose it. Then she catches sight of someone checking on Christoph.

As panic surges through her, she grabs the detective's arms. "Debra! She and Brian are in danger! Roberto is after her."

"We've got him too. He picked up Christoph at the airport earlier today, and someone spotted him and called it in. We found him a few blocks away from her. They're fine."

"And Christoph...is he dead?"

Detective Ackerman looks over at the officer tending to him for an answer. "We have a pulse. It's weak, but I can feel one."

Amber feels the weight of the world lift from her shoulders.

"Can you stand?" the detective asks.

"Probably not."

CHAPTER THIRTY-NINE

Tina's favorite room in their new home is a reading nook she took over from day one. Or at least it was her intention when she called it the day of closing. It's not uncommon to find Ashanti or Stacey in there doing homework when they're home from college. Zya likes to sit in there with her sketchbook as well.

Tonight, amidst the chaos of setting up for the wedding taking place tomorrow, they manage to carve out a few hours for themselves in this cozy room to celebrate their first anniversary.

Tina spent the afternoon preparing a beautiful Charcuterie board with thinly sliced smoked ham, prosciutto, pork tenderloin paired with terrine, and a salmon pate. Small dishes containing figs, olives, roasted almonds, and dried apricots. A separate tray has five different sliced kinds of cheese from pale white to the darkest of orange, and an assortment of crackers. Fine china plates with cloth napkins and pure silver forks await their appetites.

Zya walks in with a bottle of Cristal Rose and two flutes, admiring Tina's afternoon handiwork.

"Cheers, sweetheart. To the first of many happy, wonderful years together."

"Thank you for making all of this so easy for me," Zya says.

"You're thanking me. It's you I should thank. Look at this wonderful life we're living and everything you risked for me. You took a chance on us. I can't imagine my life without you."

Zya pulls her toward her and kisses her deeply—passionately. "I never knew love could feel like this. You make my heart skip a beat every time I look at you. I get butterflies just before I know I'm going to see you."

"You get butterflies? I remember the first time I saw you across the bar in Key West, my stomach did a flip. It still does to this day. I love you so much."

They kiss again, this time deeper and with more passion. They would have bypassed the food and champagne had Tina not pulled back.

"Wait here," she says as she jumps up and runs out of the room. She comes back with a large, flat package. "Happy anniversary babe."

Zya grabs it and rips into it like a kid at Christmas.

Inside are two napkins from the Tiki Bar at Holiday Isle with two ticket stubs from John Pennekamp Park, floating in a glass frame. The napkins have drink stains on them, and the stubs still bear stains from wet fingers holding them.

"What do you get the woman who has everything? And what she doesn't have, she can get."

"Are these the napkins from that day? And the stubs?"

"They are. I had a feeling about us."

"This is so perfect," Zya says as her eyes water. "Dominque was so funny. She couldn't understand why all these hot guys were coming onto you, and you kept brushing them off. What did you say to her? Do you remember?"

"I told her I could appreciate the opposite sex; I just chose not to play with them."

Zya snorts and says, "We laughed so hard."

"And then you—the next day with those fish. It petrified you to go in the water."

"Barracuda—they are some ugly and scary looking slimy suckers."

"If I remember correctly, it was your daughter who finally got you to try it; and you liked it."

"What I really liked was the back rub you gave me," Zya says, teasing, rubbing Tina's back with her hand slipping around, grabbing her breasts.

Tina leans forward and grabs a fig from the tray. When she bites into it, honey-like sweetness bursts into her mouth. "Wow!"

"Good, huh?"

Tina nods as she slowly chews, savoring every bite.

"Here, let me taste." Zya kisses Tina, pulling her down on top of her, begging for the sweet taste of her lips.

☯

"Is everyone ready?" Amber asks, looking at Ashanti and Stacey, who are in charge of the flower girl, Tracey, and ring bearer, Little George.

Dominque, Tina, and Zya all nod in unison. The bridal party is ready.

The double doors are open on both sides to the back courtyard so they can exit through the house, down the stairs, then over to the gazebo where Brian and Debra will exchange their vows.

Soft peach and purple sterling silver roses adorn every nook, cranny, and corner of the backyard, and both staircases inside the house. The columns, inside and out, are wrapped in the same beautiful shades.

Amber peeks out and sees the groomsmen and Brian ready, decked out in dark purplish gray suits with matching peach shirts and purple ties. Brian's shirt is purple with a peach tie. The fifty guests are sitting in their chairs surrounding where the groomsmen have gathered.

The minister walks up and greets the five men: Patrick, Stewart, Tad, Mitch, and Brian.

The music changes to the traditional procession tune as all eyes turn toward the open doors.

Zya is the first out. Her beautiful dark skin contrasts with the mid-length light peach silk slip dress. She holds a bouquet of mostly sterling silver roses with a few peach baby roses peeking through.

Tina follows next, wearing a matching dress in a beautiful rich purplish-silver fabric, contrasting perfectly with her thick blond mane. Her bouquet has the same flowers, although the opposite colors of Zya's.

Dominque is out next, shuffling along. An escort assists her nine-month pregnant body down the steps. Her dark peach dress is in the same style; however, ample room has been made to accommodate her perfectly expanding abdomen.

The younger bridesmaids follow close behind, walking side by side—Ashanti in peach and Stacey in purplish-silver, knee-length silk slip dresses.

Amber, the maid of honor, is next in line, wearing a similar slip-style dress to Tina and Zya; only hers bears a pattern mixing the shades of peach, purple, and silver. Her flowers are all sterling silver roses; an important flower to Debra because of George. Debra didn't want them in her bouquet out of respect for Brian.

Tracey comes running out much faster than rehearsed, throwing rose petals all over the place.

The guests laugh, making her go more off script.

Stacey holds out her hand to rein her in.

Two year old Little George comes out in an identical matching outfit to Brian. No pillow in his hand. He turns and says, "Come on, Bear."

Out trots the full-grown German Shepherd puppy George made sure Tracey got at his funeral almost three years ago. Debra couldn't keep him; it was too much for her, so her mother agreed to raise him until she was ready. Today, he becomes part of the family. He's wearing a pillow attached to his collar which reads, 'Will you adopt me too?'

Brian sees the pillow, and the tears steadily flow. He started the necessary paperwork to adopt Tracey and Little George legally. He just needs the marriage license to finalize everything.

Little George and Bear, both the same height, make their way slowly to the gazebo. In the last few steps, Little George runs into Brian's open arms. His tiny ones circling his neck.

Brian stoops, petting Bear with his free hand, "Of course I'll adopt you. You're part of our family too." Prompting Bear to lick the remaining saltiness from his face.

The music suddenly changes to *Just the Way You Are*. Brian smiles. *Her favorite…Bruno Baby.*

Debra comes out in a soft peach charmeuse and chiffon floor length, slip-style gown. A soft ruffle down the left leg opens slightly as she takes each step. The spaghetti straps are perfect for the crisp spring afternoon weather. The belt surrounding the gathered waist flatters her full figure. It's not until you look from the side, you can see the bump.

The vows were exchanged and several cases of champagne served as Amber sits back admiring her friends—her family, and how happy everyone is.

Debra's glowing—so in love and pregnant with her third child. She gets shivers as thoughts of the day she pulled her gun on Roberto creep into her mind. Thinking about what could have been. Everybody thought Roberto had mental issues, and in a way—he does. Debra always insisted he loved her and wouldn't hurt her. Debra's proof came when the jeweler appraised the diamond in the ring. A three carat, natural, fancy intense yellow, internally flawless Old-Mine cut diamond—it was a treasure after all. Brian would like nothing better than if she sold it and put the money toward Little George's education. Debra, however, has decided to hold on to it. Roberto will get out of jail, eventually. She'll keep it safe until the day she can return it to him.

Zya and Tina are slow dancing. Tina's eyes are closed, resting her head on Zya's shoulder. Zya's looking at the stars, praying? Thanking God? Amber is amazed at Zya's strength. No matter how tough life gets, Zya is more resilient, her compassion and determination never wavering. She's always treated people fairly, never greedy, and never taking the easy way. She defines the road less traveled and what's possible as one of the world's most successful designers, her daughter hoping to set the medical world on fire and madly in love with her soul mate. They just found out the petition to adopt the eight- and ten-year-old siblings they've been fostering, was accepted. The paperwork goes through next week. Zya is excited and scared as they go down this venture together. The giddiness in Tina's voice as she makes plans, expanding their family, is contagious. The girls are excited the boys will be part of their clan. Boys! That was the hardest part for Zya to overcome—they know nothing about raising young men. Amber chuckles as the well-mannered, very grateful siblings run up and hug Zya and Tina's legs. The wide smile forming on Zya's face is proof she has nothing to worry about.

Dominque has overcome so much. Self-esteem issues, an eating disorder, and stage two breast cancer. And here she is tonight, glowing and *so* pregnant. She looks like she swallowed a basketball. There should be a law against someone looking that good, nine months pregnant. Tad came into her life at the perfect time. Just when she needed him. His persistence won her heart. They still laugh at her being audited. Who would have thought something everyone dreads would lead to her ultimate happiness. She's been a godsend for Zya and Tina since the boys arrived. Her foster experience has helped all of them understand many of the issues they have faced and will surely deal with. Her insight has been especially helpful for Zya to not take the boys' shyness when they first arrived, personally. Zya, being such a perfectionist, was so afraid of making mistakes. Dominque, being a sounding board for all four of them, has helped them settle in nicely. She's loving being their aunt.

Amber glances down at Dominque's beach ball belly and says a silent prayer, *Please God, don't take her anytime soon. She deserves this happiness—to be a mommy and watch her kids grow up. She's been through so much pain—she should get the chance to grow old with Tad. Please God, let her stay an angel on earth.*

Amber wipes the tears pooling in her lids as she looks at Patrick. He's chatting away with Tad; the two of them deep in conversation, then tilting their heads back in laughter. Patrick quickly catches himself, bringing it down to a chuckle, his side not quite healed from his ordeal. He was adamant he take part in the ceremony, standing like everyone else. Only those entirely in tune with him could tell by his silent weight shifts and long blinks the price he was paying.

How could I have gotten through these past two years without you? I thought I was invincible—you showed me it was okay to need someone. It seems like just yesterday I was complaining I couldn't sleep because you were tormenting— teasing me in my dreams.

The tears flow freely as Amber gets up and joins the men— she can't wait any longer. She whispers in his ear.

"Really?" he shouts. Forgetting everything else, he jumps from his seat, wincing as he wraps her in his arms.

THE END

It's bittersweet writing those last two words. I've grown to love these ladies and their extended family—they've been a part of my daily life for years.

- Are you curious about Mitch and Ashanti's future?
- Amber and Patrick's wedding date is April 2020. Due to COVID-19, weddings were cancelled. Do we want to see how that plays out?
- Debra is holding the family heirloom diamond Roberto gave her with intentions of giving it back when he's out of prison. That could make for a great book.
- Dominque and Tad…we want them to live happily ever after—and they should. But what if Dom's cancer comes back when she's pregnant with their second child?
- Zya & Tina now have two young boys living in their home. They raised girls—it could be mayhem.

Thank you for escaping with me and trusting me with your precious time. My favorite part of being a writer is when my readers share their thoughts. Would you please take the time to write a review of *C'est La Vie*? If you purchased your book from a book signing, or other location, you can still write a review at Amazon, Goodreads and other retailers. Be kind. Be honest, but please be kind. When given constructively, and in a positive way, I'll always welcome your suggestions. I know I can't please everyone, however, I try. Leaving a review is one of the nicest things you can do for an author—thank you for reviewing *C'est La Vie*.

I would love know your thoughts. If you'd like to see a spin-off as mentioned, or maybe you've got one of your own, please send me an email. Melody@MelodySaleh.com

Below is the link to "Stay Tuned" and get sneak peeks into my next projects. Some pieces will be available only to my subscribers; my way of saying THANKS! Other special offers and giveaways will be made available only to my readers as well. Your information will never be shared or sold. I appreciate my privacy as much as you do.

https://www.MelodiousEnterprises.com/unbroken-readers.html

BIO

The inspiration for the Unbroken Series originally came from *Sex in the City*. The hit series and blockbuster movies *Fifty Shades* added additional creativity. The opening chapter in *Facade* was written many years ago, she had no idea where her characters were going to take her. "The story basically wrote itself. It was like a movie projector playing in my mind," is how she describes her experience. It soon became apparent, their voices were not to be silenced, hence the "Unbroken Series" was born. *Facade* was published on December 31, 2019 followed by *Deja Vu,* released June 23, 2020. *C'est La Vie,* the final book in the trilogy was released December 1, 2020.

Melody lives with her husband in her native home state of Florida. She's blessed to be alive today after two cancer diagnoses and enjoys watching her grandchildren grow up. Something she never takes for granted.